The Peveretts of Haberstock Hall

Meet the philanthropic Peverett siblings: unconventional, resourceful and determined to make a difference in the world.

Raised at Haberstock Hall, Anne, Thea, Thomasia and Rebecca know that they have the means and the knowledge to help those less fortunate than themselves. Each with their own mission, they won't be dictated by the patriarchal confines placed on them. But is the world ready for the sisters to make their mark?

Generous in spirit and heart, can these women find men who will be their advocates rather than adversaries?

Meet the men worthy of these kindhearted women in:

Anne and Ferris's story
Lord Tresham's Tempting Rival

Available now

And in Thea, Thomasia and Rebecca's stories

Coming soon!

Author Note

You will have met Ferris briefly in my Allied at the Altar series; he's one of the older brothers of Fortis Tresham (*Captivated by her Convenient Husband*).

Ferris's story is a Christmas story that tips its hat to Dickens's *A Christmas Carol*, but not in the usual way. This is not a ghost story, although Ferris does battle with ghosts. Nor is it a story about a miser whose joy in the season is renewed, although Ferris's belief in love is indeed restored. Like *A Christmas Carol*, and other stories Dickens told, this is a story about the importance of a charitable heart. Ferris is a man who is conscious of the benefits his station in life provides him. He is also a man conscious of the injustices and inequities in Victorian London as he strives to provide health care to the less fortunate. But he is also a broken man who has invested his life in his work and repairing others instead of repairing himself. He is afraid of loving again and he holds himself back from forming full-fledged emotional attachments, until he meets Anne, who inspires him to overcome those fears.

Ferris Tresham's story is about miracles. He's a man who makes Christmas miracles for others and finally gets a miracle for himself. What miracles will you make for others during this holiday season and throughout the year?

Happy holidays!

BRONWYN SCOTT

Lord Tresham's Tempting Rival

HARLEQUIN
HISTORICAL

HARLEQUIN®
HISTORICAL™

Recycling programs
for this product may
not exist in your area.

ISBN-13: 978-1-335-40744-3

Lord Tresham's Tempting Rival

Copyright © 2021 by Nikki Poppen

This edition published by arrangement with Harlequin Books S.A.

For questions and comments about the quality of this book,
please contact us at CustomerService@Harlequin.com.

Harlequin Enterprises ULC
22 Adelaide St. West, 40th Floor
Toronto, Ontario M5H 4E3, Canada
www.Harlequin.com

Printed in U.S.A.

Bronwyn Scott is a communications instructor at Pierce College and the proud mother of three wonderful children—one boy and two girls. When she's not teaching or writing, she enjoys playing the piano, traveling—especially to Florence, Italy—and studying history and foreign languages. Readers can stay in touch via Facebook at Facebook.com/bronwynwrites, or on her blog, bronwynswriting.blogspot.com. She loves to hear from readers.

Books by Bronwyn Scott

Harlequin Historical

Scandal at the Christmas Ball
"Dancing with the Duke's Heir"

The Peveretts of Haberstock Hall

Lord Tresham's Tempting Rival

The Rebellious Sisterhood

Portrait of a Forbidden Love
Revealing the True Miss Stansfield
A Wager to Tempt the Runaway

The Cornish Dukes

The Secrets of Lord Lynford
The Passions of Lord Trevethow
The Temptations of Lord Tintagel
The Confessions of the Duke of Newlyn

Allied at the Altar

A Marriage Deal with the Viscount
One Night with the Major
Tempted by His Secret Cinderella
Captivated by Her Convenient Husband

Visit the Author Profile page
at Harlequin.com for more titles.

For all my PEO sisters who make
miracles for women all year long.

Chapter One

London—November 1853

Dr Ferris Tresham was definitely *not* in the Christmas spirit. He was quite the opposite, a man beyond angry and burning with fury as he strode through the early evening streets of Knightsbridge. Not even the bright shop windows filled with speciality items tempted his attention. He did not feel like celebrating, not when winter was going to be difficult and, for some, deadly. All because the board of governors at St Erasmus's Hospital had rejected his proposal to bring healthcare to those who needed it most. How dare they!

The righteous indignation in his step set the skirts of his wool greatcoat swirling about his boot tops while his shortened alpenstock slapped at his side. The words of the Hippocratic oath flamed through his heated mind. *I will keep them from harm and injustice.* How was refusing to take care of those in need keeping people safe? How was it just? His mind railed silently even now when there was no one to hear.

He'd put that question to the board ten different ways today. When that had failed, he'd thrown the words of Maimonides the Physician at them. If they wouldn't keep the Hippocratic oath, he'd thought to compel them with the pointed reminders of the Oath of Maimonides.

May neither avarice nor miserliness, nor thirst for glory or for reputation make me forgetful of my lofty aim of doing good to thy children.

Those words, too, had fallen on deaf ears and blind eyes.

The board did not see themselves in violation of the oaths that bound the profession of medicine. Sir Bentley Dandridge had actually had the audacity to spout scripture at him. 'Does not Jesus say, suffer the little children to come unto me? Are we not keeping the teaching of the gospels by opening our doors to all who cross our threshold? Is not everyone welcome to avail themselves of our services?' There were caveats, though: *if* those availing themselves of services could pay; *if* they had the ability to walk the distance from their slums to the hospitals. But Sir Bentley and his board conveniently overlooked those limitations. The offer of care was not the same as access to care.

The gaslights of Knightsbridge gave way to the gaslights of Chelsea as Ferris turned south towards Number Fourteen Cheyne Walk, the terraced house that acted as both his office and his personal quarters in a less affluent part of London. He was acutely aware tonight of the luxuries his person possessed that allowed him to undertake the three-mile walk in comfort against the elements—the sturdy quality of his boots, the wool warmth of his greatcoat and muffler, the leather gloves on his hands, the black felt top hat on his head, the pointed end of his alpenstock a useful weapon if needed—all of which conspired to keep him warm and safe as he travelled the streets, while others around him shivered as they hurried past.

He was cognisant, too, of the power of choice afforded to him by the coins in his pocket, coins that allowed him to choose whether to make the walk at all. He could just as easily have taken a cab and, like the board of governors, conveniently ignored the despair around him. But one could not entirely avoid the poverty of London. It surrounded a man everywhere he went, even when his journey took him to the West End. Not even Mayfair was completely immune.

Chelsea certainly wasn't, which was why he'd chosen to open his practice there. Amid the bohemian collection of writers and artists who peopled the terraced houses, there were also the workers from the Chelsea china factory and the brickyards, the poor living cheek by jowl with those of some, often, mercurial incomes. An artist's or writer's income and fame was by no means a source of guaranteed security.

There was also the appeal of the close proximity to the Royal Hospital Chelsea at the end of his street, allowing him easy access to treat retired army pensioners, something he felt deeply compelled to do in honour of his younger brother, Fortis, who was serving England abroad in the Danube. Still, Ferris wished to do more.

His measly efforts hardly made a dent in the health needs of London's poor and ailing, especially in winter, a season notorious for loss—the season he'd lost her.

Ferris lengthened his stride, trying to shake the fingers of memory that reached for him. He couldn't give in to it. He beat it back with thoughts of the evening's work. He had notes to write and patients' files to update. Work was an effective antidote against despair. He was eager to be home as darkness fell and the infamous fog of London rose with its grasping, ghostly grip.

He made the last turn, dusky alleys on one side, the hiding spots of pickpockets, and the Thames, deep and deadly, on the other. It was not unheard of for a man to lose his way in the foggy dark and end up in the river. Between the cold, the fog and the memories, it was no wonder winter was his least favourite season—the season that had taken Cara while he'd been away at medical school, too far away to save her. All he could do now was save others.

Business for a doctor was brisk in winter, too brisk. He could count on a waiting room full of catarrhs and agues from November until April. Not that summer was much better for the poor. Summer brought fevers and cholera. Regardless of season, London was determined to be a seething cesspit of inescapable disease for those without the protections of location and finances.

He could do nothing about the fog and winter weather, but he could do *more* for those who suffered from them, if only the hospital would support him, which made today's rejection doubly disappointing. There *was* help, there *were* solutions, people were just unwilling to deliver them. He gave his alpenstock another hard, frustrated *thwack* against the folds of his coat. How dare those with means turn their eyes from those without! Wasn't this the season of giving?

He hated, absolutely *hated*, feeling impotent. Medicine, science—these were the most powerful tools against impotence he knew. With them, he could cure the ill, save the weak, prevent disease, hold back death. He could do for others what he'd not been able to do for Cara, and he had, for eight years since returning from his Grand Tour with his older brother, Frederick. Good lord, had it been that long? It would be twelve years in January since he'd lost Cara. Time flew and he had so little progress to show for it.

He was a short distance from Cheyne Walk when he heard the cry, the pitiful sound of a child's wail. Down a dark alley. He was immediately alert with suspicion. It could be a trap. Such manipulation was no more unheard of than a man accidentally falling into the Thames. Street criminals were not above using a child to lure a kind-hearted citizen into the dark, only to relieve him of his worldly possessions and sometimes his life. Yet, his oath as a physician demanded he investigate on the chance that it wasn't a trap. Ferris went towards the sound, his alpenstock at the ready, its metal spike pointed forward.

Precautions were unnecessary. He found two children huddled against a brick wall, a boy with his arms wrapped comfortingly, protectively, around a small girl. In the dark it was hard to guess their ages. They were thin—children out at this time of night always were. Thin. Cold. Scared.

'We ain't done nothing wrong, guv'nor.' The boy's voice held a touch of defiance. Good. The boy still had some fight left in him. *Left?* He didn't sound as if he could be more than eight. Ferris's heart twisted. Eight-year-old boys should have plenty of swagger to them. He remembered himself and his brothers at eight. Swaggering handfuls they'd been. But it was different on the streets. By eight, a child was either a whipped dog or a rabid one. The only difference between the two was how much fire he had in his belly.

'You're not in trouble.' Ferris took a final look around to ensure his safety and knelt beside them. 'Where are your parents? Why are you out here?' He could guess the reasons, but it was best to hear them from the boy before he could decide what to do, and it was best not to judge. He'd learned that, too, in his years serving the poor. Not everyone had choices, parents included.

'We've nowhere else to go, sir,' the boy offered and then hastily added out of fear of being taken to an orphanage or workhouse, 'leastways nowhere to go tonight when Pa is drinking his pay. It's best for us not to be in the house when he comes home.'

Ferris nodded. It was just after seven of the clock now. The two children would have a long night ahead of them and a cold one. There was no mention of a mother. Ferris thought it best not to ask. The little girl coughed. He didn't like the dry sound of it or the racking that seemed to shake her entire body. He liked even less what it was proof of: this was not the first time they'd been out in the London air in nothing but rags. It likely wouldn't be the last.

Ferris rose and swept off his greatcoat, feeling the cold and damp leach into his skin immediately. The children must be freezing. Some of the rage he felt towards the hospital board transmuted towards the unseen father who preferred drink to keeping his children safe. He gave the coat to the boy with careful instructions. 'This will keep you both warm tonight.' As long as no one stole it from them. He pushed the thought away. 'In the morning, take it to a second-hand shop. Sell it for cash and two coats, one for each of you.' He paused, thinking. 'Cut off the brass buttons first. You can sell them one by one later.' That would keep them in some warmth and funds for the next time they were on the street. 'Hide the money well. Don't let your father find it.' Or it would go for drink. The children wouldn't see a penny of it. That reminded him of one more thing. He felt in the pocket of his waistcoat for his coins. 'Take these for supper tonight. Get something hot to eat and drink.'

'Thank you, sir,' the boy said, mystified at their good fortune. His sister coughed again. Dear lord, he did *not* like the sound of it, but these children didn't belong to him. The last thing he needed was a drunk man accusing him of kidnapping, should he notice his children missing.

'There's a card in the coat pocket. It has my address on it,' Ferris said. 'If her cough worsens, come see me. My practice isn't far from here.' It was the best he could do tonight. He left them, searching his mind for more options. What else could he have done? They had warmth, food and some funds for the night.

He was damp and chilled by the time he reached home. At least he had assurances of warmth and hot food. Supper would be waiting for him on the stove, courtesy of his housekeeper, Mrs Green. He had certainties those children did not.

At Number Fourteen, the customary lamp burned welcomingly in the front window, a beacon against the fog and a reminder to all that saw it that help was in sight. All they had to do was knock. His sign hung over the door in promise that someone would answer, day or night.

It was a relief to be inside. Ferris shut the door behind him, already feeling the benefits of warmth and home. He could smell Mrs Green's stew, savoury and delicious, and hoped the children had found warm food as well. He stepped into the front room that served as his waiting room-cum-office and halted. He had an unexpected guest.

'Brother, what brings you here? Are the boys and Helena well?' A knot of worry took up residence in his stomach. What could have brought Frederick out unannounced?

Frederick Tresham, Lord Brixton, the heir to the Duke of Cowden, turned from the glass-fronted bookcase with an easy smile, already dressed for the evening beneath the folds of his Inverness coat. 'The children are fine, at least they were when I left them. One never knows with four boisterous boys under the age of six on the loose.' There was glowing pride in every word. His brother adored his wife and sons.

'Have you forgotten? Mother said you would.' Frederick laughed. 'I'm here to fetch you.' His brother gave him a scrutinising stare. 'Where's your coat? Don't tell me you've been without it in this weather?' He paused and gave a knowing smile. 'You gave it away again, didn't you?'

Ferris shrugged. 'I gave it to some children on the way home from St Erasmus's.' He dismissed the remark with a wave of his hand, while his mind searched frantically for his oversight. What was he being fetched for?

He found the answer hiding among the crowded events of the day: the hospital meeting, the children in the alley, his morning patients, Mrs Fitzsimmons's encroaching due date and a hundred other things. Ferris groaned. 'It's tonight, isn't it? Mother's annual charity ball for the children's home and the governess hospital.' The Duchess and her fellow patronesses would spend the evening currying favour and coaxing donations from the guests in exchange for the opportunity to dance in the evergreen-festooned Cowden ballroom with its famed Venetian chandeliers. The event was the unofficial kick off to the festive season in town.

'Precisely.' Frederick arched a censorious brow. 'And we're late. Come along. I'll help you change. We're going to have to hurry.'

Anne needed to hurry in order to make her final stop of the day and still get home in time. Already, she was running late. She'd promised her sister she'd attend a hospital fundraiser with her tonight. She found the last apothecary on her list for today—a narrow, unassuming shop on Webber Street.

Anne drew back her hood as she stepped inside the dimly lit interior. She took a quick survey of the sparsely populated shelves and noted the lack of customers. She also noted the shop. For all its dimness and lack of inventory, it was neatly swept. Someone was making an effort. Perhaps that someone was the woman behind the counter, a woman who was doing her best to also keep herself neat in clean but worn clothing and who bore the signs of hard work and hard living on her face and hands.

Good. Anne would far rather talk to a woman than a man, especially a man who believed there was no place in the ranks of medicine for a woman. It was hard enough being an herbalist—also being a woman made her task doubly difficult. But she was a very determined one. The past two weeks since her arrival in town had tested every ounce of that determination. Progress had been slow.

Anne approached the counter with a smile. 'I'm Miss Anne Peverett, an herbalist from Hertfordshire. I have remedies I'd like to share with you in the hopes that you might stock them on your shelves.' Anne set the basket on the counter and drew back the cloth cover, displaying small round jars of salve, linen packets of root compounds for teas prettily tied with a pale green ribbon, along with amber vials of tinctures and oils, all bearing a small, neat label done in her own precise hand.

'I'm Sally Burroughs,' the woman replied warily,

but her eyes couldn't resist the basket. 'Oh, they're so…
lovely.' Her interest was apparent as she leaned forward
to peer inside. Anne wondered how long it had been
since the woman had seen something pretty up close,
let alone had something nice for herself.

'They smell good, too.' Anne quickly took up the
conversational opening, encouraging the woman to
smell a vial of lavender oil. She let the soothing scent
fill the space between them. 'Lavender is good for re-
laxation and headaches. It's much better than laudanum.
It is certainly less addictive and more affordable.' She
reached for a linen-wrapped packet. 'I have blackberry
root for loose bowels. It's especially effective and safe
for small children.'

'Do you have anything for hand cramps?' the woman
asked tentatively. 'In the winter, the damp and cold
make it so I can barely get my hand around a pen long
enough to write a receipt.'

'May I see your hands?' Anne took the woman's
roughened hands in her own. She turned them over,
noting the chapped redness on their backs. Carefully,
she manipulated the woman's wrists, studying the slight
crabbing of the fingers, a sure sign of early rheumatism.
She looked fifty, but Anne thought it likely the woman
was in her forties. Hard city living aged people early.

Anne searched the basket for a small jar of salve.
She opened the lid and applied the salve to the backs of
the woman's hands, explaining as she massaged, 'This
is made from angelica root, horse chestnuts and green
walnut hulls. The latter two are good for healing worn

skin. The angelica root is good for the soreness. How does that feel?'

The woman stared at her hands as if she'd never seen them before. 'Why, it feels wonderful!' She flexed her fingers. 'My skin is so soft.'

'It will take a few days before you'll feel lasting results,' Anne said. 'You'll need to use it regularly for full effect.' Sometimes people didn't understand that.

The woman's face fell. 'How much is the jar?' Anne could already see her counting pennies behind her eyes, wondering how much a jar might cost, perhaps thinking it was too small to cost much, that maybe with economies she just might be able to afford this one thing for herself. This was a woman who'd spent her life making economies, usually by sacrificing her needs for those of others.

'It's a gift,' Anne answered swiftly, handing the woman the jar. She hadn't come to London to make money, but to help people. Those who could pay, did. Those who couldn't, would not be denied. That was her father's motto and it would be hers as well.

'A gift? Are you sure?' The woman looked sceptical, fearing the coveted jar was a lure for larger purchases. 'I don't know that my husband will want to purchase anything. We make our own stock in the back.' She gestured to a place behind the curtain.

'These aren't drugs,' Anne said calmly. 'They're herbs. They're natural remedies. They don't come from chemicals, they're different. I don't want to sell you anything. I just want to leave a few things for the shelves. Perhaps you could recommend them to your customers? I have instructions to leave with you as well.' She had pamphlets and receipts at the bottom of her basket for clients who could read. Anne smiled. 'Just think how pretty they'd look on the shelves.' Shelves that were nearly empty. Clearly, the husband wasn't an ambitious apothecary.

Anne pulled out some of the simpler, more versatile items, like the lavender, which had myriad uses. Her hand paused on a linen packet of angelica, the same ingredient as the salve. 'Does your husband drink, ma'am?' It was a delicate question, but she thought it was likely given the state of the shop and the woman.

'A bit,' the woman confessed and then hurriedly excused it. 'All men do.'

'Certainly,' Anne acceded empathetically. She pressed the packet into the woman's hand and lowered her voice in friendly conspiracy. 'When angelica root is brewed as a tea, it can dull the taste for alcohol. Perhaps you might know others who could make use of that.' Anne smiled, knowing full well there would be in this part of town. There were women here who needed her help if she could just reach them. An idea sparked.

'Perhaps you know women who might like to gather? I can show them my products and how to use them. It would just take a half an hour in the afternoon or late morning.' Anne picked a time when the menfolk would be off to work and less of an impediment to women attending, assuming the women weren't working themselves. It also seemed unlikely Sally's husband would be around to interfere that time of day. 'It would bring people into your shop,' Anne added.

There was an answering spark in the woman's eyes as the opportunity occurred to her—people in her shop and a product they would come back to buy. Business would be helped. 'All right, come the day after tomorrow. I'll see what I can do.'

Anne stepped outside, filled with a warm triumph. This was what she'd come to London for, to reach people like Sally Burroughs, to teach them about self-care remedies, to give them ways to keep their families healthy without paying the prices of London's doctors and medicines, even if it meant she and her sister would be late for the ball.

Chapter Two

The price for the privilege of dancing in the Duchess of Cowden's festively decorated ballroom was a hefty tribute to the Duchess's two favourite charities: the governess hospital on Harley Street and the Foundling Hospital in Bloomsbury. It was the one night of the year where anyone with enough money could swan among the *ton* regardless of their credentials.

Ferris looked around his mother's glittering, *crowded* ballroom, decked early for the season with evergreen boughs swagged along the wainscoting and tied at intervals with elegant red velvet ribbons. He took note of the wealthy merchants who'd taken advantage of the opportunity to rub elbows with the *ton*. He also took note of how many of them had brought their daughters along, just in case there was an unmarried duke's son or two in their midst. He nodded neutrally as a clutch of pretty girls passed on their mothers' arms, blushes hidden behind lacy fans.

'Don't give them too much encouragement,' Helena,

his brother's wife, commented, irony evident in her tone as she took up a place beside him. 'They'll think you're an iceberg, Ferris, when nothing could be further from the truth.' She laughed and leaned close. 'I think some of the guests come to the event more in the hopes of catching you than supporting the hospitals.'

'Then they are bound to be disappointed. I am not for the catching, Helena.' Ferris took a flute of champagne off the tray of a passing footman. He was not eager to have this conversation with his sister-in-law, who wanted everyone around her to have the same marital bliss she had.

'You don't make it easy on them. First, you hide away from society, coming out so exclusively that it's a grand occasion when you do, and then...' she paused with a roll of her eyes '...well, you know what you do then.'

'You talk about scurvy and scrofula until the poor young things are green with nausea, not envy.' Frederick took up his position at his wife's side, a proprietary hand at her waist, adoration in his eyes. 'Are we scolding Ferris again, my dear?'

'Yes, he just froze two blushing maidens with his nod.' Helena smiled at her husband. 'How are the boys? I am guessing you've come from the nursery?'

'They're tucked in for the night. All four of them.'

Ferris wondered if his two urchins were tucked in safely beneath the folds of his greatcoat. Was it enough? How unfair that he should be swilling champagne from crystal beneath chandeliers whose cost could feed and house ten families for a year while innocents shivered and starved.

'You're grimacing, Ferris,' Helena admonished.

'Be easy on him, dearest. He's had a setback today with his clinics—' Frederick came to his aid '—and another on the way.' He directed a cautionary nod over Ferris's shoulder. 'Brace yourself, brother, here comes Mother, guests in tow.'

Ferris turned, readying a polite smile on his face, his gaze tolerant. He'd never be rude, but neither would he be encouraging. One day his mother would recognise what he already knew. No debutante wanted a husband who was called away at all times of the night, who spent his funds on a clinic for patients who couldn't pay. The *ton*'s debutantes were not raised to live in such lowered circumstances.

His mother beamed as she made the introductions. 'Ladies, allow me to present my son, Lord Brixton, and his wife, Lady Brixton, and my son, Dr Lord Ferris Tresham. This is Miss Nightingale, who is the superintendent at the Harley Street hospital, and her friends, the Misses Peverett, Thea and Anne.'

The ladies curtsied and Ferris felt himself relax as he greeted each of them in turn. These were not husband-hunting debutantes. He knew Miss Nightingale by reputation, a woman as married to her work as he was to his. The dark-haired woman, Miss Thea Peverett, seemed of the same ilk, sensibly but neatly dressed in a navy blue gown devoid of ruffles and lace. There was nothing to guard against here, at least not until he looked into the alert gaze of Miss Anne Peverett of the coppery curls and green eyes.

A bolt of unlooked-for and long-absent awareness

speared him, sharp and hot, as he bowed over her hand. She wore a well-made gown the colour of sage, devoid of furbelows like her sister's, with a black sash about the waist and matching black trim at the bodice and hem. Miss Anne Peverett was a beauty—perhaps not the way the *ton* thought of beauty, not with her copper curls and lack of fancy ornamentation, but she was a natural beauty. A man would have to be dead not to notice her loveliness. From his reaction, he was definitely not dead, something he'd not been reminded of for some time. He was more doctor than man these days. This rather masculine reaction was the note of a moment, nothing more. The sensation would fade when she moved on. Only she didn't.

His mother had other ideas about the company Miss Anne Peverett should keep and that company was him. 'Oh, a waltz is starting! Ferris, be a dear and dance with Miss Peverett while I introduce her sister and Miss Nightingale to some of our largest donors.'

There was no time to muster a suitable excuse before his mother moved off with her guests. It seemed the sensation she roused in him was going to last a little while longer, not that his body appeared to mind. He made her a small, gracious bow. 'Miss Peverett, would you do me the honour?'

By rights, the honour was all hers. Ferris was aware he was one of the most coveted partners in the ballroom this evening *and* that he had yet to take to the floor. One had only to follow the interested eyes of the young girls and their mamas as he led Miss Peverett out for the waltz to know he'd been negligent of his duty. Even at a November charity ball, dukes' sons were in season.

Ferris placed his hand at her waist, conscious of her own hand firm and warm at his shoulder. He'd not reacted to a woman like this since Cara. But Anne was not the usual fare of nervous girls who were in raptures over his credentials until they discovered he was more interested in being a physician than claiming the privileges due a duke's second son.

Miss Peverett's bold gaze met his as he moved them into the dance, her eyes refusing to look off into space over his shoulder. Close-up, he could see flecks of gold amid the green—she had tiger's eyes that sparked with life as she laughed up at him. 'Thank you for dancing with me. It is kind of you. Your mother wasn't entirely subtle about needing to pawn me off so she could conduct business.'

Ferris laughed, too, feeling a smile creep across his face at her direct manner and her honesty—two things often lacking in debutantes of his experience. This was refreshing. 'Thank you for accepting the offer. My mother was also not subtle about her desire to see me on the dance floor.'

'Do you not like to dance?' she asked as Ferris manoeuvred them around another couple. One would think this was the height of the Season with a crowd this size on the dance floor.

'I like to dance well enough.' As if to demonstrate his aptitude, he chose that moment to take her quite competently through a turn. His hand at her back drew her closer and his pulse jumped. Good lord, his body was acutely attuned to how well they moved together. She was a confident dancer. He found that confidence appealing, perhaps even more appealing than her attractive features. That confidence suggested she was comfortable with herself and, by extension, comfortable with him.

'Ah, I see. Then I must apologise for causing you trouble. You will be besieged by mamas afterwards.' Miss Peverett flashed him a wide, confident smile that made him feel they were somehow conspiring together against those matchmaking mamas. 'London or Hertfordshire, it's much the same everywhere when there's an eligible bachelor among the hens.'

He liked the instant feeling of togetherness she engendered in him. He didn't usually feel a connection with people, as if they had something in common. More often than not, he felt apart. His *ton*nish friends didn't understand his need to work and, by definition, patients weren't friends. 'Actually, you are doing me a favour. If I must dance, I'd rather be dancing with someone who is straightforward than a dissembling debutante.' It was true, Ferris realised. He didn't begrudge Miss Anne Peverett the dance. He found himself enjoying it and her in a way he'd not enjoyed female companionship for a long time. Probably because she wasn't hunting him. 'So, there are matchmaking mamas in Hertfordshire, too? I'll make a note of it,' he joked. Small talk came easily with her. 'Is that where you're from? What are you doing in town this time of year?'

'My sister and I came with my brother in October,' Miss Peverett explained. 'He enlisted as a doctor so that he could assist in the Crimea. My sister wanted to go, too. They're twins, you see. But the military isn't taking nurses.' Something sparked in her eyes as if she disagreed with that decision. 'So, she accepted Miss Nightingale's invitation to work at the Harley Street hospital.'

'You're from a medical family?' Ferris asked, intrigued. The brother a doctor, the sister a nurse. It wasn't all that uncommon. Medical families often intermarried and begat more medical families, much like ducal families intermarried to beget more dukes. He was quite the exception to the rule on both sides. Ducal families didn't usually have doctors and doctors usually weren't from ducal families, although being a second son had brought him the freedom to choose his path.

'Yes, my father is Dr Albert Peverett of Haberstock Hall. My brother studied at Oxford. Where did you study, Dr Tresham?' She manoeuvred conversation as adroitly as she danced.

'Edinburgh,' Ferris answered in mild surprise. He couldn't recall the last time a dance partner had been interested in where he'd got his degree.

She gave him another of her wide smiles. 'Edinburgh. I'm impressed. It's considered by many to be the best medical school in Britain and in Europe.' It spoke well of Miss Peverett that she recognised the import of it. Too few doctors actually held a diploma from a university. At his last count, only something like four percent of the doctors listed on the rolls had a degree. Usually, it was an issue he didn't hesitate to hold forth on, but it was hard to keep his mind on such things when Anne Peverett's green eyes were looking up at him, bewitching him with her intelligence. Perhaps the evening wouldn't be a loss, after all.

A brief furrow formed at her brow. 'Forgive me for not knowing, Dr Tresham, but do you have a practice here in Mayfair?' He was immediately on alert. Was she fishing for how deep his pockets were? Or how successful he was by worldly standards? He tensed, instinctively bracing against disappointment as he offered his answer.

'I have a practice in Chelsea on Cheyne Walk.' He tossed the words out like a dueller tossed down a gauntlet. Would she be interested in him now that he'd clearly indicated he wasn't a wealthy society doctor? But Miss Peverett seemed more interested than ever.

'That's near the soldiers' hospital, isn't it?' she quizzed, her brow furrowing once more as she recalled the London streets.

'Yes, I make rounds there weekly, so the location is convenient,' he offered cautiously, still waiting for disappointment to cross her fine features. But none came. If his answer had dissatisfied her in anyway, she gave no sign of it.

'How wonderful. It is too bad you didn't meet my brother. He would have enjoyed talking with you about the effects of war on the psyche. It is something of a speciality of his.' Her green eyes were lively with interest, but he didn't want to talk about himself. He wanted to talk about her, about Anne Peverett of the medical-minded Peveretts. There was so much he wanted to know about her and so little time in which to know it. The usually long waltz suddenly seemed too short. There was no time to redirect the conversation. The dance was over and he was nowhere near ready to let her go, but a second dance was out of the question.

He acted quickly, eager to keep her with him. 'Would you care to stroll the portrait gallery, Miss Peverett?' One could not stroll the gardens in November. The portrait gallery was the best he could offer and hope it wasn't overly crowded by like-minded people.

She smiled. 'I would love to, if only to hear more about your practice, Dr Tresham, and your work with the soldiers.' A thrill of elation jolted through him. Was it from her smile or her interest in his work? Perhaps both. What a heady combination that would be. Too heady. He was careful to tamp down on that thrill. He knew full well he should proceed with caution until he knew her better. Was she merely playing at being interested or did she feel it, too, this remarkable connection between them?

Ferris guided her down the long gallery of Cowden dukes, portraits on one side, long glass windows to let in the light on the other, with large square plush benches in the centre of the corridor for sitting and viewing. It was quiet in the gallery. There was time to study her as they strolled: the deep round apples of her cheeks that lent her face its expressiveness, the bold green eyes, the wide, sensual perfection of her mouth, where his gaze lingered far too often. Sweet heavens, he was acting like a green boy with a crush. Where had such a reaction come from?

There was time to listen to her as well, the softness

of her laughter, the intelligence of her questions. There was no doubt she was a doctor's daughter, an extraordinary find in the rarefied circles of the *ton* where only peers' daughters dared to tread. In response, something that had long lain dormant inside Ferris began to stir, to dream, restless at first, surprised to be roused from its dormancy in the middle of a ball of all places.

Here was a woman who understood his life, who would understand his choices, who had not lived a *ton*-nish existence herself, but instead was acquainted with the demands of a doctor. Here was a woman who would not mind his devotion to work, who would encourage it, who might even work alongside him in some capacity and who might fill the hole in his life left by Cara.

He'd not thought to find such a paragon again. He'd not dared to dream of a wife, of a family of his own again. Love hurt too much. He'd buried those dreams alongside Cara, but tonight, being with Anne Peverett resurrected old hopes.

Steady, old chap, it's too soon to draw such conclusions, his careful conscience warned, but his heart was barely listening. His heart and his tongue were tripping over themselves in a mad rush to impress Miss Peverett.

'I must conclude, as your brother does, that treating a soldier these days is more about treating his mind than his body,' Ferris summarised, coming to the end of what had become a lively dissertation on his part about soldiers and mental health. He chuckled. 'There, I've gone and done it. I've said too much. You're a very good listener, Miss Peverett.'

'It's easy when the topic is so engaging.' She smiled.

'I must confess I was not looking forward to coming tonight. I find myself feeling hypocritical swanning around a ballroom full of pompous rich men who would pay so much for an evening with a duchess, no offence to your mother, but who won't spend a farthing to offer direct help to so many in need.'

'A hypocrite, yes, that's exactly it. You've put it perfectly, Miss Peverett.' How often had he felt that way? Warmth spread in his chest. Talking to her was like coming home. This was too good to be true and yet he detected no insincerity in her. Hadn't he thought this very evening that this was the season for miracles? Wasn't he entitled to a Christmas miracle of his own?

It was a heady thought but his mind was braced for it, ready with a rebuttal.

Do you really want a miracle, old chap? Have you forgotten how it hurts to love and lose? You know you're better off alone, with your work.

But the argument didn't carry the weight it usually did, not when Miss Peverett was staring at him with those green eyes and that smile as if he could talk all night or, the horrid thought came, as if he *had* talked all night. Perhaps she'd merely been polite earlier. He had to ask, just to be sure. 'Have I bored you, Miss Peverett?'

Chapter Three

Bored her? Heavens, no. Is that what he thought? 'Not in the least, I am sorry to have given that impression.' She sounded flustered to her own ears and she was. It wasn't a feeling she was accustomed to, especially around men. She'd taken their measure and found them narrow-minded and lacking. But not Dr Ferris Tresham. He fairly stole her breath in looks and words. Whatever *he* was, he was definitely not boring.

'I'm not used to talking about my work with such a receptive audience. It has been a treat for me. I believe I got carried away.' His blue eyes sparkled like sapphires, winking in the light as he gave a self-deprecating chuckle. Here was a man confident enough to joke about himself, a man more concerned about his conversation partner's enjoyment than his own need to put himself on display like a puffed-up peacock.

The quality was as appealing to her as his looks, although it hardly mattered if he was appealing or not. She was not hunting a husband—that was something she'd given up for the best over a year ago after 'The Great Disappointment' with Robert. Still, she was not immune to what other women in the ballroom saw in him—a handsome man whose thick, wavy dark hair looked like it would spring to curls on a moment's provocation and whose blue eyes were at once both shrewd and kind, set against the sharp angles of his face. That face was enough to ensure a woman's attraction. His height and broad shoulders only served to enhance his appeal.

Then all that handsomeness had opened his mouth and Anne felt her resolve to avoid romantic entanglements teeter after a year of adherence to her own strict rules: no men. They were dangerous to her freedom, to her dreams, even when they meant well, even when they professed to understand her. Robert was proof of that. And now, here stood an engaging, confident man who was interested in her.

That interest was there in those intent blue eyes, circumspectly studying her as they strolled. He was interested not just in her looks, but in her conversation. It was another potent level of his appeal and one she shouldn't keep encouraging with her questions.

They'd reached the end of the gallery. It was darker down here and they were quite alone. She ought to run as fast as she could. Instead, she found herself saying, 'I couldn't help but overhear part of your discussion with Lord and Lady Brixton as we approached. Something about clinics? It sounded intriguing.' So much for not encouraging him.

He shook his head. 'It's complicated and, as of today,

it's likely over, or at least deferred until I can change some minds.' She arched a brow, inviting further comment, and he indulged her, perhaps a sign, she thought, of how much he needed to talk about this subject, even if it was to a woman he'd barely met. Perhaps it was a sign, too, of how much the subject meant to him. His passion for it was evident, in his voice, in his face, as he explained his plan for mobile health clinics to go in to the poorer neighbourhoods where people did not have access to adequate care and were unlikely to walk the distance to seek it out.

'I think it's a brilliant idea,' Anne said when he finished. 'It's exactly what is needed. Why did the hospital board refuse?'

Dr Tresham gave an exhalation of disgust for the board, a sharp light in his eyes underscoring his position on the subject. 'The board believes the poor don't count.'

Anne laid a comforting hand on his arm out of reflex, wanting to console this man who felt so deeply for others. 'Perhaps you need a different sponsor? My father always found hospital boards too political for his tastes. He prefers country practice to the contretemps of town.' She thought for a moment, cocking her head as she ran his problem over in her mind. It seemed odd that the son of a duke would lack for funds, and it wasn't as if his family was against such charitable endeavours. His mother was hosting a ball for such needs. 'Would your family act as sponsor?'

Dr Tresham offered her a soft smile. 'They would, but I can't take money from them. My father has offered in the past to make donations to the hospital, with influential strings attached, of course. Frederick and Helena have offered to support the clinics outright and bypass the hospital altogether.'

His smile turned rueful. 'With either offer, I become just an eccentric rich man with a hobby. Such a reputation doesn't establish a precedent for long-term care or a consideration for the poor that goes beyond me. I don't need my family to acknowledge the poor—they've already done that. It's the rich, the hospital boards, whose acknowledgement the poor need. When the board refused me today, they refused to recognise the less fortunate. The board remains blind to the realities that these people cannot take time off work to walk the distance to clinics in middle- and upper-class neighbourhoods. The board is content to adopt an attitude of out of sight, out of mind and leave them to the care of charlatans and whatever passes for doctoral expertise in the slums.'

Anne nodded in agreement. On her own rounds, she'd seen what he spoke of first-hand. Reliable physicians didn't practise in St Giles or the East Docks. Yet she wondered if Dr Tresham was being too stubborn in refusing family help. 'I'd hate to see such a grand idea as your clinics foundering for the sake of pride, Dr Tresham.' What would he make of her boldness? Would he think she'd gone too far in seeking to advise him? 'What does it matter where the money comes from as long as it allows you to begin? Right now, you don't even have that. If you could just get started, who knows what might develop in the future? Surely the project is worth swallowing your pride and asking your family for funds,' Anne reasoned.

Dr Tresham shook his head. 'I appreciate your thoughts on the matter, but I think there's still a chance I can convince the board if I am able to show them the actual numbers of people who will take advantage of a mobile clinic and the good it can do. With physical proof in front of them instead of a hypothetical idea they won't be able to fall back on their old arguments about there being no need.' He offered her a hopeful smile. 'After all, it's nearly Christmas, the season of miracles and giving, where anything is possible and hearts grow softer for a short time.'

'But how might you do it without funds?' Anne asked, genuinely curious.

'I think I might be able to arrange my budget in order to afford a dray and a horse. I'd hoped to set aside funds for more medicines this winter, but if I forgo that, I could effect a start.' He smiled, his eyes resting on her with genuine warmth and appreciation. 'Thank you, Miss Peverett, for reminding me that sometimes our biggest obstacles are our own pride.'

Anne smiled in return, feeling the electricity of a connection spark between them. He was a remarkable man, not only in his calling, but in his openness to taking advice from a woman he barely knew. 'Here's to making a start, then. I'll be interested in hearing how it goes.' She regretted the words immediately. She was practically inviting him to call on her, when that was the last thing she wanted. She was in London exclusively for work and it needed to stay that way.

Dr Tresham gave a low laugh in the dimness, a sound that was entirely too intimate on short acquaintance. It should have served as a warning, not a welcome. 'I've not met anyone like you, Miss Peverett, for a very long time.'

'Nor I, you,' Anne whispered softly, barely daring to breathe the words. What would happen if she gave them life? If she acknowledged the connection that drew them together, that kept them talking in the gallery far past the time it took to make a strolling tour and return to the ballroom as so many other couples already had. *Anything.* That was the answer. Anything might happen here in the unchaperoned dark, where the promises she'd made herself waited to be broken.

A slow smile took the lines of his mouth and her body responded with decadent want. She wanted to taste that smile, drink from those confident lips. Her breath caught as he reached a hand to her cheek, cupping her jaw in a gentle caress, a prelude to the slow capture of her mouth with his. The press of his lips sipped from hers and she opened for him, welcomed him. A soft moan escaped her. He was a sure, deliberate master of the kiss, his exploration unrushed, and, against her better self, she was enjoying this moment out of time in his arms right up until her mind rebelled.

Kissing Ferris Tresham was the height of foolishness! She turned her face away, breaking the kiss, her hand flying to her lips in shock, as if her mouth had acted independently and she could hardly believe what it had done. She was cognisant of the confusion in his eyes as she stepped back from his embrace. She'd not meant to hurt him, but she had to save herself.

'I shouldn't have! I don't want to give you the wrong impression.' She looked about hastily, thankful for the isolation of their situation. A kiss in public was a dangerous thing. If they'd been seen, she might have ruined everything. She bobbed a hasty curtsy, her flustered mind wondering how one took leave of another after a clandestine kiss. 'I must beg your pardon.'

'Wait.' Dr Tresham reached for her, perhaps to comfort her in her distress, to assure her, but she moved beyond him. She was the only source of assurance she could trust.

'I must go, my sister will be looking for me.' She was already on the run before she finished her sentence, leaving Dr Tresham alone in the dark. She would be safe now, from her own foolishness and from the temptation of him. He would not chase her and risk causing a scene. Her heated mind started to formulate a plan. She would collect Thea from the ballroom, pleading a headache, and go home.

Anne's mind was still reeling as she and Thea settled in the hired hack, putting distance between them and the ball. What had gone wrong? How had she forgotten her promises so easily, so quickly, and with a man she barely knew? Hadn't she learned her lesson?

She was thankful the darkness of the hack's interior hid her mortification from Thea. It helped that Thea was too absorbed in reliving the evening to note her silence.

'I thought you were having a good time, too?' Thea

remarked, coming to the end of her commentary. 'You looked happy dancing with Dr Tresham, or should we say Lord Ferris Tresham?'

'I'm not sure he sees himself as a peer,' Anne corrected absently, her thoughts too ready to reflect on the man who'd laid out his plans for a mobile clinic, who'd talked so passionately about serving those who needed him the most. 'He's quite dedicated to his work.' She'd found that dedication appealing, relatable. He spoke of his work with the same passion she felt towards hers. He lived for it as she lived for hers.

He was a man who'd broken from his expected path in life to take a path less often trod, as had she. She'd chosen her work over Robert, a home and family. Like recognised like. Perhaps that was why he tempted her, a woman who knew better than to be taken in by a man. She'd been to London once before, during the Season years ago. She'd met medical men in the past, the sons of her father's friends, and learned they were no different from other men when it came to a woman's status in society.

Her history with men hadn't been all that successful. Men wanted to stake claims, wanted to dictate her life no matter what they said early on. Even Robert Eisley, whom she'd nearly married, whom she'd thought had known her better than anyone, hadn't truly understood. He'd thought her healing was a hobby, something to dabble in until she could marry and devote herself to a husband and family. It was what he'd expected. But not her. She expected to lead a *life* of healing. She'd not been willing to give it up for him or any man.

She and Thea—Florence, too—were alike in that regard. At twenty-three and twenty-five, she and her sister were proof women could lead meaningful lives without men and families of their own, that not having those things didn't diminish their worth.

'You're quiet, Annie. Are you thinking about your handsome Dr Tresham?' Thea nudged her with a slippered foot. 'Or is your head plaguing you? It's not like you to have a headache.'

'My headache is better,' Anne offered. She didn't want Thea to worry, especially over a lie. 'I think it was just the noise and having been out all day.'

'Or it might have been your handsome lord. You left the ballroom with him, don't think I didn't notice.' Apparently, Anne wasn't fooling her with the headache excuse. 'You were gone for a while.' There was curiosity behind those words, but no censure.

What a wonderful while it had been. Meeting him had been an undeniable bright spot in an evening she'd not been looking forward to—too bright a spot it turned out. He'd shown himself to be a man of skill and compassion. He would have attracted her eye on looks alone, but it was his conversation that had drawn her heart. In the short span of time they were together, she'd felt as if she'd met her soulmate, a man who shared her values, then he'd kissed her, a long, slow kiss that had turned her knees to blancmange and caused her blood to heat. It was the kiss that had done it. She'd known if she didn't stop it there, she would be tempted towards disaster. In the end, men disappointed. Men were not all they seemed or protested to be.

'Will you see him again?' Thea asked quietly.

'No, there's no reason to.' Nothing could come of pursuing a connection with him, professional or otherwise.

'But you liked him?' Thea pressed.

'That's not a reason,' Anne replied firmly. She would leave London eventually and return to her work in Hertfordshire. Socially, she was beneath him, a country doctor's daughter of comfortable means. She didn't have the qualifications or the dowry to be an acceptable match for a duke's son.

And yet he'd kissed her.

Her heart would not let her forget that one salient detail. But she must. It would be best to set it aside and focus on the upcoming gathering on Webber Street at Mrs Burroughs. *That* was what she was in London for. But her heart wasn't as ready as her mind to put the matter to rest.

It whispered one last temptation: *you could find him if you changed your mind. He told you how. Cheyne Walk, the soldiers' hospital.*

She wouldn't change her mind, Anne told herself firmly. That's all there was to it. She'd already learned this lesson. Robert had taught it to her most exquisitely, and she'd always been a fast study.

She heard Thea draw a breath, about to ask another question she didn't want to answer. She cut her sister off. 'Enough about Dr Tresham. He was an evening's highlight, nothing more. There's something else I want to discuss.' Anne tried to recapture the enthusiasm and excitement she'd felt upon leaving Mrs Burroughs's

earlier this evening. 'I want to tell you about my outings today and an idea I have to get my herbals into
people's hands.'

If she could concentrate on her project, her mind
would soon forget about other hands, hands that belonged to a blue-eyed doctor who, for a moment, had
almost tempted her to throw it all away on a waltz, a
walk and a stolen kiss in the dark.

Chapter Four

The impetuously born idea of a women's gathering was an unmitigated success. Mrs Burroughs managed ten women for the first gathering, and twenty had shown up for the next. Anne quickly saw the merits of the new model; it helped her circumvent talking to male apothecaries who were sceptical of herbs *and* women, which made for difficult persuasion. The new model also served to put her products and information directly into the hands of customers.

Anne duplicated the gathering at Mrs Burroughs's in the other neighbourhoods she visited throughout November, each session drawing a larger crowd than the last until it was difficult to fit everyone inside the little shops. Best of all, she was able to establish a rotation of sorts, visiting each place twice a week and laying the early foundations of relationships.

Some women were happy to pay for a product after her demonstrations. For those who could not, Anne simply gave. Giving was the credo of Haberstock Hall. Her parents had raised all five of the Peverett siblings on it. She'd learned it at her mother's knee along with herbology. She'd seen it in practice when she accompanied her mother on her rounds as soon as she was old enough to walk the five-mile circuit.

Anne packed up her basket at the end of another session, this one held at a shop in Southwark. The basket was much lighter these days and she made a mental note of the items she was running low on. Replacing them would be tricky. She had money enough of her own and from the items she did sell to buy ingredients for more products, but the ingredients wouldn't be fresh this time of year and she had no place to work other than the table in the rooms she shared with her sister. It wasn't the most ideal of conditions, but it would be better than what passed for workrooms and laboratories at the back of the apothecaries she visited. Still, she was missing her herbal room at Haberstock Hall.

The good news was that her dwindling supplies were a sign of her efforts. Word was getting out. People were being helped. On those grounds, she was a success. On other grounds, however, she'd been less successful. Focusing on work had failed to completely drive out thoughts of Dr Tresham from her foolish heart. She found herself wondering how his mobile clinic was getting on. Were people lining up for his services? Would the hospital be convinced?

Such thoughts were harmless enough, but not all her thoughts were about business. She wondered, too, if he had danced with anyone else. Had he smiled at another with that sensual mouth and those blue eyes? She told herself it didn't matter if he had. He was only a one-night fantasy. He could be nothing more. She'd made her decisions. She had no room in her life or her heart for a man. What mattered was that she'd come to London and seen her project succeed beyond expectation.

He'd failed beyond all expectation. Ferris stared at the blank ledger as he sat atop the bench of his new wagon. He'd had his movable clinic, comprised of the horse, wagon and the last of his quarterly funds, for nearly three weeks now. What he didn't have were signatures to show for it. Suddenly, in the midst of winter, when colds and coughs abounded, there wasn't a sick person in sight.

It made little sense and it was proving problematic. How was he to convince the hospital board there was a need for his proposal when he couldn't show them an outpouring of patients clamouring for his services? Even his regular clients were a bit thin on the ground. They came by to visit and celebrate his new wagon, but they didn't need refills of their medications when Ferris knew they should have nearly exhausted their current supply.

By the time Mrs Fulton stopped to admire the wagon, his curiosity was fully piqued. There was nothing for it but to ask her straight out why she was in no hurry to renew the prescription for her ageing father's arthritis.

'His hands feel ever so much better,' she enthused nervously, wanting to hurry on to other conversational topics. For a woman who usually went on ad nauseum about her father's ailments, it was a telling gesture.

'You do understand, Mrs Fulton,' Ferris said, 'that the medicine won't keep working if you stop using it. It must be used always—there is no curative for your father's condition.'

'Yes, I understand that.' The matron blushed furiously, indicating some level of embarrassment. Was it a matter of money?

'If it's a question of affordability, you know I would extend your family credit,' Ferris said. Quite often he never collected on that credit. No one was turned away on his watch. But the offer offended Mrs Fulton, who puffed up with flustered indignation.

'No, Dr Tresham, it's not a matter of payment—it's a matter that I don't need it. I have a different salve for my old father now. It's from a healer. She makes everything herself and it's all natural.' She added the last rather proudly, as if his medicines were somehow abnormal.

It was enough to set alarm bells off for Ferris while Mrs Fulton fairly oozed with admiration for this new paragon. 'She's got teas and tinctures, salves and lotions, root compounds wrapped in linen and tied with a pretty green ribbon.' Mrs Fulton was quite possibly more taken with the presentation of the products than their actual functions. 'She's an herbalist.' The term obviously impressed Mrs Fulton.

An herbalist? Ferris was less impressed. This was alarming indeed. There was a hierarchy in the medical world, tenuous as it was. Doctors, reputable ones at least, earned degrees from universities. Chemists and apothecaries had to be licensed before they could practise the making of medicines. But herbalists were under no such regulation. Anyone might be a self-proclaimed herbalist, even a woman, which was explicitly excluded in the Hippocratic oath. *To regard the offspring of my mentor as equal to my brothers in male lineage and to teach them this art.* All one needed to be an herbalist was a garden and a pestle, gender notwithstanding.

'How do you know the product is safe, Mrs Fulton?' Safety would resonate with Mrs Fulton if the distinction of degrees did not.

Mrs Fulton answered confidently, 'She shows us how to steep the teas and mix the tinctures so we don't use too much. There's so much to learn.' Mrs Fulton was positively alight with excitement. 'I had no idea there was such bounty to be had from the land aside from crops. Take mushrooms, for instance.'

'One must be very careful with mushrooms, Mrs Fulton,' Ferris cautioned. Did this country herbalist have any idea what she'd unleashed? A little education in the wrong hands could be a dangerous tool. 'How many ladies attend these meetings?'

'There were ten to start, but now we often have as many as thirty women, more than the apothecary can hold. We meet once a week. But Lady Grey—that's what we call her because of her grey cloak—goes everywhere, not just our neighbourhood. She goes to other neighbourhoods like ours where the need is great. When someone can't afford a product, she gives it for free.'

'She meets in apothecaries?' Where Mrs Fulton saw a saint, Ferris saw a Trojan Horse. There was a clear motive behind giving things for free. Did Mrs Fulton not see it, perhaps blinded by the charismatic 'Lady Grey'? Give it for free now and then have the customer come back to the apothecary to buy it the next time, where she no doubt had an ongoing arrangement for shelf space in exchange for a commission for the apothecary. Everyone would make money. Very savvy, especially around Christmas when people might be willing to part with a few extra coins or purchase a gift. Well, that explained where his clientele had gone in such a short time. This herbalist must be charming indeed to win everyone's trust so quickly.

No, not everyone's trust. The *women's* trust. This herbalist knew her best audience. It was the women who looked after a family's health. Men were stubborn and unobservant. They barely looked after their own health, let alone the health of their spouses and offspring. The women would feel an affinity for her as a fellow female. No wonder they found her so appealing, so approachable—perhaps more approachable than a male physician who was so far above them in station and all ways.

'She understands us,' Mrs Fulton affirmed. Oh, she probably did understand them, too well. That's what worried Ferris. He didn't want his patients taken advantage of. Nor did he want their trust destroyed by a charlatan after he'd done so much to convince them to trust medicine. This woman could undo all his hard work over the last several years. This was a worrying development for not only his patients, but for himself as well, and it was horrid timing coming on the heels of his petition to the hospital board.

Ferris smiled through gritted teeth to hide his irritation. 'Perhaps I could come to your next meeting. I would like to meet this…herbalist.'

Chapter Five

He wasn't the only one who wanted to meet the herbalist. Ferris eyed the cramped apothecary's shop through the window. It was standing room only inside and this was as close as he was going to get for now. Although it did appear that the gathering was beginning to break up. Women were moving about and a few began to trickle out into the street with excited chatter.

It was hard not to eavesdrop as he waited for a chance to enter the shop, nor was it hard to notice the little jars the women twisted lids off of and held up to their noses for long, deep inhalations before replacing the lids and slipping them into pockets like precious treasures. One woman held a thin linen bag tied with a sage green ribbon to her nose before passing it to a friend to smell. The colour of the ribbon called to mind too readily his elusive Miss Peverett, who'd been in his arms one moment and gone the next. Even after the three weeks since the ball, she was still on his mind.

He blamed himself, of course. He'd frightened her

off, moved too boldly, urged to such actions by a rare moment of uncharacteristic emotion. It had been ages since he'd felt such an immediate connection to another person and the experience had been overwhelming. He must have been hungrier for companionship than he'd thought to have opened himself so completely, to have allowed himself to feel that way again.

He'd acted rashly and it had cost him. He might even now be squiring her about town, enjoying conversation with her, if it had been otherwise. He had toyed with the idea of tracking her down through her sister at the Harley Street hospital, but that smacked of desperation. He would not embarrass her by stalking her. Ha! As if he had time for such pursuits. He had a case to make to the board of governors, a cause to promote and a herbalist to take to task for passing herself off as a legitimate healer.

A pair of women giggled as they passed, too absorbed in their recent purchases to notice him even though he tipped his hat. 'She's a wonder, she is! She knows everything. I bet she knows how to prevent a babe.' The woman gave her companion a sly look, her hand on her stomach. 'What I wouldn't give not to be popping one out every year.'

The comment riveted Ferris's attention. It was nearly as dangerous as Mrs Fulton's mushroom comment yesterday. Fabulous. A female herbalist was on the loose empowering women to self-diagnose and take abortifacients. There were other comments, too, like the woman who had claimed to a friend they needn't worry about affording a doctor now that they could do it themselves.

That did it. He needed to confront this woman. What she was doing was dangerous and misleading. It was people like her who gave the profession a bad name. He needed to do this for these women's own good. He recognised far too many of them as patients who'd sought out his help before, although today they hardly noticed him. Ferris forged towards the door, the stream of exiting women having slowed. Mrs Fulton came through just as he reached the entrance.

'My dear Dr Tresham, you came after all.' She smiled kindly. 'Come with me, I'll introduce you. Our Lady Grey is just packing up. What a turnout we had today. Isn't it exciting? We're becoming doctors like you.'

Hardly. The idea was nearly insulting, but they didn't know the difference and he couldn't bring himself to ruin Mrs Fulton's excitement. She led him to the counter where a woman stood with her back to him, the hood of a grey cloak pulled up over her head as she packed her basket. She appeared quite ordinary. Without Mrs Fulton, he might have missed her. She might have walked past him and he would have been none the wiser.

'Miss, I've someone I'd like to introduce you to.' Mrs Fulton touched the woman on the arm, all easy familiarity with this newcomer; a familiarity, Ferris noted, that had taken him quite a while to earn from his patients. Envy pricked at him before he could dismiss it. He wasn't supposed to be his patients' friend. What mattered was that he was competent and reliable.

'It would be a pleasure, Mrs Fulton, to meet one of your acquaintances.' The woman's friendly voice froze Ferris. He knew that open, easy tone, or was his mind playing tricks? It couldn't possibly be... The woman's hands went to her hood, drawing it back as she turned to greet him, revealing coppery curls and sharp green eyes. His heart plummeted.

Dear God, it was *her*, the woman who'd made him feel alive, who'd awakened old dreams again and had inspired new ones. He might not have purchased his wagon without Miss Peverett's encouragement. How was it possible that the same woman who'd motivated him was the herbalist encouraging the sacrilege of empowering the uneducated to self-diagnose, the person who was undermining his efforts to establish a mobile health clinic? How could the world be so cruel?

Abject betrayal roared loud in his ears. He was aware of Mrs Fulton making introductions while he madly grappled with the unfathomable depths of perfidy. All this time, he'd been yearning for her, feeling he'd found a soulmate, but it had been an illusion. His dream was in actuality a nightmare. His perceived kinship could be nothing further from the truth. She stood in *absolute* opposition to all he valued. What could an unlicensed herbalist have in common with a doctor?

This was why he'd eschewed emotional attachments after Cara's death. Love hurt, love disappointed. Love failed. Science and logic were the only truths a man could count on. Perhaps it had only been a matter of time before he was reminded of that yet again. A familiar cold hand closed around his heart as he found his voice, iced with derision to hide the betrayal he felt deep in his gut. 'So, you're the snake-oil woman.'

* * *

Snake-oil woman. The words paralysed her. It was
the most derogatory term one could use to describe
what she did, but she'd heard it before. What stunned
her was the man uttering the words. Whenever she had
allowed herself to fantasise about being reunited with
him, it was not like this, not as enemies. The man who
condemned her now was a man she'd allowed herself to
feel kinship with, a man whom she'd let herself believe
shared her values. That same man was now dismiss-
ing her as a charlatan and the betrayal was stultifying.

'For the record, I prefer the term "herbalist",' she corrected frostily when she found her words. The upward
arch of his dark brow suggested he didn't think there
was much of a difference between the two. Of course
not. She should not have expected otherwise. Men were
forever trying to fit her into their pigeonholes: mother,
Madonna, mistress, saint, spinster, witch, whore. It was
unfair that a woman might be only seven things when
a man could be anything.

Witch. That was the box he'd put her in. She could
see it in his eyes. Her instincts had been right the night
of the ball, after all, once she'd got past being bowled
over by him. It was a good thing she'd run when she
had the chance. Only there was no running now. She
was pinned beneath the hard blue of his condemning
stare. No matter, this was a fight she was prepared for.

It had only been a matter of time before a doctor
came poking around. If she'd learned anything as an
herbalist it was that confrontation was inevitable. Mrs
Fulton, sensing the tension between the two of them,

had taken herself discreetly off to confer with Mrs Burroughs. Anne had the field to herself. She would defend her craft, her heart *and* her ladies.

Her ladies. She'd become protective of them in the time she'd been here. She knew their names, their families, their situations and their secrets. They'd shared the most intimate details of their lives with her. She was touched by their trust and she was determined to prove worthy of it. As such, she was immediately on the defensive at the thought of *any* doctor invading this feminine space, but this one especially. She'd felt an unmistakable connection with him. She'd thought he shared her beliefs. Anne tamped down hard on the hurt ricocheting through her. Her emotions would only hinder her here. She needed to think efficiently, logically. She could tend her emotions later.

Dr Tresham nodded towards the table holding products she'd not packed up yet. 'May I?' He was testing her.

'Please, help yourself,' she said stiffly, aware that she could only accede if she didn't want to fail that test. To deny him the chance to look at her work would make her appear suspicious, which was no doubt what he wanted or expected. Besides, she had nothing to hide. Her products were pure and reliable when used properly.

He selected an amber vial and sniffed like a sommelier with a fine wine. He had the nose for it—a long, slim, elegantly masculine affair. She ruthlessly pushed aside thoughts about his handsomeness. Those thoughts had no place here. She didn't want to remember that her blood had warmed for him with something other than anger. His eyes were closed for maximum concentration as he inhaled. She recognised the gesture. She did that, too, when she needed to focus all her senses on a scent. But, no, that was yet another thing she didn't want to recognise. She wanted no reminders of any similarity between them. He was the enemy now.

He opened his eyes. 'Larkspur.' It was said definitively. He was not asking for clarification. 'And whisky,' he added with condemnation. She knew what he was thinking—that the medicine was meant to be an excuse to imbibe alcohol—but the thought was ridiculous in the extreme. This was a vial; it hardly contained enough alcohol content to get anyone tipsy, let alone addicted, even if alcohol had been the main ingredient.

'Only what is required for preparing the tincture,' Anne corrected. 'I'm not in the business of turning my clients into drunkards. The alcohol is hardly an ingredient of note. You have an astute nose if you can sniff out the barest whiff of alcohol.' Too bad that talented nose belonged to such an arrogant man.

He eyed her and reached for a salve. 'You'd be amazed at what I can sniff out.' There was a warning in that for her. She knew what he implied. He wouldn't find any of *that* scent here. He inhaled the salve and thought for a long moment. 'Chickweed, green walnuts and horse chestnuts,' he announced, although there was the faintest upward inflection on the last. Anne took a moment of irrational pride in having almost stumped him. The man knew his herbs. She'd be impressed if he wasn't here emanating suspicion. The conversation had become a duel between his pronouncements and her sharp retorts.

'Chickweed is good for skin irritations and rheumatisms, although angelica is beneficial for rheumatism as well.' Anne began to gather up the remaining samples, making it clear this was to be a *short* conversation.

'And the tincture of larkspur?' he quizzed.

'Head lice.' That should deflect him more permanently. At the least it should send a hand to his head in a reflexive scratch. 'It's quite popular with the mothers and effective.'

'As is a good shave and a scrub with carbolic soap.' Dr Tresham's hands remained fixed at his sides.

'Larkspur is less abrasive. It's a gentler, but equally effective treatment,' Anne countered. She covered the basket and put it on her arm, wanting to be done with this conversation.

'You mean alternative.' Tresham's eyes narrowed in objection to her use of the word treatment. Ah, this was the true crux of his argument. He didn't object to herbs unless they were used in lieu of 'real medicine', no doubt supplied by 'real doctors'. Men.

'I do *not* mean alternative. The word assumes it is a secondary remedy, something that is lesser than the preferred option, when it's not secondary at all.' Anne refused to relent, refused to apologise for the sharpness of her tone. She was swamped with disappointment and anger. He was like all the rest, too set on his own knowledge and degrees to consider anyone else's less traditional education.

'Larkspur is dangerous, though,' he pressed. 'It's

considered too potent to be consumed and its seeds are poisonous.' Again, there was that flash of knowledge. Most medical men she met preferred their chemistry to nature. But she could not let herself forget he wielded his knowledge like a blade by which to cut her down.

'Well, thank goodness the tincture is for hair and not stomachs, then,' Anne shot back, but Tresham wasn't ready to concede.

'Still, if someone, say a child, were to get a hold of this tincture and drink it, the results would be disastrous.'

'As it would be for drinking any inappropriate medicine and just as unlikely to occur.' Anne made to push past him. She didn't have to justify herself to him. 'You'll have to excuse me. I need to go.' She had a hundred things to do once she got back to her rooms. There were roots to pound, notes to record, this unpleasant encounter to forget.

Tresham stepped in front of her. 'Perhaps we might continue this conversation elsewhere? There's a tea shop across the street.' He had audacity in spades, or was that simply just more arrogance? Did he really think she'd sit down to tea with a man who insulted her?

'I must decline. I am not in the habit of keeping company with a man who condemns me as a charlatan.' Her tone was decisive, drawing a verbal line in the shifting sands of understanding between them. She would not allow him to attack her integrity and get away with it.

'And *I* am not in the habit of allowing someone I am not familiar with to treat my patients.' *Not familiar with.* He dismissed her so easily, as if the ball had never happened, as if they'd never kissed, never burned for one another. Oh, she'd had a narrow escape indeed. 'These ladies you've been selling to are *my* patients. I need assurances of their welfare, and we need to move our discussion so that Mrs Burroughs can get on with her day.'

His patients? How territorial. She could argue with that, but she couldn't argue with the latter. Mrs Burroughs was looking decidedly nervous that she wouldn't be gone before Mr Burroughs showed up, and this conversation was not finished. There were things to be settled between them and Anne had a perverse sense of curiosity that begged to be satisfied. How could she have been so wrong about him? Surely, after Robert, her instincts were better honed. It posed the question— who was the real Dr Tresham? The man she'd met at the ball, or the man who challenged her now? If she wanted answers, she had to accept his invitation.

Chapter Six

'It's to be interrogation by tea, is it?' Anne speared Tresham with a knife-sharp look as he held her chair out in the tea shop. It would take more than good manners before she forgot he'd called her a snake-oil woman.

Dr Tresham took his seat and made no apologies for his intentions. 'It is my business to know what is going on with my patients. When they don't come for their usual medicines and check-ups, one wonders what game is afoot, and it seems the current game is you.' The implication was clear. There'd been 'games' before and he'd been victorious against them. They were gone and he was still here. He was warning her she should not expect it to go differently for her.

He gave her one of his stern blue-eyed looks. 'I will not have a charlatan peddling sweet-smelling salves and potent potions for pennies while undermining the trust in scientific medicine I've taken years to establish.'

Anne matched him with a stern stare of her own. She could be equally as affronted. 'I must take issue with your choice of terms, Dr Tresham. In the short time we've been together today, you've insulted me *and* my profession, referred to herbology as akin to snake-oil elixirs and myself as a charlatan. Those terms offend me deeply. If my gender were other than it is, I think you would not dare use those terms at all, knowing full well a *man* would be within his rights to call you out. As a woman, I have no recourse but to sit here and be maligned.'

Except that she did have a choice. She could leave. It would be at the expense of getting her answers, though, or maybe she already had them. Maybe sitting here just prolonged the inevitable conclusion: Dr Tresham was no different from other men, no different from Robert. Anne gathered her basket and rose, her tone edged with irritation at him for not being different and at herself for thinking he could be. She'd been foolish to have hoped for more. 'Good day, Dr Tresham. It seems I don't have to sit here, after all.'

A look of surprise crossed his fine features as he registered she would actually walk out. His hand reached for her, sending a jolt of awareness down her arm. It was the first time he'd touched her since the ball and the warmth of the old connection surged, unwanted. She did not want to be reminded of other touches, other reactions. Something flickered in his eyes. Perhaps he didn't want to be reminded either.

'Please, sit down. I only seek to better understand what you hope to accomplish here.'

She did not want to give him the satisfaction of obeying. The immediate gratification of walking out warred with the more practical choice of staying and winning her argument. Here was a chance to perhaps win him over. Marching out would make an enemy of him, and that would complicate her work should he choose to overtly oppose her. Although, lingering in his presence complicated her emotions instead and to no purpose. It was clear now they could not be soulmates—they were different ends of the spectrum, *not* two peas in a pod.

His interest in her today was vastly different from the interest he'd shown at the ball. That night, he'd been interested in *her*. Today, he sought to protect his patients from her. She'd become the enemy, not a woman he was interested in as a man. His attention now extended solely to making her leave his neighbourhood. Anne sat as decorously as possible, aware they'd drawn the stares of other customers.

'Thank you.' His tones were quiet as he refilled her cup with fresh, hot tea, a strong Assam. 'Now, why don't you tell me about yourself? I only know your name and that you take your tea with a bit of milk.' A brief smile took his mouth. For a moment, there was a hint of the man she'd met at the ball, gallant and observant. Kind. Not the hard man who'd confronted her at the apothecary.

'You know more than that.' Her tone held an accusatory edge. Had he really seen so little of her the night of the ball that he was willing to believe the worst of her now? 'You know I'm the third child of five, the daughter of a doctor from Hertfordshire.' She ticked the facts off her fingers, still prickly and refusing to be softened by his attention to the details of her tea.

Tresham interrupted. 'Those are not the type of things I want to know.' He leaned forward and lowered his voice to a fierce growl. 'I want to know what you're doing *here*.' How different those low tones were from the ones he'd used in the gallery right before he'd kissed her.

'I am here to help people learn to care for themselves with natural remedies.' She was boldly defiant in her answer. She was having success with her work at last and she would not let this man steal that from her.

'Those are dangerous goals, Miss Peverett. Self-education has consequences,' he said when she'd finished. She knew he included her in the mention of self-education. She lacked his fancy degree. Anne bristled at his judgement, his hypocrisy doubly hurtful. At the ball, Dr Tresham had spoken against hypocrites. It only deepened her sense of betrayal that he was one of them in his own way.

Tresham wasn't done yet. 'People running around self-diagnosing and dosing for whatever malady they perceive they have, or going out to the heaths to pick plants on their own, invites trouble. Just recently, Mrs Fulton was telling me about mushrooms. I had horrid images of her picking them at random, believing any mushroom would do. It's a lesson I'd rather not see her learn at the expense of losing a family member. Not everyone can be a doctor, Miss Peverett. There are reasons for that.'

It was an unmistakably personal jab. Not everyone could be a doctor, especially not *her*. She was all too aware of the 'reasons' why. Anne waited until he had taken a sip of hot Assam before she made her reply. 'Penises, Dr Tresham. The reason for that is penises.'

'I beg your pardon?' Tresham struggled to swallow his tea with any amount of aplomb sans choking.

Anne leaned across the table and explained with deliberate slowness, 'The reason everyone can't be a doctor is because doctors can only be male. The Hippocratic oath is nonsense.'

Oh, that got to him, a direct hit at last. He stared at her, his gaze scalding. She could read his thoughts behind furious blue eyes. How dare she sit there and call the oath he revered and lived by a piece of nonsense?

His voice was heated with barely leashed fury when he spoke. 'Now, let *me* explain to *you*, Miss Peverett. Doctors are trained. They undergo years of study in order to diagnose illnesses and prescribe remedies. *We* go to university, *we* study all our lives. Your father is a doctor, surely you know this. *Our* learning doesn't end with a diploma. It goes beyond that as we must stay up to date on all the new advancements. We have degrees, we have professional organisations so that we may devote ourselves to the lifelong pursuit of knowledge in our field.'

We. Our. He made the in-grouping distinction abundantly clear. How like a man to cloak himself in such exclusionary protections. Anne was boiling. 'Is this about your patients or about your own ego, Dr Tresham? You can't bear the thought of not being the gatekeeper, of not determining who gets what knowledge, of not being able to tell people what to do, of not being able to play God with other people's lives.'

She watched his jaw work, his voice low and dangerous. 'If you knew me at all, miss, you would know how utterly wrong you are.' He sat back in his chair and placed his napkin on the table, signalling he was done with this impertinent usurper who encouraged recklessness in the form of people picking plants and treating themselves. He made a show of checking his pocket watch. 'If you'll excuse me, I have an appointment.'

Anne rose with him. 'You were the one who wanted to know me. It's up to you to decide when the interrogation—I mean the interview—is over. Do you know enough?'

'I know you're here,' Tresham growled. 'I know you're a danger to my patients.'

Dangerous! How dare he! 'If *you* knew anything about *me*, you would know that's not the case.' Therein lay the truth. They were not kindred spirits. The supposed similarity that had called to them that one magical night was an illusion. Beneath the surface, they were polar opposites. Despite that reality, Anne couldn't shake the sensation that for better or worse, she'd never met a man quite like him, and it left her reeling. He wasn't just dangerous to her work. He was dangerous to *her*.

Chapter Seven

'I've never met a more arrogant man. He practically suggested I *leave* as if *he* had ownership of the neighbourhood and could decide who came and went.' Anne wielded her pestle with an obliterating ferocity that reduced her roots to a fine powder. It was one way to vent her frustration.

She glanced at Thea, who sat beside the fire in their rented rooms, pretending to read. Anne didn't think the pages had turned in the last half hour. Anne pushed a strand of hair out of her face. 'No, I take that back, Thea. He did not *suggest* anything. That would imply some subtlety.' She went back to pulverising with her pestle. 'Did I mention he was arrogant?'

'About five times.' Her sister set her book aside, giving up on the pretence. Thea was distracted tonight and not because of her tirade about the doctor.

Anne finished with the roots. In her frustration, she'd ground far more than she needed. She gathered her things and went to sit beside Thea. 'I'm sorry. Here

I am going on about Dr Tresham and you're thinking about William.' Anne placed the work basket between them, a subtle invitation for Thea to join her in filling linen bags. When one was worried, having something to do with one's hands often helped.

'William will be there now. It's been three weeks since he left and the journey itself only takes about two.' 'There' being the Danubian principalities. *Where* their brother was exactly they didn't know. He could be in Constantinople, in the Dardanelles or the Black Sea with the British Navy, or any number of places they hadn't even known existed this time last year. Hopefully, he would write soon.

Anne worried for her brother, too, but he was more than just a brother to Thea. He was her twin, and they'd not been apart like this ever except for the years when William had studied medicine at university. Still, as Thea liked to put it, going to university and going to war were two very different things. One could come home from university whenever one liked. The military wasn't as lenient or as safe. But William had insisted he felt compelled to serve as a military doctor and do his part to protect British troops abroad. So, William had gone to war and Thea and Anne had come to London, each with their own dreams and intentions.

'How was the hospital today?' Anne asked, tying a length of green ribbon around a linen sack of hickory root. Thea always loved to talk about the governess hospital.

Thea reached for a bag to fill. 'I *do* enjoy the work, and Florence has such incredible insights into the role of cleanliness and one's environment when it comes to health and wellness. It seems to me that she's likely right. Our patients are thriving and it's the cleanest hospital I've ever seen.' Thea gave her a smile. 'I *am* glad I took Florence's invitation to come to London and work.' Thea had struck up a correspondence with Florence two years ago over some mutual medical interests, and their professional friendship had grown from there, resulting in the invitation to work at the hospital.

'But?' Anne prompted, hearing the unspoken caveat in her sister's tone.

Thea put down the bag and gave Anne an honest gaze of longing. 'But it's not enough. There should be more for me to do than care for retired governesses. I'm a horrible person for saying it, for thinking the work isn't noble. Helping another person no matter their station is always noble.' Thea shook her dark head. 'But I want more. I've trained for more. I can do more. Florence feels the same way.' She let out a long sigh. 'We'd hoped to go to the Crimea, but the military took no nurses. I don't know how they'll manage. It seems the height of foolishness to set off for war with only doctors and surgeons. They'll be short-handed. They always are.' The strength of her gaze wavered. Instinctively, Anne reached for Thea's hand.

'I wanted to go with him so badly, Anne. He'll be alone for Christmas,' Thea confessed with a tremble in her voice. 'I could help. I could protect him. You know how William is, always the first to rush in. He'll get himself shot, and if he did, at least I'd be there to care for him.'

'William will be fine,' Anne assured her. It wasn't often that Thea's confidence and strength showed a chink. Sometimes it was hard to remember Thea was human like the rest of them, so rarely did it happen. Growing up, Anne had admired her older sister and had done her best to emulate her. There wasn't a problem Thea couldn't solve, a circumstance she couldn't handle. Thea was competence personified. Anne could only imagine how the current situation must gall her. There was simply nothing Thea could do about it. It was not unlike her own situation, both of them tethered to the limits society placed on women.

'Perhaps the army will change its mind once they see the need,' Anne suggested optimistically. In reality, there was as little chance of that as there was of Dr Tresham changing his mind about her. Both were so set in their ways.

'This wouldn't be a problem if I was a man,' Thea groused. 'I could have gone. I would have had my degree, too. William and I could have graduated together. Wouldn't Papa have been proud? His two *sons*, both doctors.' But Dr Albert Peverett had been blessed with one son and four daughters instead.

'Gender has never stopped Mama and Papa from training us to be the best healers possible according to our talents and interests,' Anne gently reminded her, but she couldn't ignore the echoes of her conversation earlier today with Dr Tresham coming back in Thea's own arguments.

There are reasons not everyone can be a doctor.

'It's the unfairness of it all that I don't like.' Thea returned to work, tying a ribbon around a linen bag. 'William got to go to medical school and I had to stay home.'

'You got to study side by side with Papa, the finest doctor there is,' Anne argued. She gave her sister a sly smile. 'I remember the day you delivered Mrs Putnam's baby. You were so proud and so was Papa. I also remember the day you stitched up Henry Latimer because Papa was away and Henry had cut open his hand with a hunting knife.' Thea had taken charge, ordering hot water and bandages, whisky and needle and thread as if she'd known what she was doing. Of course, she *had* known what she was doing. Thanks to Thea, Henry Latimer had recovered full use of his hand. 'You are as good as any man,' Anne said confidently. 'If not better than most.'

'But I don't have a diploma to prove it.' Thea was refusing to be mollified tonight. 'Because of that, I have to stay home.' She relented for a moment. 'Do you think that makes me ungrateful or prideful?' Those were two of the three greatest sins according to their father. Peveretts were raised to be grateful and humble, using their station and education to help others, not to glorify themselves. What would arrogant Dr Tresham think about *that*? The man at the ball would have agreed, but not the man who'd interrogated her over tea.

'No, dear Thea, it doesn't. I was saying much the same thing to Dr Tresham this afternoon. Why should men hold all the power? Why should they be the gatekeepers to wisdom when it comes to healthcare? There's no rationale for it.'

'Yet I don't think those limitations make Dr Tresham himself a bad man,' Thea prompted with a sly look. 'He's making a name for himself with his work with soldiers after they return from war. Florence said he's a regular fixture at the soldiers' hospital in Chelsea.' She shrugged as she shared the news, but the gesture couldn't hide what Thea had done. She'd made enquiries.

'I don't care what he does. He's arrogant and he's no different to other men,' Anne said staunchly, hoping to quell any further quizzing.

'No different than Robert, you mean?' Thea corrected with a scolding purse of her lips.

'Tell me I'm wrong,' Anne challenged. Even after a year, Robert was still a difficult topic to discuss. 'He taught me a very important lesson—that even well-intentioned men are blind to a woman's potential beyond being a wife and mother. I thought he was different and he wasn't. I almost built a life with him based on lies. All the hurt would be in vain if I forgot that.' She tied another bag, feeling a sense of satisfaction at the mounting supplies in the work basket. They would help replenish her depleted stock. 'My work here and at home is what matters, Thea. Robert never understood that, not even when I thought he did.' That was what had hurt so much, the realisation that Robert had never grasped the fundamental core of her, the need to serve and to heal.

Healing was a chance to change lives. For those whom London overlooked, she hoped she could make a small and lasting difference with her herbs and roots. She would not be deterred by the Roberts of the world who thought she had no place, or the Dr Treshams who thought her careless. Tresham didn't respect her. He thought she was reckless in teaching people to self-diagnose and medicate, that she was a threat to people's well-being when nothing could be further from the truth. The only thing she threatened was his male ego.

'She's a threat to my entire project,' Ferris lamented to Frederick over quiet brandies before the fire at Cowden House. They had the place to themselves tonight. Helena and the children had left that morning with the Duke and Duchess to prepare for the upcoming Christmas at Bramble, the Cowden family seat in Sussex. Frederick would follow later once the current session of Parliament adjourned.

Frederick gave him a grimace that said he thought his brother was exaggerating. 'If you're so worried about her, show her to be a fraud and be done with it. Your patients will come back when they realise what she is.'

'That's just it. I don't think she is one.' He'd looked up her father when he'd got home. Dr Peverett was a well-respected physician. He presented papers regularly, but preferred living in the country. 'She's not wrong in her instruction, just misguided in her application.' Extraordinarily misguided. 'She wants people to self-diagnose and medicate, people who are not best equipped to do that.' They loved her, too. He'd seen first-hand the way the women had flocked to her today. She'd get his numbers up for the hospital, Ferris thought begrudgingly. After all, she was the reason those numbers were down at present. Perhaps instead of fighting with her, he ought to join her. His mind paused on what had been intended as a sarcastic idea. Maybe he ought to take the idea more seriously.

'What are you thinking?' Frederick broke into his thoughts. 'You were gone there for a moment.'

Ferris tried the idea out. 'I was thinking that if I can't fight her, I should join her, or rather, I should ask her to join me.'

'But?' Frederick prompted, and Ferris leaned forward, elbows on his knees as he worked through the dilemma.

'It's the ethics of it. I don't believe what she is doing is sound, but if I join forces with her I am in essence condoning her message. It could make things difficult if the hospital found out.' Although there was little chance of that. The hospital board at St Erasmus didn't rub elbows with the people of Webber Street, and it only need be for a short time. Once he had his numbers and his mobile clinics, he could cut ties with her.

Frederick was thoughtful before replying, 'Perhaps the ends would justify the means. Making war with her gains you very little and could jeopardise your project. But making peace gets you the numbers you need. In addition, you could keep an eye on her. You win all around.'

'I wish it were that simple.' Ferris sighed and leaned back into his chair. 'There's also the issue of whether she'll take my offer after today.' He paused and cast about for the right phrasing. 'We were not kind to one another. After today's fireworks at the tea shop, the odds seem small she'd want to join forces. I called her a snake-oil woman and she called me arrogant, a God-player who wants to control other people's lives.'

There was more to it than that, though. The words wouldn't have hurt so badly if he hadn't liked her. He'd felt utterly betrayed when he'd seen her in the shop. The shock had ripped through him with a visceral intensity that had only grown as she cut him down to size with her categories: arrogant, self-serving, controlling—all the things he prided himself on not being, all the things the oaths he held dear counselled against. It had stung and he'd struck back in full fury.

Even that defence had not been enough protection. From the moment she turned around and revealed herself, a piece of him had been lost just as it had been at the ball. He was unmistakably attracted to her even as she raged at him and threatened his project. That part of him recoiled at the thought of bringing her down. His mind's eye could see her as she'd been today, so full of righteous indignation as she railed at him, those green-flecked tiger eyes filled with fiery intelligence. She'd not shown him any quarter. Her passion, in all its forms, made her beautiful. Most of all, it made her *alive*, unlike the young women his mother was constantly parading in front of him. He did not want to destroy that. Quite the opposite—he wanted to preserve it, just not at the expense of the things he'd worked so hard for.

Did he dare invite her into his work? If he did, what else might he invite her into? It could be a very dangerous proposition on several fronts. If he wasn't careful, he'd end up hurt, personally and professionally. He'd promised himself years ago he'd not open himself up to that sort of hurt, that sort of loss, after Cara died. He'd stuck to that promise faithfully and he'd been safe, even if life had taken on a certain flatness to it, all his energy spent on work, on making better lives for others. Until now. The idea of working with Miss Peverett found an empty corner of his mind and began to set up house.

The brothers sat before the fire, each lost in their own thoughts. What a pair they were tonight, Ferris thought, watching the firelight dance in the facets of his tumbler. He with his worries over his project and his brother, whose thoughts were quite obviously with his family over the miles between London and home. 'You're missing them already,' Ferris mused.

'The house is too quiet.' Frederick chuckled. 'One gets used to the constant noise of four boys. Sometimes I think I'd give anything for just one sane moment of peace and quiet and then, when I get it, I don't want it. All I want is the noise back. I never want my life to be that quiet again.'

It was on the tip of Ferris's tongue to offer the automatic assurance that it wouldn't be, but something held him back. More than temporary loneliness was plaguing Frederick tonight. 'Do you think it could be quiet again, Frederick?' he asked softly.

Frederick gave him a strong look full of blunt honesty. 'You're a doctor. You *know* it could be. Titles and money don't protect any of us from nature, from disease, disaster, death. Titles are fictions we make up to feel better about ourselves, but a body is just a body, whether it belongs to a duke or not.'

Ferris studied his brandy. 'Is this about Fortis? Are

you worried about where he is?' The Danube was heating up. War in the Crimea was inevitable now and Fortis would be in the thick of it. But Fortis had seen action before in India and other far reaches of the Empire. Their brother knew how to handle himself.

'Yes,' Frederick confessed. 'Our little brother is off to war again. I know Mother and Father are worried. I want you to come to Bramble for Christmas, Ferris. I think our parents need to be surrounded by the family this year. I think Avaline needs it, too.' Avaline was Fortis's wife, a pretty, young woman whose estate abutted Bramble. Fortis had married her and promptly left her. She hadn't seen her husband since and that was nearly six, or was it seven, years ago? Ferris couldn't understand how Fortis could treat a marriage in such a cavalier fashion when Frederick worshipped his, when once upon a time, Ferris would have, too. There'd been nothing he'd wanted as much as a life with Cara, serving others.

'You know I can't do that.' Usually he spent Christmas Eve and Christmas Day in town, making it bearable for those less fortunate who could not escape the yellow fog and perpetual winter of their lives. As he liked to remind people, medical needs and babies didn't run on a calendar.

'Can't come or won't come?' His answer didn't suit Frederick. 'This is about Cara, isn't it? She's been dead for years, Ferris. Don't let her ghost keep you from coming home.'

It would always be about Cara. He'd loved her, he'd lost her. She'd been a part of his childhood, a part of growing up at Bramble, of coming into adulthood, of planning for the future, and then it had been taken from him. He wasn't sure he could face it. 'The last happy Christmas I had at Bramble was with Cara,' Ferris said quietly. 'We celebrated our engagement.'

'I remember.' Frederick nodded with a hint of a smile. 'Every year, Mother still puts out the lacework Cara made for her. It lays on the piano.' Cara had loved the piano at Bramble. She'd played carols every Christmas while they sang.

'I can't, Frederick.' Ferris shook his head. How could he be there, seeing her everywhere, and knowing she was nowhere? Bramble at Christmas without Cara would hurt too much.

'Think about it, Ferris. You can't stay away for ever and our parents won't be here for ever, either,' Frederick said sternly before softening. 'Bramble at Christmas is different now with the boys running around. There are children in the halls again like when we were growing up.'

'I'll think about it,' Ferris offered. The idea of watching his nephews on Christmas morning was tempting, and Frederick made a good point about his parents. Of course, he knew his brother's agenda. Frederick hoped it would help him move forward, but Ferris feared it would only serve to resurrect the past.

It wasn't territory he was eager to revisit any more than he was eager to revisit today's altercation with Miss Peverett. He wouldn't apologise for feeling as he did about her position on self-diagnosis, but perhaps he could make amends for how he'd gone about voicing his disagreement. He hoped that might be enough to win her over—his project depended on it.

Chapter Eight

He was *here*. Inside the Burroughs's apothecary shop. Anne paused on the street in front of the shop window. She would know those broad shoulders anywhere, even with his back turned to her. Anne paused, taking a moment to gather herself and keep her temper in check. What could he possibly have to say after yesterday's altercation? Had he come to lay claim to what he clearly thought of as *his* territory? Or worse, had he come to lay waste to her reputation?

She couldn't allow that. Another woman might choose to return later, but Anne would not be so intimidated. She would go in and conduct her business as planned. Sally was expecting her to drop off more lavender and angelica root today. She had as much right to be there as Dr Tresham did. She wasn't going to let the harsh words and limited opinions of an arrogant man deter her from her errands. Neither was she going to let him cast aspersions on her reputation without being there to defend herself. He'd said nothing she hadn't heard before. It was only that things had started better with him than they usually did with men, which made the devolution to those harsh words more hurtful.

Anne set the bell over the door jingling, causing Mrs Burroughs to look up from her conversation with Dr Tresham. Mrs Burroughs waved her over. 'There you are. I was just telling Dr Tresham I expected you today. He was asking after you.' Mrs Burroughs smiled—she did that a lot more these days. She was a far happier woman than the grim-faced one who had greeted her weeks ago. The angelica root must be working on her husband's drinking. The apothecary looked better, too. The little shop seemed brighter, the windows cleaner, the shelves fuller, the place busier with customer traffic.

'He was?' Anne asked the question of Mrs Burroughs instead of Tresham, ignoring him entirely as she sat her basket down on the counter beside Tresham's worn leather bag. She set out the amber vials of lavender. 'These will have to last a bit until I can figure out how to put up another batch,' she told Mrs Burroughs. 'I can pound roots in my rooms, but distilling oils and tinctures requires time and more sophistication than my rooms offer.' She'd have to go home to Hertfordshire to make more and she was loath to leave London just when she was having success. She was even more loath to leave and give Dr Tresham the impression that she'd ceded the field to him.

'Yes, Miss Peverett, I was asking after you because I had a proposition for you.' Dr Tresham turned to face her, refusing to let her talk about him as if he weren't present.

'A proposition? That sounds wicked indeed, Dr Tresham.' She flashed him an arch look, more aware of his nearness than she'd like to be.

He's arrogant. Arrogance is not handsome in any guise, she told herself even as another reminder came from the depths of other memories. *He cares for the poor and kisses as if he had all the time in the world to explore your mouth. Behind that arrogance is a man who shares your goals, if not your methods.*

No. She pushed the thought away. She'd believed the best of a man before and it had nearly cost her freedom. She could not open herself up like that again only to be disappointed.

'I would appreciate the chance to speak with you after you finish your business with Mrs Burroughs, if you could spare me a few moments?' He made her a small bow and took himself off to browse the shelves under the guise of giving her privacy to conduct her transaction. It was politely done. He was *asking* for permission to talk with her instead of assuming he had the right or, worse, outright interrupting. Today, he was more like the man she'd met at the ball. Calm, kind. *Dangerous.* She could argue with ferocious prejudice. Arguing with politeness was far more difficult, nearly as difficult as resisting her own curiosity. What could he possibly want with her?

She finished with Mrs Burroughs and approached Dr Tresham with wariness. They'd parted on poor terms, after all, and his opinion of her had been quite clear. 'Dr Tresham, I find I'm curious to hear your proposition. I did not think we had anything left to say to one another.' She kept her tone formal, making it obvious there was distance between them after yesterday.

'I looked your father up last night in the annals. He's well respected,' Tresham said. She was alert now for different reasons. She'd not expected this.

'Is this the beginnings of an apology, Dr Tresham? Because if it is, it's going very poorly.' It was also very oblique. How like a man to take shelter in another man's ethos. She wanted acceptance on her own merits, not her father's.

His eyes were a steely blue as he held her gaze and the faintest quirk of a smile twitched on unrelenting lips. 'No, it absolutely is not. An apology would suggest I was wrong in some regard and I am most assuredly not wrong, not yet at least.'

'Oh, yes, heaven forbid you be wrong,' Anne said smartly. It sounded more like a justification of his opinion. 'I have no wish to rehash yesterday.'

'Neither do I. May I finish, Miss Peverett?' Her frosty tone had not frozen him. 'It did occur to me that it is unfair to dismiss you without closer observation, Miss Peverett, simply because those who have come before you have failed to win my approbation.'

'The words "closer observation" sound a lot like "second chance",' Anne mused aloud. 'Who would need such a chance, I wonder? Me or you?' And for what purpose? She was not so easily beguiled into thinking his reconsideration was all about doing her a favour. Why would he offer such a thing? What did he need from her that would prompt him to approach her? He *was* working hard for this, coming to the shop, enquiring after her, putting on a display of fine manners now that he'd found her.

The door slammed open, the bell jangling wildly as a child burst in, his unruly arrival claiming all their attention. 'Mrs Burroughs, it's my ma! The baby's been coming since dawn and she's bad off.'

'It's Mrs Fitzsimmons,' they muttered simultaneously.

Tresham was already striding forward, bag in hand. 'I'll go to her at once, Davy.' He had a firm hand on the frightened child's shoulder, steadying him.

'I'm coming, too.' Anne fell into step beside him, snatching her basket off the counter as she passed. 'I didn't like how she looked yesterday at the seminar.' She berated herself silently for not having said something. She should have insisted the woman stay off her feet.

Tresham shot her a look. 'There's no need for both of us to go. I can handle this. She is *my* patient. She's been under my care for the entirety of this pregnancy.'

Anne entrenched. Did he really think he could handle this with only a single pair of hands? 'She has four children underfoot.' She'd gone with Thea to several country births where the best help she could offer was keeping people out of Thea's way so her sister could do her job unimpeded. And she'd be on hand for more significant help if that was needed as well. Already, Anne was running through the contents of her basket. There was the lavender, of course. It would be of use in calming, and there was the Nerium tincture, which might be useful if labour had been prolonged.

* * *

The Fitzsimmons lived two streets away and Anne was breathless, running to keep up with Tresham's long strides. She followed him up the steps and into the tiny rooms that belonged to the family. The two rooms were dim and dingy. The youngest girl had the toddler with her in a front room that did triple duty as a kitchen, parlour and sleeping quarters for the four children. The oldest girl was with their mother in the one bedroom.

Anne took immediate action, setting the worried children to work boiling a kettle of water over the fire and searching out spare linen. She doubted they'd eaten all day. She would see to that next, but first, the sick-room needed to be in order. Her father had taught them all a healer was only as good as their supplies and support.

Anne took the clean linen and fresh hot water into the bedroom. Tresham's coat was off, his sleeves rolled up over his elbows revealing strong forearms dusted with dark hair, and the room held the familiar medicinal scent of chlorine lime as Tresham laid out soap for washing in preparation for a clean, healthy birth. He nodded his thanks, a note of appreciation in his eyes, as she set the hot water down.

While Tresham washed, Anne turned her attention to the patient. Mrs Fitzsimmons lay on the bed, sweaty and exhausted. Anne went to her with a cool cloth, smiling reassurances. 'The children are doing beautifully in the other room. You're to be commended, they're so well behaved,' Anne complimented to ease the woman's mind, pleased to see the woman smile.

Tresham, hands cleaned, did a quick assessment of the labour. 'The baby hasn't turned, Mrs Fitzsimmons,' he explained in even, unpanicked tones. 'That's why your efforts haven't produced any results, which is for the best actually. Breech babies need assistance. We wouldn't have wanted this baby to come on its own. You were right to send Davy.' Gone was the arrogant man who had argued with her yesterday. This man was all compassion and assurance as he comforted the woman. 'I'll need you to relax as best you can and we'll see what we can do.'

Anne reached for her vial of lavender and tipped a few drops into the water, letting the sweet herbal scent of it fill the room, overriding the smell of chlorine lime. 'Breathe deep, Mrs Fitzsimmons. The lavender will help.' The new smell would at least give the woman something else to focus on.

Anne took the woman's hand and kept up a stream of chatter, telling her how well she was doing and how there'd be a beautiful baby to hold very soon. People needed hope in situations like this, a chance to see beyond the moment, a reason to keep going.

'We should see progress now,' Tresham offered optimistically, his efforts completed. Anne was impressed. His manner made it easy to believe this man with his confident reassurance. How could anything go wrong with Dr Ferris Tresham on duty?

But despite Dr Tresham having turned the child into a more favourable position and the presence of regular, exhausting contractions, the Fitzsimmons baby made no appearance as the afternoon passed into evening. Even Dr Tresham's confidence couldn't dispel the sense that things were quickly degenerating. Anne sensed Tresham might need a moment alone with Mrs Fitzsimmons. She excused herself before he was forced to ask for privacy. Asking for privacy in front of a patient often panicked the patient, who feared the request foreshadowed bad news.

She put soup on for the children's dinner and sat with them for a short while, assuring them all would be well. When she returned to the bedroom, she rooted through her basket for the Nerium tincture and hoped Tresham wouldn't be too stubborn to listen to her. 'Try this.' She came to stand quietly at Tresham's shoulder. 'It's Nerium. Use it externally. It should hasten the labour,' she instructed in low tones.

Now was not the time for him to stand on ceremony. Mrs Fitzsimmons was exhausted and worried as her hard labour approached twelve hours. Who knew how long the woman had been labouring unofficially before deciding to send for Dr Tresham? Babies often took a long time making their appearances, but Anne also knew dangerous exhaustion when she saw it.

Tresham's gaze lingered on her, an unspoken understanding passing between them, eyes speaking words that could not be said out loud.

This needs to work. We're down to last things here.

It will work. You need to trust me. You have no other suitable options left. She will die if you don't.

In this moment, they weren't adversaries—no longer the prideful physician and the herbalist from Hertfordshire, they were united in the common goal of safely delivering this baby. They were a team, working for a common good.

Tresham's hand closed around the vial and relief swept Anne. Trust was no small thing to give and she knew what it cost him to give it after the hot words that had passed between them. Trust had to be earned and she liked to think she'd earned a modicum of it from him today. If given the chance, she could earn more.

She took up her position at the woman's side, letting the woman take her hand in a bone-crushing grip as another contraction swept Mrs Fitzsimmons's tired body.

A half hour later, the sweet first cry of a baby filled the lavender-infused room as Mrs Fitzsimmons gave a final push. Tresham was swift and competent, holding the squalling, red infant up for the mother to see moments later.

'It's a boy, Mrs Fitzsimmons, and he's perfect,' Tresham announced with a beaming smile that transformed his stern face into joy as if this were his first delivery. He was striking in his dishevelment. The warm room had turned his wavy hair to dark, errant curls that stuck out at odd places, dislodged from perfection by hours of labour. Evening stubble shadowed his jaw and his shirt was wrinkled, but he stole Anne's breath as he worked, handsome, proud and reverent, as if the child he held was his own.

A child of his own. The thought did queer things to Anne's belly. What a father this incarnation of Ferris Tresham would make! She remembered how he'd stead-

ied Davy this afternoon, knowing instinctively the reassurance the worried boy had needed and *how* Davy
had needed it—a manly clench of the shoulder. He'd
not treated Davy as a child.

Tresham wrapped the newborn in clean linen and
brought him to his mother, his gaze resting softly on
both mother and child for a moment before turning
away to wash his hands and finish with the business
of delivery. In that moment, Anne saw his thoughts
exposed.

Tresham wanted children.

It begged a host of questions. Why didn't he have
them? She guessed him to be in his thirties, certainly
old enough for a family. It also begged the question of
why would a man who wanted children hold himself
apart from marriage? His comments at the ball suggested he was not interested in it.

Anne supposed she ought to pay more attention to
the babe after it had taken such effort to bring it into
the world, but her attentions kept sliding to Tresham
as he moved about the cramped bedroom, washing his
hands once more, washing instruments and tidying. He
was careful and fastidious. Her father would agree with
his choices. Hygiene was paramount in safe childbirth,
a realisation that had only gained significant purchase
over the last ten years. But that wasn't why she watched
him. Her mind was alive with one singular question:
Who was the real Ferris Tresham? The man who'd ruthlessly confronted her yesterday? The man she'd met at
the ball? The man who'd delivered this child?

Tresham had been a revelation this afternoon. Confident, competent and compassionate. Never once had he passed his own worry on to Mrs Fitzsimmons. Never once had he questioned her input, or her right to be there. This was the man she'd danced with at the charity ball, the man who'd made her blood thrum dangerously, who'd kissed her, who'd thought like her.

He came to stand with them, his chores completed. 'What shall we call him, Mrs Fitzsimmons?' He took the baby and held it in his arms as if it were the most natural thing in the world to rock a child. He should have a horde of them, Anne decided. But what did she know? She once thought she'd have a pack of them, too. She had believed she could have a family and her work until Robert had made her choose. She'd picked the greater good of serving others over the indulgence of a family of her own. Had Tresham, too, come to that conclusion? Was that the reason he'd not married? A man didn't need to make the choice, though. A man could have both, so why didn't he?

'We'll call him Thomas, after my husband's father.' Mrs Fitzsimmons smiled, weary and content.

'That's a good name,' Tresham said approvingly, handing the baby back to its mother. 'Put him to the breast as soon as possible, he'll be hungry. You've done well, Mrs Fitzsimmons. Mr Fitzsimmons will be pleased when he gets home tonight. I'll have the neighbour look in on you until then and I'll be by tomorrow to make sure all is still well, but I'm sure it will be.'

They gathered their things—Tresham his bag and she her basket—and stepped out into the November evening. Anne was conscious of his hand at her back

as he escorted her down the dark steps of the building and out on to the street—a street darker than she
was used to. Harley Street was well lit until midnight,
and she was home long before that. But here on Webber Street in the early evening, lamplight was sparse
as they made their way to a hack stand. Anne was glad
for his strong presence beside her. She would not have
felt safe otherwise.

Tresham helped her inside the rented hack and took
his seat, clearing his throat as the hack lurched into
motion. 'Might I offer you supper, Miss Peverett? We
could continue our discussion about my proposition.'

Ah, he hadn't forgotten, then. Her early wariness
began to creep back in, dimming the revelations of the
day and reminding her that the man she'd seen today
was also the one who'd challenged her work. It reminded
her, too, that her instincts weren't wrong. He definitely
wanted something if this was still on his mind after such
an eventful afternoon. Truth be told, her curiosity over
the proposition was still there as well, helped along by
what she'd observed this afternoon. She wasn't ready to
say goodnight to this conundrum of a man who had so
many faces. Which one was the real one? Her cautious
mind and her curious heart wanted to know.

Why does it matter? What do you hope to discover?
Do you dare trust your instincts after they failed so
miserably with Robert?

Just as she'd thought when she'd accepted the invitation to tea, she would never know if she didn't go.
That decided it.

'Yes,' Anne breathed before she could change her

mind. 'Dinner would be lovely. Do you have a place in mind?' London was littered with small restaurants and inns where a couple might find a dinner.

'At my practice on Cheyne Walk. Mrs Green, my housekeeper, will have a hot meal waiting. She will stay and act as chaperon, of course. I can send a messenger with a note for your sister, and I will see you home safely afterwards.' *This* was the thoughtful man she'd met at the ball, but in truth, he'd been thoughtful during the interrogation over tea as well, following all the rules of good manners. Even angry Ferris Tresham had been a gentleman.

'How can I refuse, Dr Tresham, when it seems you've thought of everything?' Anne smiled as an awkward silence settled between them. What were they now, after today? Certainly not enemies, not soulmates either, but somewhere in between. Perhaps they were two professionals, carefully feeling their way together? Or perhaps something more? She was aware of him in the silence of the hack. He smelled of lavender and chlorine lime, and beneath that lay the clean scent of his soap and sandalwood cologne.

'What a day, Miss Peverett,' he said, easing the little thrum of tension that permeated the small space. 'That's the exciting part of being a doctor. One never quite knows what the day will bring. There's always an adventure.' He chuckled and then sobered. 'Thank you, for coming and for your suggestions. The Nerium worked wonders. If not for it, things may have gone very differently.' He paused before adding, 'We made a good team today.'

It was probably the best olive branch she was going to receive—not an apology, but an admission. It did wake a niggling suspicion, though, as to what had prompted his change of heart. 'Doctor Tresham, you were quite adamant yesterday over tea that herbalists were unlicensed quacks. Yet, you accepted my advice and assistance today. Why was that?' Anne put the bold question to him. She had to know. It would tell her where she stood with him, his pretty compliment about being a good team aside. 'Did you believe my advice on the strength of my expertise or on the strength of my father's name? Or was it simply desperation?'

She felt his gaze on her and heard his resigned sigh in the dark. 'Miss Peverett, do you always specialise in asking impossible questions? You do understand there's no good way for me to answer that, especially when we're both operating on empty stomachs.'

Ah, that was answer enough. Anne stifled a sigh of disappointment. So, she hadn't earned his trust entirely. For all that he'd revealed about himself today, he still had his doubts about her. And she still had doubts about him. In the dark, Anne imagined she heard the olive branch crack as the hack arrived at Number Fourteen Cheyne Walk.

Chapter Nine

Ferris tried to see the clinic through Miss Peverett's eyes as he gave her the brief tour. Would she see a place of healing and hope, or just a converted house where the front parlour was a waiting room, where the adjoining doors that led to his exam room really only led to a transformed dining room?

'There are three rooms upstairs, two of which I can use for overnight patients should the need arise.' He finished the tour as they approached the back of the house and the smell of hot food.

'It's very impressive, Dr Tresham. You've made good use of the space, truly.' She'd been quiet on the tour, but her sharp eyes had taken everything in—from the locked glass-fronted cabinets with their bottles and equipment in the exam room to the little space he had set aside for his lab.

He wanted her to like it. It would go some way in swaying her towards his proposition. Originally, he'd hoped the space in general would impress her, but after her conversation today with Mrs Burroughs about needing workspace, an idea had occurred to him.

'There's one more room I'd like to show you before we eat. It's part of my proposition.' Ferris opened the door to what would normally have served as a lady's sitting room. He stepped back to allow her to enter first. 'The room gets good light in the morning and it's close to the kitchen. It's warm and clean.' He paused, holding the lamp up high so she could take it all in. 'A person could pound a lot of roots in here and the stove is close by for doing teas and distillations.'

Miss Peverett's alert gaze rested on him, consideration flickering in it. 'What are you suggesting, Dr Tresham?'

'I am offering you a place to work. I divined from your conversation with Mrs Burroughs today that you might be in need of one.'

Her gaze shifted to take in the room one last time before returning to him. 'You would just *give* me a space in your practice after calling me a charlatan? That smacks of suspicion, Dr Tresham.'

'Some might call it generosity,' Ferris corrected as they stepped out into the hall. He wasn't used to having gifts rejected, although he should have prepared himself for it given their pattern of mercurial conversations.

He shut the door behind them and ushered her towards the kitchen and Mrs Green's supper. Ferris served them both, ladling servings of hardy beef stew into bowls and cutting thick slices of Mrs Green's rosemary bread. He pulled the cork from a bottle of red wine that Frederick sent over with regularity and poured two glasses. It wasn't a fancy meal with four courses, but it was good food, hearty, healthy and practical. That pot of stew on the stove would feed him for three days and there'd likely still be enough for Mrs Green to take a pail of it home for her family.

'The food smells delicious, Mrs Green,' Miss Peverett complimented before the housekeeper took herself off to the front room to knit and take up her post as a nominal chaperon. 'The rosemary bread is especially good, very fresh. I have a recipe for an herb bread you might like to try. I can send it over.'

'Or you can bring the recipe with you when you set up your herbarium.' Ferris took advantage of the suggestion to steer the conversation back to his offer.

Miss Peverett eyed him over the rim of her goblet, assessing. She was always so alert. Was it only with him or had something happened that caused her to be suspicious in general? 'You're very sure that I'll take the offer. Some might call your gift a Trojan Horse. You've got something hiding inside, wrapped up in all this seeming "generosity", as you put it. Why play games, Dr Tresham? Just tell me what you want badly enough to give me a space in your practice when you think I'm a fraud.'

They were back to that awful question she'd asked on the way over and to the harsh words he had hurled at her in anger yesterday. He was regretting that profoundly now. He'd been reeling with betrayal, seeing nothing but dreams of his mobile clinics being jeopardised by a woman who was peddling potions, and he'd reacted defensively. But he had a chance tonight, with the day's success behind them, to put that to rights.

Ferris set down his napkin and fixed her with a stare. 'I trusted you with a woman's life today. That hardly suggests I think you are incapable. You misunderstood my concerns yesterday. My primary concern was the encouragement to self-diagnose and medicate. In that regard, you expect too much of these people. Most of them cannot read the instructions you leave.' He believed that still, no matter how capable she was.

'Perhaps *you* expect too little, or perhaps you don't *want* them to think for themselves? That would undercut your power.' She was less acerbic this evening, the comment thoughtfully posed.

'My *power*? The only power it undercuts is my ability to treat them at the right time instead of treating them too late, after they've delayed seeking help when it might be most useful.' Ferris buttered his bread in slow reflection, seeing himself for a moment from her position. 'You think I am pretentious, Miss Peverett. I would suggest that I am *protective*. I assure you, I do not revel in the chance to play God.' He knew doctors who did, and while he found comfort and order in the control science offered, he did not think it extended as far as to create a desire to be godlike.

'Tell me, Miss Peverett, do you label every man as arrogant who simply disagrees with you?' He watched her stop chewing, her thoughts assembling like troops behind her eyes. There it was again, that innate defensiveness. Miss Anne Peverett was always building her walls, always defending them with pointed barbs made all the sharper because of the insightful truths behind them. The wonder came again as to where and how she'd learned such truths. She was well beyond the age of London's debutantes, perhaps in her mid-twenties, but still quite young to have acquired such cynicism.

'Now who is asking questions for which there are no good answers?' she parried, taking another swallow of wine. She set her glass down with a decisiveness that signalled she'd come to a conclusion. 'All right, Dr Tresham. I'll take your room,' she said as if she were accepting a wager. 'I think it will suit us both. You want to keep an eye on me and I want to prove you wrong. I am not a reckless healer and these people are worthy of being empowered to manage their own health.'

Ferris felt a smile take his mouth. Of course she wanted to prove him wrong. Anne Peverett was as stubborn as he was. Tonight, her stubbornness suited him. He was halfway to getting his project back on track. It suited him in other ways, too, ways that had nothing to do with his mobile clinics and everything to do with simply enjoying a quiet dinner with this woman who'd helped him deliver a child today under difficult circumstances. Anne Peverett had been more than up to the challenge.

'There is something more, Miss Peverett. On your fine suggestion at the charity ball, I purchased a wagon and horse. Would you like to travel the neighbourhoods with me?' This way, he could keep an eye on her attempts at encouraging people to self-medicate and her clients could be his clients, their names in his ledger as proof to the hospital.

He'd managed to stun her. She was speechless for a long while, her gaze studying him. 'The offer is very... generous,' she said at last.

'I don't care if it's generous, Miss Peverett. Is it *tempting*?'

He wanted her to say yes, despite the voice inside whispering a warning, *You are tempting fate.*

She nodded, but her words were wary. 'Yes, it is.' She was still suspicious.

That voice inside was more insistent now. *As well she should be—you are concealing your true purpose from her.*

Ferris refilled their glasses, ignoring her suspicion and his twinge of conscience. 'A toast, then, to a new partnership.' The idea of having her here should not please him as much as it did, nor should the thought of his undisclosed agenda sit so poorly with him. He didn't like the feeling that he was misleading her.

Anne had summed up his offer correctly. He did want to keep an eye on her and she needed the space. There was just more that he'd omitted telling her. Perhaps the omission wouldn't matter in the long run. They both had what they wanted and people would be served by the arrangement. But the 'ends justifying the means' reasoning didn't quite assuage his conscience as well in practice as it had in theory.

'To teamwork,' Anne replied, clinking her glass against his.

'Now that's settled, tell me about the Nerium. It was an inspired choice. There was a space of time when I thought we might lose her.' He thought he detected a slight blush on her cheeks from the indirect compliment. He hoped so. He found he liked the idea that sharp, alert Anne Peverett had at least one soft spot.

'Oleander works best, but my mother and I only grow Nerium. It's what the soil in the south of England will tolerate. But I have hopes some day of obtaining oleander from Australia and growing it in a conservatory.' She smiled suddenly, her eyes sparking as she leaned across the table. Some of the sharpness faded from her. 'In fact, I have grand hopes of having a conservatory full of herbs and plants from all over the world: India, Africa, the Caribbean, the Mediterranean. Not just plants that ships' captains can trade for in ports, but plants that live in remote, untouched corners of the world. Who knows what properties I could discover in them, what cures are out there that we haven't begun to uncover?'

Ferris stared at her for a long moment, letting his gaze take in the flame of the lamp playing across her face, catching the light in her eyes. In that moment she was the woman he'd danced with, strolled the gallery with, shared part of his own dreams with, whom he'd kissed in the shadows. This woman who spoke so passionately of her love of herbs and who'd saved a life today was not his enemy. Was that the real Anne Peverett?

She gave a little laugh in the silence. 'Have I made you cringe, Dr Tresham?'

'On the contrary, I'm quite inspired,' Ferris admitted. 'I dream of curing people by travelling the neighbourhoods of London, but you seek to travel the world. I must dream bigger.' Ferris paused, ignoring the warning in his head to keep her at arm's length, where he kept everyone else. 'If we're to be partners, though, perhaps you should call me Ferris,' he urged in an uncustomary fit of recklessness.

'Then you must call me Anne.' She raised her glass to his once more.

'Cheers, Anne. Partners it is.' He drank the toast, waiting to feel relief, fulfilment. He had everything he wanted, his project was back on track. So, why did he feel as if the wheels were about to come off his wagon?

Anne could not shake the feeling that it was all too good to be true. The feeling followed her home and stayed with her long after Ferris had seen her to her door. It kept her up late talking with Thea. She'd got everything she wanted in coming to London: a space to make her herbals, a wagon from which to distribute her products. No more relying solely on the good will of shopkeepers for presentation space, no more walking long distances and hiring hacks to wind her way from Harley Street to the neighbourhoods she frequented.

There was more she now had, too—the shield and ethos of Dr Tresham, second son of a duke. Surely he understood the intangibles he offered by presenting her with a partnership. People who scoffed at women participating in medicine, or at herbals as legitimate treatments, would not be allowed to scoff at her now without running afoul of him.

Thea gave her a sharp stare when she finished. 'What does he get from all this generosity?'

That was the question, wasn't it? She'd asked it of herself and of Ferris, yet here she was with her sister, packing up her herbals late into the night for a move to Ferris's clinic tomorrow. 'He says he gets a chance to keep an eye on me. He fears I expect too much from these city people in terms of their ability to provide their own healthcare.'

Even as she said the words out loud, new doubt came to her, doubt that she'd overlooked or pushed aside in lieu of focusing on other things at the time—wine, lamplight, good food and a day spent bringing a new life into the world, all with the enigmatic Dr Tresham at her side, not antagonising her, not challenging her, but working with her. They had been a team today.

'Is that all he gets? It sounds like very little in exchange for what he's giving.' Thea's words made the new doubts concrete. 'Is he not the same arrogant man today that you spoke of yesterday, when that was his defining quality as I remember?'

'Yes, it was. And, no, today he wasn't arrogant. I can't figure him out, Thea,' Anne confessed, wrapping a set of glass bottles in old newspaper. 'He was a…revelation.' She met her sister's eyes. 'We delivered a baby today, unexpectedly. Thea, you should have seen him.' She couldn't stop seeing him in her mind: those powerful forearms, his calm manner, his confidence in knowing what needed to be done. 'He had to turn the child.'

Thea frowned and wrinkled her nose. 'He didn't use the podalic version, did he?' Only untrained country midwives and old-fashioned physicians still used it.

'No, he was more sophisticated than that.' Anne

laughed. 'Like you.' She added, a little shyly, 'He used the chlorine lime like Father.' He was like Father in a lot of ways—she'd seen that today, although she rather wished she hadn't. It made it more difficult to keep her defences up.

'So today, our arrogant Dr Tresham is a good healer,' Thea surmised.

'He was.' She would give credit where it was due. Ferris's words had stung this evening that she conveniently labelled all disagreeable men as arrogant. Did she do that? It made her sound like a narrow-minded shrew.

Thea wrapped the last of the herbs. 'And now you're ready to throw your lot in with him. Well, be careful. He might be a healer, but he's also a duke's son. He doesn't have to do anything he doesn't *want* to do.'

Thea's words continued to bother her as Anne made ready for bed. Ferris *wanted* to do this, wanted to take her out on rounds with him, *wanted* to give her space in his clinic to work with her herbs. Why? Anne slid beneath the covers and blew out her lamp. Too bad she couldn't blow out her thoughts as easily. She needed her mind to quiet, but it insisted on sifting through the other things Ferris wanted as well: he wanted to live outside Mayfair, wanted to focus his work on the downtrodden, wanted to live more simply than his station required. His work was his life.

That was something she'd noted as he'd toured her through his home. His work was everything to him. There was no physical division between work and privacy in his home. Every room had been turned to some medical purpose. Even the guest rooms upstairs had been labelled as hospital rooms.

How a man used his physical space was indicative of how he interacted with the world. It was clear Ferris saw himself not as a duke's son, but as a doctor. It was reflected in every inch of his home, in the way he chose to dress, how he chose to live—not as a rich man, but as a man who put caring for others ahead of personal luxury. Her father would like him. She *could* like him. The man Ferris had been today was a man worthy of her liking, but only if he could come to fully respect *her*— therein lay the rub. Liking him wasn't part of her plans.

Chapter Ten

It took Ferris two weeks to realise the flaw in his plan—he *liked* having Anne at the clinic. One wasn't supposed to *like* the competition. Ferris looked up from his journals, his attention drawn from his work in the office by the sound of feminine voices engaged in pleasant late-afternoon conversation in the kitchen. He smiled at the chatter. It was only one small way Anne had changed things since she'd been here, her days spent either working in the clinic or out with him in the wagon. His practice was livelier, homelier, for having her here, and for taking her out with him when he drove the wagon. The ledgers lying open on his desk were proof of that.

They'd served twenty people yesterday from the wagon's visit to Southwark and fifteen the day before on the East Docks, bringing their total for this week to fifty. Last week, they'd gone out only twice, due to rain, and had served thirty-five. It was a great relief. With numbers like these, he could present the journal of names to the board of governors right before Christmas, proof that there was need for his mobile clinics. By the new year, he could have the funding he needed for more wagons and more doctors.

All thanks to Anne. That was the fly in the ointment. Each day they went out with the wagon, he was keenly aware of her contribution and of his little deception. She had no idea his offer to work with him was motivated by the need to get his numbers up for the mobile project. Ferris shut the journal of names in the hopes of tamping down his conscience before it awoke, but he was too late.

You should tell her, it whispered. *Who knows, she might not mind. She might agree the ends justify the means.*

He doubted it, not after how she'd cut up at him that day at the tea shop.

That was another issue—he owed her an apology. He'd judged her prematurely and from a place of anger. He'd watched her these weeks and been impressed with the way she handled her clients, making careful diagnoses and taking time to thoroughly explain how to use the herbs she gave them.

She's not just good with patients, she's good with you, too. Admit it, the two of you make a good team and not just professionally. His conscience was on a roll today, calling forward all the vulnerabilities he liked to keep hidden away. *You'd like having her here even if it wasn't for work. You've never got over that kiss. If it had been nothing, you wouldn't have offered her a partnership, you would have driven her from the neigh-bourhoods.*

His conscience drove him from the office. He rose and headed towards the kitchen, hoping to leave his conscience behind. It was damnably awkward trying to reconcile himself to the growing realisation that his attraction to Anne had only been rekindled by her constant presence in his life. The differences in their opinions over empowering patients to treat themselves had not proved to be a staunch barrier against that attraction, especially now that they'd joined forces and the threat she'd posed had been diminished.

Ferris leaned against the door jamb in the kitchen, watching Anne at work at the stove. Auburn tendrils curled at her temples, her face flushed from the steam. What a delightful mess she was when she worked. 'What are we brewing today?' Ferris strode towards the stove to take a sniff. 'Rosemary, is it?'

Anne smiled and wiped her hands on the big apron she wore. 'I'm making a rosemary tincture for Mrs Grant's boy. He has terrible acne and I'm nearly out.' She passed him a wooden spoon. 'Here, you stir.'

Ferris took the spoon and stirred, leaning over to breathe in the aroma. The hot brew sloshed against his hand. 'Ouch!' He drew back in sharp reflex, shaking it to dispel the burning sensation that shot through him. 'Oh, sweet heavens, that's hot!'

'What happened?' Anne was beside him instantly, taking his hand in hers. 'Come sit, let me look at it.' She led him to the worktable and sat him down. 'The aloe please, Mrs Green.'

'It's nothing.' Ferris felt immediately foolish, and immediately cognisant of her touch. *This* was what his conscience was talking about, this constant awareness of her. The simplest of touches could set his body aflame.

Anne gave him a stern look as she manipulated his hand, turning it gently. 'It's not nothing. A doctor's hands are the tools of his trade. You'll have a blister, but the aloe should help.' She took the lid off the jar and dabbed the aloe on to the back of his hand, working it in softly, her fingers moving in small circles. Had anything ever felt this good? To be touched, to be cared for… When was the last time someone had done something like this for him? Oh, good heavens, he was in trouble here.

'How does that feel?' Anne put the lid back on the aloe. Ferris wished he could put a lid on his rampant feelings as easily. He was not used to attraction, not used to being drawn so irrevocably to someone.

He flexed his hand and looked about the kitchen. They were alone—Mrs Green had gone upstairs for a moment. 'It feels better, thank you.' Ferris took advantage of the privacy. His gaze lingered on her face. He let the silence stretch between them until it became awkward for them both. She looked away and made to return to her rosemary. 'Wait, Anne.' He stalled her with a gentle hand, savouring the brief contact. Would she always affect him thus? His voice was low when he spoke. These were words meant for just the two of them. 'There's something I need to tell you.'

A crease formed between her brows. He'd not meant

to give her concern. 'I owe you an apology, Anne. I judged you unfairly that day at the apothecary's and I was unduly harsh.'

Another woman might have been flustered or flattered by the words, might have offered some diminishment of the apology, or excused it with words like 'it's all right', but not Anne. She knew what he'd called her that day wasn't all right. She held his gaze with her customary steadiness and took the apology with the gravity it deserved. 'Thank you. What changed your mind?' It was another of her blunt, impossible questions that required a man to make himself entirely vulnerable.

'*You* did, Anne,' Ferris offered truthfully. 'Watching you with our clients, watching you work here at the clinic. You are a very gifted woman.' Ferris reached for her hand before he could think better of it. 'What I am trying to say is that I like having you here and I am glad you trusted me enough to accept the offer.'

'I like being here,' Anne replied. Her succinct tones disappointed him. He'd just laid himself bare. He supposed he'd expected a bit more in response. Instead, she withdrew her hand and retreated to the stove with a little laugh. 'It's back to work now, this tincture isn't going to stir itself.'

'Yes, back to work.' Ferris rose, knowing when he'd been dismissed, but hating the feeling. 'I should be heading out for rounds at the soldiers' hospital.' He knew that strategy—it was one of his own. He'd buried himself in work for years now so that he didn't have to feel on a personal level. His emotions were reserved for others, he saved none for himself. It was safer that way. There was no risk of being hurt.

He plucked his hat and the new greatcoat, courtesy of Frederick, from the pegs by the back door. Did she use that strategy for the same reasons? People who were afraid of being hurt were afraid because they'd been hurt before. Had Anne been hurt before? The urge to protect surged. Surely she didn't think *he* would hurt her? Did that mean she felt it, too, this connection between them that wouldn't go away?

'Anne...' He cast about for the right words as he did up his buttons, but finding none, he opted instead for, 'There's a concert of carols at St Luke's tonight to benefit the soldiers' hospital. Would you come with me? We can walk over after dinner.'

'Is this part of your apology?' Anne didn't turn from the stove. He wished he could see her face. Was there a hint of wariness beneath the words or did he imagine it because he was wary, too? Wary of what lay between them and what could be done about it.

Or perhaps, old chap, his conscience spoke up, *she doesn't think about you like that at all.* Now, his conscience was just being mean.

'No, it's not,' he assured her. 'You've been busy with work here and you haven't had time to enjoy London at Christmas. You should see some of it.' Would she see right through him to the truth? That he simply wanted to spend time with her?

'Perhaps you should get out and enjoy some of it, too.' Anne turned from the stove, her green eyes soft, and Ferris felt a stab of desire shoot through him—

desire for her, for what she represented in his fantasies: a home, a family, hope, an end to the grieving.

Do not look at me like that, like you could be the answer to my dreams.

'When was the last time *you* took a night off?' she teased, and the teasing felt good. He liked that she joked with him. Not many did. 'A night off might do us both some good.'

Ferris nodded, feeling a boyish jolt of excitement go through him at her acceptance. 'Then it's settled. We can eat when I get back, and go from here.'

You're tempting fate, sharing meals, attending concerts. You know where such things lead.

Yes, he did indeed. Perhaps he should not have issued the invitation. It would only prompt more temptation. He flexed his hand as he grabbed his bag. He was playing with fire. He even had the burn to prove it.

Ferris's hand rested at her back, his touch searing for all its lightness as he ushered her through the queue at St Luke's. At the donation box, she reached for her reticule. 'Allow me.' Ferris's voice was low and deep at her ear, private for her alone as it had been this afternoon in the kitchen. 'This is my treat.' He smiled and guided her through into the church and towards an empty pew. 'Will this do?'

He was charming tonight. He was dangerous like this, so solicitous and generous, which meant he was dangerous all the time. She should not have accepted the invitation, just as she should not have stayed for dinner. It would send the wrong message, not just to

Ferris, but to herself. She was conflating business with pleasure. She'd promised herself no entanglements and here she was, out for a night of Christmas music with Ferris Tresham, a man who had the power to ignite her with a look, a touch. She'd put herself in a vulnerable position and not unwillingly. How much longer would she be able to enjoy his company while still resisting his charm? Perhaps the better question was how much longer would she *want* to resist? Especially when she *knew* what it was like to be in his arms?

He offered her a look at the programme. 'We'll get to hear the organ tonight. It fills this hall. It gives me chills, in the best of ways.' He smiled warmly at her and Anne's restraint lost another battle.

'I love Christmas music. We have an organ at our church in Hertfordshire and the organist gives a Christmas Eve recital, but it's nothing like this.' St Luke's was grand in the most Gothic sense of the word, an impressive feat of engineering that made the most of modern technologies while capturing the grandeur of the old style. But as grand as it was, Anne's gaze slid too often to the man beside her as they talked before the concert began. He was full of information regarding the church—the reredos painting behind the altar, the east window and the coat of arms over the west door. But nothing could compete with the simple pleasure of watching his face come alive as he told her about the church. This was his community, a place he'd helped build with his clinic.

It was easy to let her imagination run away with itself as he talked. This was what it would be like to be with him—to have the sum of his attentions not just as a work partner. This was what it would be like to be courted by him, to always have his steady hand at her back. It was a heady path to let her thoughts wander down and they led to a more dangerous fantasy—one where she imagined them as husband and wife, working together by day and stepping out together by night. That was the impossible fantasy, a fantasy she'd given up. As his wife, he would, no doubt, expect her to give up her work, as Robert had.

His wife? Dear heavens, she really had grown fanciful. It was what came of working in such close proximity, of developing a routine and a sense of teamwork. And yet, the fantasy had a point. It served as a reminder that nothing could come of this, that she would be better off not to encourage it for both their sakes.

The choir filed on to the risers and the organist took his place. There was no more time to think, there was only time to feel as the first resounding notes of Handel's 'Joy to the World' filled the church. 'Oh…' she breathed, overwhelmed by the magnificent chords of the organ. Ferris was right, chills indeed. She glanced at him and he caught her gaze, a silent message of appreciation and awe passing between them. His hand closed over hers where it lay in her lap and they were swept away, lost in the music together.

'That was just lovely. It feels like Christmas now,' Anne enthused as they stepped out into the cold evening. She tucked her arm through his as they began the short walk back to the clinic. 'I love all the Christmas songs.'

'I'm glad you enjoyed it.' Ferris smiled as they strolled. He'd enjoyed it, too, and the sight of his own pleasure warmed her. 'I had a patient today at the soldiers' hospital I wanted to talk over with you.' That warmed her in a different way entirely. He was seeking her advice, proof that his apology today had been heartfelt and genuine. This had been an intoxicating day—an apology, the recognition she'd set out to earn from him, a concert and now consultation. This was tempting ground—toying with what it would be like to be partners in work, partners in life.

'My patient suffers from night terrors. He was in India and saw a comrade mauled by a tiger. I haven't been able to help him.' Ferris sighed. 'I can mend a broken bone, but I can't seem to mend a broken mind. Any thoughts?'

'I'd like to see him, of course, first, to assess his situation. But offhand, I'd recommend a lavender tea before bed and a massage with lavender oil if possible. Both are useful for relaxing and falling into sleep peaceably with a quiet mind. I'll go with you next time if you like.' She offered it casually, but her heart was hungry for this kind of acceptance. How long had she waited to be taken seriously? For a man to see her as a healer? And here was a man doing just that.

'Thank you, I will take that offer.' Ferris put his hand over hers where it lay on his sleeve and her heart skipped a beat.

Be careful, her mind warned. *He will disappoint*

you in the end. All men do. He's already disappointed you once.

But he apologised. He admitted his error. Her heart leapt to his defence despite the reminder she'd given herself in church just an hour ago. *Ferris could be different.*

Different? Do you really know him so well after a few weeks? Do you really trust your instincts? After all, you were wrong about Robert.

'The men are lucky to have you looking after them,' Anne said.

'It's the least I can do. I wish there was more.' Ferris shook off her praise. 'We're raised to believe men are made for war, but they're not. War changes a man. I look at those men at the soldiers' hospital and I can't help but think about my brother, Fortis. I have not seen him in nearly six years. Neither has his wife. Would either of us recognise him? I mean, recognise him on the inside? What nightmares does he carry? Or perhaps he carries none, and that says something about him, too, that war has hardened him beyond the horrors.'

'The two of you are an interesting combination. He's a warrior and you're a healer.' Anne cocked her head to take in his profile, the long, elegant nose, the mussed waves of his dark hair and the consideration of his gaze. 'You miss him. I can tell from your voice.'

'I *do* miss him. Family is everything and I would prefer to have mine safe, especially this time of year. Families should be together.'

'Christmas will be difficult this year, for both of us, it seems. William won't be home. For the first time in twenty-five years, the Peveretts won't all be together.' The evening was starting to mellow and it felt good to be with someone, to not be alone.

'Will *you* be home for Christmas?' Ferris asked as they turned the last corner home.

No, not home, she corrected. *To the clinic.*

'I think Thea has plans to stay in London. The hospital can't spare her. I'll stay with her. It's been hard on her with William gone. The ranks of Peveretts around the long oak table at Haberstock will be severely depleted this year. Just Thomasia and Rebecca will still be at home. God willing, we'll all be together next year, though. We've had a lot of Christmases together, we can all stand to weather one apart.' Anne smiled and tried to put a bright face on it. 'Thea and I will send gifts from the city, of course. They'll be the talk of Christmas Day. What of yourself? Will you stay in town?' Did she imagine a shadow on his face or was it the gaslight playing tricks?

'I usually do, but this year I think I might go down to Bramble. My brother felt there was some need for it with Fortis on the front at the moment.'

'Ah…' Anne fought back a wave of disappointment—unrealistic disappointment. It would have been nice to have spent Christmas with him, perhaps invited him over to their rooms and had a small Christmas supper, just the three of them. But that was nonsense. Of course he'd go home. She was forgetting who he really was—a duke's son. He needn't spend Christmas in middle-class quarters with two women from the country.

A knot of unlooked-for envy tied itself in her stomach, overriding the disappointment. There would be Christmas parties at Bramble. It would be merry and lively. Ferris would be sought after by the neighbourhood hopefuls. There'd be no medical practice to distract him. He would dance with those hopefuls, maybe steal kisses beneath a mistletoe bough. He was entitled to. She had no claim on him. Tonight, today, changed nothing, no matter how many butterflies they had set fluttering in her stomach.

And that was for the best.

Ferris was married to his work. She was married to hers. She would not give it up for any man, neither would she give up her mission of helping people treat themselves, something Ferris was rankly against even if he did respect her skill. It would be better to not start something that was doomed to fail from the outset. It would save her hurt in the long run.

They approached the door of the clinic, the lamp burning welcomingly in the window. 'We'll check in with Mrs Green to make sure no one stopped by needing anything and then I'll take you home in a cab.' Ferris paused before he opened the door, the full force of his gaze lingering on her face. For one long moment, she thought, *He is going to kiss me again.* And for another long moment, she wanted him to. 'Thank you for a splendid evening, Anne.'

There was going to be no kiss. Something inside her deflated even as she knew it was for the best. 'I'll put some more aloe on your burn before we go.'

Inside, Mrs Green was waiting for them, wringing

her hands in worry. 'I'm so glad you're home. There's a boy to see you, Dr Tresham. He's in the kitchen. I've fed him, but he insists he must speak with you…' Mrs Green hardly finished before a child barrelled out of the kitchen, running straight for Ferris.

'It's my sister, Meggie, sir. You must come with me at once, she's terribly ill. I've come like you said if she got worse.' Anne exchanged a worried look with Ferris and in that instant the euphoria of the evening vanished. It was time to get back to work.

Chapter Eleven

'Tell me everything.' Ferris knelt and put an arm about the boy. Anne wondered if he saw it, too—the purplish blush of a bruise along the boy's jaw. Ferris looked up over the boy's head—another glance passed between them. Yes, he'd seen it.

Tears welled up in the boy's eyes at the touch of comfort and his restraint broke. 'We sold your coat, just like you said, sir. But Meggie's cough didn't get better and now she has a fever and can't get out of bed. She can't even take a bit of gruel. Pa says there's no money for doctors, especially for girls. But please, you have to come, I need you to help her. I promised my ma I'd look after her, you see, before Ma went to Heaven.'

Another glance. 'Anne, will you bring your basket?' They were speaking in code.

Will you come? I will need you.

'I'll get your things as well.'

Yes, I will come.

Something swelled inside her; perhaps it was her

heart, or maybe her pride. He'd *asked* her to come, just as he'd asked her for her opinion on the soldier. He needed her.

Anne was already in motion. She gathered Ferris's bag and her basket, adding an extra blanket as a precaution. Who knew what they'd find? The boy's story boded ill—a sick sister, an abusive father and not enough of anything to go around from the looks of him, for he was painfully thin.

Ferris spared her a final look.

Are you sure, Anne? It might be dangerous.

She answered him back with a short nod.

I am sure.

Whatever awaited them, she wasn't going to let him face it alone.

The boy lived a little under a mile away in Turk's Row, past the soldiers' hospital, and a hired cab made quick work of the distance, but the boy might have lived in another world far from the orderly, respectable houses that lined Cheyne Walk. Turk's Row was a potent reminder of how closely the London poor lived to the pockets of London's rich.

Turk's Row was lined with one-room cottages, packed together and without any notable sanitation. Such poorly kept density was a breeding ground for disease. Ferris catalogued those conditions immediately, his trained eye noting the slops thrown into the street, the coal smoke spiralling into the fog from homes lucky enough to afford heat at the price of diminished air quality. Prostitutes and drunks populated street corners, reminders that the slums never slept.

Ferris slid a glance across the cab to where Anne sat, the boy, Peter, snuggled against her. She'd wrapped the blanket about him and the boy had become an immediate admirer. Had he done right by asking Anne to come? She had seen the poor parts of London, but working with impoverished women in daylight was different from reasoning with drunk men in the dark.

The cab came to a stop and the driver called down that they'd arrived. Ferris reached for his bag from under the seat. 'You and the boy should wait here. I'll see what can be done.'

'I should come,' Anne argued. 'If it's a cough, I have herbs and teas that can help, and...' she paused '...perhaps their father might think twice about starting trouble if a woman is present?' She had a point. There might be an advantage in that.

'I should come, too.' Peter sat up straight and shook off the blanket. 'I can carry the blanket. Meggie will need it and a stranger might scare her.'

In the dim interior, Ferris could see Anne's mouth quirk in a knowing smile and he knew he was beaten. 'Very well, we shall be in and out in no time, but I will need both of you to follow directions.' Whatever those directions might be. He wasn't certain what exactly his plan was as they alit from the cab and made the short trip to the door. Was he here to treat the little girl or to extract her? The bruise on Peter's cheek indicated treatment might not be enough. One night of treatment certainly was no guarantee of cure either, and a drunk father was hardly a reliable caregiver. 'Stay close, both of you,' he muttered as he knocked, not that the knock signified anything beyond a courtesy. He was going in regardless.

A hulking, unkempt brute of a man answered the knock, reeking of cheap drink and sweat. Ferris instinctively put his own height and breadth between Anne and Peter and the man. 'I've come to help your daughter.' Ferris strode inside the one-room cottage with a confidence that caught the man off guard, Anne and Peter behind him before Peter's father could do more than sputter objections.

Peter ran to where Meggie lay on a cot before the fire. 'I've brought the doctor, Meggie, and a blanket. You'll be better in no time now.'

The word 'doctor' seemed to galvanise the brute at the door. 'We don't need no doctor.' The man glared at Peter, his voice menacing. 'I told you, boy, your sister just has a cough. Everyone has a cough this time of year.'

Ferris reached for the little girl's tiny wrist, feeling for a pulse, finding it shallow and weak. Her skin was hot and her eyes were glazed. A cough took her, racking and rattly, like bones in a dice cup. This was not the same cough he'd heard weeks ago in the alley. He exchanged a look with Anne. This was more. 'How long has she been ill?' he asked the man, but it was Peter who answered.

'Since last week, sir. That's when she started not getting out of bed.'

'Don't talk to him, boy, or I'll show you the back of

my hand. Your sister is lazy and that's why she won't get up,' the man growled, words slurring.

'She is not! She's four and she's sick!' Peter railed, anger and hatred, impotence and sadness fuelling his thin form as he charged his father.

Ferris was faster, grabbing the boy by the grimy collar of his shirt. 'No, you don't, lad. Whatever pleasure it might bring you in the short term, the punishment later isn't worth it.' There'd be more bruises, perhaps worse. A drunk man didn't countenance a loss of face easily, especially not being called to task by an eight-year-old in front of strangers. Ferris steered the boy in Anne's direction for safekeeping. If there were to be any fisticuffs tonight, it would be between him and the big man. His mind was made up. He couldn't leave the children here.

'Your daughter is very ill.' Ferris tried to keep a courteous tone, but it was deuced difficult when every bone in his body begged to pummel this man for not caring, for not providing for his children, for being a drunk instead of being a father. And yet, his cooler mind cautioned, he did not know this man's past. What had turned him? Had he always been this way? Likely not. If practising medicine had taught him one thing, it was that everyone had a story. Still, Ferris could not turn a blind eye to the rampant neglect he saw here, no matter what the reason. 'I want to take her to my clinic and treat her there.'

'Do you think I'd let you take my child and experiment on her?' The man staggered towards Ferris. From the corner of his eye, he saw Anne give her basket to

Peter, already divining what needed to be done. Her hands were free. She could snatch up the child and make a run for the hack waiting outside.

'I'll want the boy to come, too, to help look after her,' Ferris pressed. He could not leave Peter here now. His gaze narrowed on the man. Drunks were uncertain fighters with no sense of reason and that made them quick to pull knives.

'Over my dead body. These are my children. I say where they go and who they go with,' the man roared, his fist taking a mad swing, but Ferris was ready. He dodged and swung, forgetting his blistered hand long enough to land one well-placed punch to the solar plexus. The big man went down, the wind knocked out of him. Ferris stepped around the gasping man and scooped the little girl from the bed. Anne had her arm about Peter, ushering him towards the door.

Inside the cab, Ferris settled Meggie on his lap, stunned by how little she weighed. She was four? Helena's boys at four were heavier than this. 'We have rooms for you and hot food, if you're still hungry,' Ferris assured Peter, who sat in wide-eyed silence beside Anne. He could only imagine what the boy must be feeling tonight. 'We have medicine for your sister.' He would not lose this precious child who'd been given so little in life. He and Anne would do their best.

Would his best be enough? The question haunted Ferris as he stood in the doorway of the bedroom where he'd put Meggie. Anne had seen the little girl bathed and into a clean nightdress, although she reported the girl had shook the entire time. That would be the fever talking. Anne had seen her fed, too, although she'd not eaten very much of Mrs Green's mutton stew.

A pot of willow-bark tea sat at the ready on the bedside table for the fever, and the room smelled of soothing lavender underlaid with something else. Ferris sniffed. 'Is that onion I smell?' Or was it just remnants of dinner?

Anne turned from the bed with a tired smile. 'Yes, an onion poultice to draw the cough and any infection she might have. I'll stay with her tonight to make sure she gets the willow-bark tea,' Anne said. 'If you could send word to let my sister know I won't be home?'

'I can stay up with her, you needn't do it,' Ferris offered—it wouldn't be the first all-night vigil he'd kept. 'You've already done so much. I shouldn't have asked you to go tonight.' There'd been violence. Anne could have been hurt. How would he have explained that to her family?

'I want to stay,' Anne said firmly, coming to stand beside him. 'You might have your hands full with two children who are sleeping in an unfamiliar place for the first time.'

'Thank you.' The offer overwhelmed him, made his throat thick with emotion. They were in this together now. How many women did he know who would voluntarily give up their night to nurse a sick child, especially one who wasn't theirs? He motioned that she should step out into the hall with him.

'How is your hand?'

'It hurts,' Ferris admitted once they were outside Meggie's room.

She arched a brow. 'What was it you said to Peter about the consequences of short-term satisfaction? And then moments later what did you do? You have to agree, the irony is hilarious.'

Ferris managed a short chuckle. 'Are you teasing me?'

'You need to be teased once in a while.' She smiled and then sobered. 'Is Peter settled?'

'Yes, I've just come from seeing him to bed. He wanted to stay in the room with his sister, but...' Ferris shook his head '... I can't possibly risk that. If she's contagious and he doesn't have it then we need to keep him away.'

'Contagious? It's not just a catarrh, then?' Anne asked in low tones.

'I don't think so. When I heard her cough, there was a "kink" sound to it, and, given her build and background, she's a prime candidate for whooping cough.' That concerned him greatly. Mortality from whooping cough was high among children.

'You're worried?' Anne touched him gently on the sleeve and he took comfort from it.

'Yes. She had a cough when I first met them. They were fending for themselves in an alley.' Ferris offered a brief smile, his mind going back in time. 'It was the night of the charity ball and one of the reasons I was late.'

'Five weeks ago,' Anne supplied as his own mind did mental, medical maths.

'She was coughing then, but whooping cough takes two weeks to manifest, which makes it hard to catch early.' Ferris sighed, filtering back through Peter's comment that she'd come down sick a week ago. That made sense. 'It's hard to know the difference between it and a catarrh in the early stages.' Not that it would have changed anything for Meggie.

'You couldn't have known that night in the alley,' Anne offered softly. 'You're tormenting yourself, Ferris. You couldn't have known,' she repeated. 'Doctors don't have crystal balls and they are not infallible.'

But he wanted to be. Ferris nodded absently, his mind focused on what-ifs and might-have-beens. What if he'd done something more that night? What if he'd had his mobile clinic up and running sooner? What if children had access to healthcare? So little was written about care for that tender population. None of that could help Meggie now. How did he go forward? 'Can you take the first watch, Anne? I want to review my notes on whooping cough.' Perhaps there would be answers in his medical books.

'I am happy to take the first watch, but you should sleep. Research can wait until morning,' Anne countered.

'I couldn't sleep right now. My brain is too awake.' Ferris shrugged off the suggestion. 'I'll send a note to your sister and have the bedroom readied for you.' He paused. 'Anne, thank you for going with me tonight to Turk's Row and for being here now. I had no right to ask it of you. It's certainly not how I thought the night would end.'

She shifted on her feet and shook her head. He'd made her uncomfortable with his praise. Despite her sharp edges, Anne was a humble woman. 'We are healers, Ferris. It is what we do. We go where we are needed, otherwise we wouldn't be of much use.' She smiled. 'Go and do your research. I'll check on our patient.'

Chapter Twelve

It was a good note, the *right* note, to end their conversation on, a professional note that overrode the little frisson of awareness that had haunted them in the kitchen today and followed them home from the concert.

Anne pulled up a chair beside Meggie's bedside, pleased to see that the lavender was working. The little girl was asleep and restful. Anne settled a cold rag on the girl's brow and began her vigil. The squalor of the cottage tonight had been eye-opening in ways working with the women at the wagon or in the shops was not. She heard their complaints, but she'd not seen first-hand the situations in which those complaints existed. How was a child to thrive in conditions that did not feed the mind, the body or the soul? Where food, shelter and safety were daily insecurities and clothing a luxury beyond that? It made her mission in London even more important. Health was the cornerstone of change. Peter and Meggie's poor conditions were proof of that.

This child was lucky to have Ferris Tresham on her

side. He'd been a man on fire tonight, his passion for healing unleashed. He'd fought for this child with words and, when those had failed, with his fists. She did not condone violence as a way to resolve problems, but she could not deny there'd been something very virile about Ferris tonight, taking on the drunk, protecting them, seeing all of them to safety.

And not for the first time. Confess, you've always been attracted to him, came the whispered reminder.

Even when he'd treated her like the enemy and likewise she him, he'd still been a *handsome* boor.

They weren't enemies any more. He'd apologised— more than that, he'd readjusted his thinking as needed, and that was problematic. One *could* be attracted to one's friend, or someone with whom one shared a significant similarity. There was no longer any denying the attraction between them, that went beyond professional appreciation. It put her on very dangerous ground, at risk of breaking the promises she'd made herself and at risk of setting herself up for hurt again.

Anne leaned forward and placed a fresh rag on Meggie's brow. Being attracted to Ferris didn't change the outcome, though. Anything long term with him was out of the question. There would only be disappointment when they discovered neither could truly be what the other needed. But what of the short term, before they could disappoint one another?

It was a wicked thought, but temptation was relentless tonight, catching her at her most vulnerable after a whole day spent with Ferris. This was a new argument that slipped beneath her defences.

What if you both recognise the limitations of the long term?

In the past, she'd thought of relationships with only one outcome: marriage. She'd been taught a woman had two choices: marry or pursue her own calling. She'd always thought that was fairly liberal of her parents. Most girls in Hertfordshire were taught there was a single path, that one's life ended if one did not marry.

What if there was a *third* path? What if a woman could follow one's calling *and* pursue short-term, meaningful relationships with no expectation of a permanent outcome? She'd not viewed *affaires* in that regard before. She'd been raised to believe *affaires* were sinful, base things, reserved for idle society and the wicked French. But that wasn't quite true, was it? There could be meaning and satisfaction for however long the two engaged desired it. Temptation's whisper grew louder— why not? She didn't plan to marry anyway and she knew how to be careful, with her body at least. Her heart was another matter. It had been trampled on before.

Somewhere in the house a clock chimed one. She helped Meggie drink another draught of willow-bark tea and to settle back to sleep. Meggie wouldn't need her again until dawn. She could get some sleep of her own. In Ferris's room. In Ferris's bed. The idea seemed somehow less benign than it had a few hours ago, coming as it did on the heels of her more lurid thoughts. She pushed the idea away. She was a healer, a professional. She could sleep in Ferris's bed without acting like a naive debutante blushing over the smallest indication of an intimacy. In any case, she'd be sleeping in that bed alone. It wasn't as if he'd be in the bed, too.

She was sleeping in his bed, her hair a copper skein drawn over one shoulder, her face peaceful in repose. Sleep softened her. A man might mistake this sleeping beauty for a sweet, biddable woman, a benign woman. He was not that man. There wasn't a passive, biddable bone in her body, but there were kind ones, compassionate ones, proof that, contrary to current social beliefs, women could be kind *and* strong. Kindness and pliability weren't contingent on one another. Ferris chuckled. Heaven help the man who mistook Anne Peverett for a docile country miss.

Had there been such a man? The thought was a product of weariness, circumstance and the tendency of late hours to bring out such fanciful wonderings. Did Anne have a gentleman suitor in the country? It seemed doubtful if she wasn't going home for Christmas. Had she left someone behind, then? Had she broken his heart or had he broken hers? Was that why she'd run from their kiss?

The thought of some cad breaking her heart seemed unconscionable to Ferris. It made him want to do battle on her behalf. It was a ridiculous notion. Anne could fight her own battles. Anne wouldn't *want* anyone to fight them for her. She'd stood up to him readily enough.

Ferris set the lamp on the bedside table and weighed his options for sleep. He could stretch out beside her atop the blankets, which was the preferable option at three in the morning, or cobble a bed together in the clinic downstairs, which meant giving up hope of getting any amount of decent sleep. He pulled off his boots with a yawn and opted for the former. There was no harm in it. Both of them were fully clothed, fully exhausted, and there was no one to tell tales. Besides, they needed to be close to the children, especially Meggie. He was sure it was whooping cough now, which meant things were likely to get worse for her before they got better. *If* they got better.

Ferris stretched out on the bed, hands behind his head, and stared at the ceiling, the lamp casting shadows as his mind cast doubts. He'd combed the works of Buchan and Culpeper, but his findings had not been reassuring. The young and undernourished were prime victims and less likely to recover. Meggie fit that unfortunate profile and there was little to be done. Whooping cough was an ailment that had been relegated to the mercies of women's home remedies.

Not if he could do anything about it, Ferris thought fiercely. The statistics were just the statistics. There were exceptions to the numbers all the time. Surely, between him and Anne, one little girl could slip through the statistical ranks of the dead. Surely Heaven didn't need one more angel badly enough to take Meggie.

Anne shifted and rolled in her sleep, her head snuggling against the hollow of his shoulder, fitting as if it belonged there, as if she'd known he needed her. His body, his very *soul* even, reacted to the contact. He understood his reaction to her *scientifically*. His body had been alone too long without the rewards of physical comfort, without the benefit of touch.

It was the reaction deep inside him that he could not or perhaps would not explain. How could this woman he'd not even known two months ago understand him so well? Speak to the depths of him so thoroughly he felt complete with her even as he disagreed with her? Being with her had become about something more than filling his ledger with names for the hospital, and it scared him even as it tempted him. Was he ready for this? To risk everything again for a complete life?

Those were fantasies he'd not thought to spin with another woman, ever. He'd not expected to feel as he did when he was around Anne, as if all things were possible. Anne made him hope, hope that his personal and professional goals might both be realised after all, that he might dream of a family once more. Yet the opposite of hope was fear.

Did he really want to lay himself open to such depths of feeling again only to risk losing his heart, his soul? He'd been in love before—head-over-heels, blinding, blissful love that drowned out the aches of this world, a love that made everything possible and everyone invincible. How he'd soared with Cara! How he'd dreamed with her of the world they would make. And, *oh*, how he'd crashed when he'd lost her. It had taken three years of a Grand Tour to put himself back together after losing Cara, three years to see his way forward alone. It had taken nearly twelve years to *feel* again for another what he felt for Anne, what he'd once felt for Cara.

He looked down at the woman sleeping in his arms. No, that wasn't fair. This feeling for Anne was merely similar. It was not quite the same. There was an edge to these feelings, an intensity that surpassed the long-standing comfort he'd felt with Cara. His feelings for Anne had a vibrant life of their own that crackled and sparked whenever they were together.

He wanted to fan that spark, to let it catch and flame. He wanted to be burned by it, scorched until the charred remains of his old self fell away and he emerged a radiant new phoenix, free of sorrow, free of grief for what could never be, free to look forward to what *could* be. The lure was a potent one—it had to be if it was to pull him out of the complacency he'd safely cocooned himself in all these years, a cocoon where he spent his passion on repairing others instead of repairing himself.

What would she say to these thoughts? That was the risk with Anne—not that she'd die like Cara had, but that she would reject him. Lying here, with Anne tucked against him, he wasn't sure what was worse: knowing an unrecoverable loss as he'd known with Cara or losing Anne and knowing she was still at large in the world. She had a poor opinion of men. He'd like to know why. He could guess at some of it. She felt limited in her profession by her gender. But he suspected it ran deeper, giving credence to his earlier thoughts that she'd left heartbreak behind in Hertfordshire. 'I want to know your secrets, Anne,' he whispered in the dark.

He needed to know them now that he was sure. He was falling for her, perhaps he'd been falling all along, perhaps he'd never stopped.

You know what that means—you have to tell her everything; you have to tell her about Cara, about your fears, and you have to tell her why you invited her to join you. The real reason, not the reasons you tempted her with.

And he would, he promised himself, when the time was right. For now, it was enough to drift off to sleep and for once not be alone.

Chapter Thirteen

Anne stirred, sleeping and waking engaged in a tug of war for her attentions. Her eyelids felt heavy, too heavy to open. She wanted sleep to win, just for a while longer. Wherever she was, it was in the world's most comfortable bed; soft and warm. It smelled like clean linen and sandalwood, like Ferris.

Like Ferris.

She was in his bed. Her eyes flew open at the remembrance, an arm flinging wide to the space beside her. What was it looking for? A body? No body? Proof that he had or hadn't slept beside her? Her arm found proof. The bed was empty, but it was warm—he had been here, beside her. Of course he'd slept here. Where else was he to sleep when the children occupied the other two rooms?

Practical argument wasn't quite enough to dispel the sense of intimacy that came with knowing he'd lain beside her. It wasn't helped either with the growing awareness of her position in the bed. She wasn't exactly where she'd left herself on her side of the bed when she'd fallen asleep. Somehow, she'd progressed to his side. Dear heavens, what else had she done in her sleep? Drooled? Snored? Talked? Kicked him? Oh, she hoped not that. Was that why he wasn't in bed now? Or had something happened with the children? Surely he would have wakened her if the latter were the case.

Thoughts of the children fuelled Anne with urgency. People needed her. She couldn't lie abed wondering what she'd done in her sleep. Meggie would need fresh willow-bark tea, and she needed to look through her remedies for something to help with the cough. Then there was the lavender to make for Ferris's soldier with the nightmares. Her mind was awhirl with chores as she sat up in bed and froze.

Ferris wasn't gone. He was still here and he was shaving. Without his shirt on. All thoughts of lavender and lotions fled. Dear Lord, what a back he had—smooth with long, elegant muscles—and those shoulders didn't disappoint naked. Neither did his arms. It was easy to see how he'd felled Peter's burly, brick-working father last night with arms like that. He was built like an aristocrat, tall and lean, but also muscled, a man who took care of himself. The results of good diet and proper nutrition were evident in the body on display, from the breadth of his shoulders to the lean waist hugged by dark trousers, to what appeared to be the promising sculpted rounds of his... She had to stop herself there. She was *not* going to stare at his arse. But her eyes had other ideas. They wanted to feast.

'Good morning, sleepyhead.' Ferris's voice was all

low gravel. His gaze caught hers in the mirror over the washing basin and her heart lurched, her mind filling with fantasies of waking regularly to a well-made, bare-chested man shaving. Above all, it was a reminder that this could be hers for a short time if she took the leap.

'You should have woken me.' Her voice sounded groggy and as unattractive as she felt. She'd slept in her clothes, while he looked and smelled fresh. Ugh. Anne ran her tongue over her teeth. She must look and smell a mess.

'There was no need. Meggie and Peter are both asleep and it's still early. Mrs Green won't be here for an hour.' Ferris imparted the reassuring information in easy tones as if they woke up together every morning. The warm weight in her stomach intensified. She wanted to lie in bed and watch him shave all day.

He picked up a towel and wiped the shaving residue from his face. He reached for his shirt and turned to face her, shoving his arms through the sleeves, but not before she had a fair glimpse of his chest, as beautiful as his back, just as smooth and just as well muscled. While she was flustered, he was collected.

Perhaps he fell asleep beside women all the time? The thought had a dampening effect. Just because he wasn't interested in the charms of London's debutantes didn't mean he was a monk. There were other types of women who would be less demanding of him.

'There's fresh water in the ewer. I heated it myself this morning. There's a clean towel for you as well, and you can use my comb and brush,' Ferris offered, finishing with his clothes. 'I asked your sister to send over clean dresses and anything you might need when I wrote last night. You should have them by mid-morning. I'll be downstairs if you need anything.' Ferris excused himself, giving her privacy before she could even utter 'thank you'.

Anne had made quick work of tidying her hair and washing her face. She found Ferris in his office, organising notes at his desk. 'Shall we discuss Meggie?' She gestured towards the open books. 'Did you find anything of use in your search?'

'No, not particularly.' Ferris held up a battered book. 'I thought you might like a look at Culpeper's *Complete Herbal*. He recommends thyme for whooping cough. What do you think?'

'Thyme is effective against coughs. I like to add ivy leaves with it,' Anne offered, still warmed by his willingness to consult with her. It was different from the warmth generated by the sight of his unclothed back, but just as necessary. Perhaps a woman needed both.

'We can try a pipe of rosemary as well.' Ferris smiled. 'I think Meggie might get a laugh out of smoking a pipe in bed.'

But Anne saw the forced nature of his smile. 'We will try everything. There's hyssop syrup, too. We haven't tried that yet. I'll bring her downstairs for a steam treatment as well,' she assured him before dropping her voice in case Peter was awake and eavesdropping. 'Is it truly that bad?' She'd been encouraged by Meggie's deep sleep and she thought Meggie had seemed cooler to the touch when she checked on her before coming down-stairs.

'It's always bad for children like her, Anne. Under-nourishment is a key factor in the survival rate.' He gestured helplessly to the books on his desk and then returned to the tasks at hand as he had last night. It was a coping strategy for him, she realised. 'Do you have a good stock of cough remedies on hand? I might sug-gest making some more up if you don't. I am scheduled to do check-ups at the Royal Military Asylum for chil-dren today. It's located between Turk's Row and King's Road not far from where Peter lives.' Ferris sighed and held her gaze meaningfully. 'I have a hunch there will be other cases.'

'I'll pack what I have. Would you like me to come? Perhaps Meggie could spare me for a couple hours.'

'I *do* want you to come, Anne, but I need you here. Just in case.' He didn't have to say it, she knew the rea-sons: just in case Meggie took a turn for the worse, just in case Peter's father came looking for his children. 'But perhaps we can go together to the soldiers' hospital and take the lavender over later this afternoon.'

'I'd better get busy, then. We've got a full day ahead of us.' She wanted to say more, do more to ease the worry she saw on Ferris's face. He cared so deeply whether it was one little girl or a whole orphanage of them. She was tempted to go to him, to touch him, but this wasn't the time. She could hear Mrs Green enter-ing through the back door. Breakfast would be ready soon and she wanted to have Ferris's supplies assembled before he left on his rounds.

* * *

The day flew by in a whirlwind of chores. Anne barely had time to change into a clean gown and sort through the valise Thea had sent over. She and Mrs Green took turns sitting with Meggie so Anne could work on remedies. Anne kept Peter with her, busying him with tasks like chopping herbs or putting the herbs in little bags, and Mrs Green spoiled the boy with biscuits and milk. It was a joy to see the boy avidly watching her with the herbs as she explained what she was using them for and to see him take to the little tasks she assigned him.

'That's how I started, just like you're doing now,' Anne commended him as they finished filling bottles with hyssop syrup. 'I began working with my mother when I was five. I would follow her on her rounds as soon I could keep up with her.'

'My mother is dead,' Peter offered matter-of-factly. 'She died of a cough, too.' He looked at her with dark, worried eyes. 'Will Meggie die? I promised my ma I wouldn't let anything bad happen to Meggie.'

Anne set aside her chopping knife and placed her hands on his shoulders, aware she could feel every knob of bone and muscle beneath her fingers. 'If anyone can make her well again, it's Dr Tresham and myself.' She wouldn't lie to him, but neither would she worry him any further. He knew enough of the truth to know Meggie's situation was serious. She wished she had a better report for him. She'd carried Meggie downstairs to breathe steam over the stove, but it seemed to have minimal effect. Meggie had continued to cough throughout the day with less relief than Anne would have preferred.

When Ferris returned at three from his rounds at the children's home, he was grim. One look at his expression and Anne knew they were going to need all the remedies she'd put up today. 'The children have got it?' she asked without preamble. They both knew what 'it' was.

'A few cases, enough to confirm it's brewing in that part of town. I've had them isolate the cases and not permit any comings and goings for a couple of weeks in hopes we might stop the spread there. Are you ready to go to the soldiers' hospital? It's cold out, but it's not raining. I thought you might like to walk. It's not far and we could stop at the physic garden on the way home.'

Anne nodded. 'Meggie is sleeping, finally. I'll get my basket.' Some air would be just the thing to clear her head. Ferris took her basket and offered her his arm. They walked in silence for a while, Anne appreciating the opportunity to be away from the clinic and the worry that dogged her steps. She might have little control over saving Meggie, but perhaps there was something she could do for Peter.

'What will we do about Peter when this is over?' Anne said carefully. 'He can't go home.'

'There might not be a choice. His father is his guardian.' She felt Ferris's gaze slide in her direction as his thoughts caught up with hers. 'No, Anne. I can't keep him. I am a doctor. I am out all hours of the day and night. I can't watch him or raise him. I don't have a wife. I am not a family.'

'His father is hardly a "family",' Anne dismissed his arguments. 'Surely, we can find him a situation, though? He was a good helper today and he was interested in the herbs. He's eight, he could apprentice when he's older.'

'That's in six years, Anne.'

'Well, there's school until then.' Anne fixed Ferris with a hard stare. 'He can't go back to Turk's Row.'

'I'll think about it.' Ferris covered her hand where it lay on his sleeve. 'I know you mean well, Anne. But it's complicated, it's more than just taking him in.'

Anne didn't back down. This was too important to let it go. 'No, it isn't. We do or we don't. There's no middle. That's how it is at Haberstock Hall. Either we want to help or we don't. You were wondering last night if you could have done more for them that night in the alley. If you really think that, now's your chance, Ferris.'

There was nothing quite like a scolding from Anne Peverett. Friend or foe, she knew how to put a man in his place. The worst of it was, she was right. This was his moment to make a difference for Meggie and Peter. Over the years he'd had to balance detachment with compassion. He couldn't save every child living in poverty, but he knew what Anne would say to that— *But you can make a difference for these two. Let that be enough. For now.*

What an extraordinary woman she was, what a family she must have, a family not unlike his own with their bent for caring for others.

* * *

At the hospital, he introduced her to Lieutenant Garrett Stroud, the man with the nightmares, and stepped back to watch her work her unique brand of magic, charming Stroud with her wide smile and caring manner as she explained how to use the lavender.

She is like you, his mind whispered. *She cares so deeply, she wants to help people, to make their worlds better. She wants to help you—not just your practice, but you.*

Stroud was laughing at something Anne said. Ferris couldn't recall ever hearing Stroud laugh. The man was stoic during his visits despite his best efforts to bring the man out of his resigned shell and the belief that his life would never be better than it was today. Ferris had seen Anne do the same for the women they visited with the wagon. She'd been doing it even before that, with her visits to the apothecaries' shops. Listening to them, laughing with them, hugging them, offering them her strength along with her herbs and insights. She'd done the same for him whether he'd realised it or not. His mind whispered the dangerous thoughts born last night as he lay beside her.

You could make a life with her, a good one full of service and healing. She would be an extraordinary partner in all ways. All you have to do is make room for her in your heart and in your life.

In his life. That was something he'd conveniently let his heated mind overlook last night. He already had a partner—his work. There was no room now for a wife, for a family and medicine, too. With Cara, they would have grown their marriage and his career side by side. They would have stepped into both together. That window of opportunity was gone now. His career was fully fledged and all-consuming, as the late-night visit from Peter proved. As much as he wanted a family, the argument remained, there wasn't room for one any longer. Sooner or later, something would be compromised.

Some men manage it, came the rejoinder.

Anne's own father had managed a large family and an active country practice. Other doctors Ferris knew married and had families. His brother, Frederick, was a devoted family man as well as being dedicated to his work in Parliament. The recent weeks Anne had been with him had shown him how it might be different, how they might share the work and let it bind them together. But how long would Anne tolerate sharing him with his work when it took him out late at night?

Anne finished with Stroud. 'Dr Tresham and I will check in next week and see how the lavender is working. It was a pleasure to meet you, Lieutenant.'

Stroud smiled, actually *smiled*. It took years off his face. Ferris hadn't realised how young he was. 'The pleasure was all mine, Miss Peverett. Thank you for coming.'

Anne glanced over and caught him watching her. Her gaze sent an ever-present jolt of awareness jangling through him. 'What are you smiling at, Ferris?'

'You. You made quite the impression,' Ferris complimented as they walked the short distance between the hospital and the physic garden. 'You seem to have that effect on everyone you meet.'

Even him.

With a look, a touch, a word, she could chase away his doubts and make him question the decisions he'd made to keep himself safe. He'd not realised how lonely he'd been until he'd met her. She made him wonder the impossible. What if it was different this time? What if he fell and she caught him? What if this time it was for ever? Was she worth the risk of finding out?

At the garden, they turned down a row of plants, Anne's gaze going everywhere to take it all in. 'This garden is a wonder!' She was in awe and he felt exceedingly, ridiculously pleased to have brought her. 'Oh, my goodness, is this henbane? And this datura?' Anne exclaimed, taking in the surrounding plants. 'This is quite the intrepid aisle. These are all hallucinogens.' She waggled her eyebrows in a teasing gesture. 'This must be the witches' row.'

Ferris laughed. 'The garden is laid out by ailments. It makes it a good study for students. You know by the row what type and use of plant you're looking at.'

Anne spun in a circle. 'Who knew such a magnificent place existed, and it's only a few streets from your practice. You're very lucky. You can come here to walk and think any time you want, and the view of the river is soothing, even in the winter. I can only imagine how beautiful this place is in the spring and summer.' Would she be here in the spring?

Her enthusiasm was infectious and Ferris pushed the silent question away. 'If this impresses you, I'll have to think of other sights to dazzle you with.' He felt playful and light for a moment despite the burdens of the day.

'I know one.' He tugged her down the path towards a glasshouse. He held the door open for her to go ahead of him. The glasshouse was warm, quiet. Private. They had the place to themselves. His hand dropped of its own accord to the small of her back as he guided her towards the plant. 'I give you *Theobroma cacao*, courtesy of Dr Hans Sloane and his time in Jamaica.'

'Chocolate?' Anne leaned forward to examine the plant. 'It looks like a gourd.'

'He apparently discovered how well chocolate dissolved in heated milk and sold his recipe to the Cadbury Company for drinking chocolate.' For all of her sophistication and knowledge, there was an innocence about Anne Peverett.

Anne wrinkled her brow in question and Ferris supplied, 'Cadbury's is a confectioner in Birmingham.' Ferris laughed. 'Most women come to London for the shops and the parties. I've never met one who was thrilled by a physic garden.' Or one that seemed content to spend her days treating the sick poor when the delights of one of Europe's great cities was to hand. He was doubly glad he'd taken her to the concert last night.

Anne tucked her arm through his and flashed him a teasing smile. 'I am not most women, I'm afraid.'

'No, you certainly are not and I'm glad for it. I wouldn't want you any other way.' He held her gaze, letting her see how serious he was, that he was not teasing. 'Anne, there's something I've been meaning to ask since the charity ball.' There were several things he'd been meaning to ask, but he'd start with the one that was most important, the first step forward in taking the risk. 'Why did you run from our kiss?' It was time to discover her secrets, time to know where he stood, time to know if there was a chance, for him, for them.

Anne's face suffused in a furious blush. 'What kind of question is that, Ferris? And why ask it now after so many weeks have passed?' She was trying to go on the offensive with her bluster, but Ferris recognised the tactic for what it was: a defence.

'Because it didn't matter then, Anne. It was a one-night wonder, a Cinderella moment, if you will.'

He noted the wariness in Anne's gaze as she followed the logic of his reply. 'And it matters now?' Anne issued her challenge. Did she really think he would retreat? That he would not answer her?

His gloved hand cupped her jaw, his thumb tracing the delicate zygomatic arch of her cheek. 'Yes, it might. In fact, I would like it to matter, very much.' His voice was low and intimate as he bent to take her mouth with his in a slow catch that made his intentions clear. This was not an ambush, not a surprise, not the impulse of a moment. This was a declaration, and a man could not declare himself more boldly.

Chapter Fourteen

Was there a more deliberate kiss than this? A deliberate taking of her mouth, a deliberate drinking from her lips, a deliberate assault on her senses. This was a thinking man's kiss and, oh, how Ferris Tresham loved to think. He'd apparently been thinking about this for quite a while, long enough to make her tremble, long enough to make her blood heat and her hands to make fists of themselves in the wool of his coat, her body to press against his and her mouth to answer him.

A slow hunger simmered and rose. Her hands were in the thick dark depths of his hair, his hands were at her hips, at her waist. He lifted her to a potting table as he deepened the kiss, and she answered with her mouth, her body, making room for him between the vee of her thighs, where his arousal made its presence known through the layers of her skirts. The heat and hardness of him was intoxicating. Neither of them shied away from it. Anne brought her hand to the core of him there, pressing her palm against its length. A trembling sigh escaped her, that sigh proof of how lost she was in the moment. Why deny what so blatantly lay between them? Hadn't she promised to allow herself a taste of passion with him? She curved her palm, moving to stroke the length of him, but Ferris's hand covered hers and he uttered a single, shattering word. 'No.'

'No?' Anne queried with a coy stare. Her hand refused to budge. 'This feels very much like "yes".'

He was more forceful this time. He took her hand away. 'Answer my question, Anne. Why did you run from our kiss?' He certainly gave a girl no quarter—not 'my kiss' but 'our kiss'. He was going to make her accountable for her rather ardent response that night.

'It wasn't right then.' She foundered, trying to get her thoughts together. Dear heavens, it was feeling pretty *right* now, though. Perhaps because she'd made herself new promises about what she could and couldn't have? How did he expect her to answer questions at present? Ferris crossed his arms and gave her an arched brow stare. She would be required to explain further.

'We didn't know one another. We were strangers caught up in a moment and that moment showed every potential of leading to other, more decadent moments.' Like this one. They were explosive together. This was why they'd ignored and then resisted the pull between them. It was positively flammable, and fires had a way of getting out of control. 'I didn't come to London looking for an attachment. I didn't want to lead you on.' Or herself. It was easy to forget herself, and her plans, when she was with Ferris. 'It wasn't right then,' she repeated.

'Is it right now? Anne?' Ferris's low tones were

hoarse with remnants of desire. She saw in the hot blue depths of his eyes that he wanted it to be.

'It could be,' she breathed the answer, excited anticipation pulsing through her, but Ferris took a step backwards. Her answer displeased him. She saw the snare too late. Hadn't she argued earlier today that there was no middle ground, just yes or no? 'There are things that must be negotiated, Ferris.'

Ferris's hot eyes cooled. 'Negotiated? That's decidedly unromantic, Anne.' He paused. 'Is there someone else? Someone back home in Hertfordshire?' There was a tension that radiated from him as he asked, a sign that her answer could hurt him, a sign, too, of how vulnerable he'd made himself to her. She didn't want that power, the power to hurt him.

'No, not any more.' Anne slid down from the potting table. 'Nothing permanent can come of this, Ferris. It doesn't work out for me.'

'Why is that?' Ferris's eyes followed her about the glasshouse.

'I won't give up my herbs and my work for a man, Ferris. I don't plan to marry and trade my calling for a nursery and housekeeping.' There was a long silence as she strolled the aisles of potted plants, absently reading the identifying tags. Ferris was thinking, quite palpably, too. Then he swore softly under his breath.

'I would like to call the man out who put such a dilemma to you, who made you feel you had to choose between him or your passion. Of course, he was hoping those things might be one and the same. He clearly didn't understand you.'

She looked up from a plant. 'No, he didn't. But he thought he did and so did I. That's the real tragedy of the story. I nearly gave up the things I loved the most without realising it. I thought my dreams were safe with him.' She trailed her fingers through clippings of rosemary, filling the air with their fragrance. 'But he'd never even heard me.' Ferris was listening intently now; she had all his attention.

'Two weeks before the wedding, he surprised me with a house not far from my parents. All he could talk about was the nursery, how he wanted to start a family right away. There was no herb garden, no workroom. When I asked about it, he simply said I'd be too busy being his wife to dabble in such things.' Anne faced Ferris, her arms crossed in defiance. 'I broke the engagement right then and there.'

She watched him take that in, a cloud crossing his solemn features. 'I decided there was room for one or the other in my life, but there could not be both.' The conversation had got away from her. She'd not meant to talk about Robert. The topic had galloped away from them as well. They'd only kissed twice, and here she was, acting as if Ferris had proposed.

Anne sighed. 'I'm sorry, I've completely exaggerated the issue.' Perhaps this was what happened when one got carried away with Ferris Tresham. Perhaps this was why gently bred girls weren't encouraged to kiss young men before they were engaged.

'Now I really do want to call him out.' Ferris grimaced and made his way to her. He offered her his hand, but there was resignation in his tone. 'You need to apologise for nothing. Am I not in the same position? Wondering if there's room for anything or anyone else in my life? I understand. You are not ready. I do apologise if I importuned you this afternoon.'

That wasn't it at all. She'd made a hash of it and effectively signalled, somehow, to him that she wasn't interested, even though she'd had her hand on him minutes earlier. If that wasn't interest, she didn't know what was. Anne halted, forcing him to stop and look at her. 'Ferris, I *am* ready. I just need you to know from the start what you're up against and that I need you to go slowly with me.' Perhaps he needed to go slowly for himself as well. They were both burning with a recognised passion, but unsure how to pursue it and where it could lead, or, more importantly, where they would allow it to lead without leaving them in ashes when it was over.

Ferris's eyes glowed hot for a moment as he reached for her and drew her close. 'I will take it slow, Anne, starting with this kiss.'

He meant to court her, but courting was deuced difficult amid a whooping cough outbreak. After a week since their watershed moment at the physic garden, Ferris didn't think it could be going any more slowly than this. He ducked out of the rain and stepped inside a small shop in Chelsea that sold children's toys. He was on the way back from errands and a doll in the window had caught his eye. A very nice doll, the kind with a porcelain head, carefully painted eyes and a pretty dress trimmed in lace. A doll for Meggie. Perhaps it would lift her spirits. No doubt she'd never had one like it, and a little girl should have nice doll, at least once. If only once.

He pushed the thought away. He'd not wanted to leave her today, but the wagon had needed to go out. People were counting on him, and Anne was with her. The situation was quickly moving from desperate to futile. He was holding death off with steam and hyssop syrup, a paltry arsenal against what he feared was the inevitable.

'I'll take the doll,' he told the shop assistant, casting his gaze over the shelves looking for something that would please Peter. A ship? Perhaps the boy was too old for a wooden ship. There was no place nearby to sail it. Jacks? A cup and ball? Those were good indoor games for winter. He took them both. He might have himself on a strict budget, but he could afford some small gifts where others were concerned. Was this what it would have been like to buy gifts for a family, for children of his own? For the first time since Cara died, the thought did not entirely fill him with loss. Sometimes families were made in unexpected places and in unexpected ways. Anne's words regarding Peter had stayed with him. He might not have children biologically, but perhaps he might be a father figure in other ways.

'For Christmas, sir?' the assistant asked, handing him the brown-paper-wrapped packages, a reminder that Christmas was just eight days away. Eight days would seem like an eternity for Meggie. Ferris paid the assistant and headed back into the rain, determined to make another stop. Christmas might need to come early at Number Fourteen Cheyne Walk. Whenever it came, Christmas required sweets at the very least.

At the confectioner's he selected some peppermints for Meggie, liquorice drops for Peter and searched for something for Anne. What would she like? Hard sweets? Soft sweets? Then he hit on it. Chocolate. Something that would remind her of their day at the physic garden and a reminder, too, that he'd not forgotten the flame that had sparked between them even if he hadn't kissed her, hadn't courted her, since that day. 'Do you, by chance, have any chocolates from Cadbury's of Birmingham?'

'I do. They're just in for Christmas.' The shopkeeper smiled and hurried to get the bars. 'How many would you like?'

'Four, please.' He hoped Anne would understand he did mean to court her. The whole purpose of courting was to see someone, to go on outings because that was the only way to be with them. But he saw Anne every day and there was no time for traditional courting outings about town, although even in winter there was plenty to do in London. With the festivities upon them, the shops were full of treats to look at, but their minds were far from the cheer of the season at the clinic.

Whooping cough had hit the asylum hard and Meggie had worsened despite their best efforts. Anne hadn't been back to her rooms on Harley Street for several nights now, devoting all her energy to fixing syrups and potions for the children's asylum and to caring for Meggie. Where a crisis might have served to drive others apart, it had served the opposite between him and

Anne. There was a new sense of unity between them that transcended the physicality of their attraction and the stilted nuances of courtship. They took turns driving the wagon out so that one of them was always with Meggie. They understood what the other needed without asking; unspoken messages flew between them.

I will take the first watch tonight. I will wake you if anything changes.

They shared his room and his bed with a natural ease born of exhaustion and circumstance, but also born of growing comfort.

They never went to bed together, by design and by necessity, one of them always staying up with Meggie, who needed them more and more often. But there were a few hours towards the end of the night when he might slide into bed beside Anne and enjoy the warm proximity of her. Fully clothed and on top of the blankets, of course.

He was a gentleman, after all, and a man, too—a man who was very aware that she was a woman to whom he was powerfully attracted. He would not tempt fate any further than he already had, although there were a few mornings when he'd awakened as he had that first day, with her in his arms, or his arm draped about her quite unintentionally, his body and hers calling to one another in spite of their best efforts for restraint.

You could make a life with her.

It became a daily mantra. He saw the proof of it in everything she did. If only there was time to do this right. It struck him as unseemly to fall in love in the midst of an outbreak. He supposed one could not choose when one fell in love. Between the outbreak, approaching Christmas and his trip to Bramble, he was running out of time. It might be weeks, well after the new year, before he could properly court her, and he found he didn't want to wait.

He'd been waiting years to feel this way again—not that he'd been *actively* looking to feel this way. He hadn't. Instead, he'd been actively avoiding it, perhaps for this very reason—there simply wasn't time for it. But it had pushed its way in nonetheless. He needed to make time for it, to see where it led, to see if he could persuade Anne to trust again. Surely if he could try again, she could, too.

Ferris gathered his packages with their gay ribbons tied about the necks of twisted paper. He made one more stop before heading home—the little market near Cheyne Walk where a man hauled a wagon of evergreen boughs in from the countryside each day for those in the city who wanted to decorate. He must have looked comical, walking the last few streets juggling the boughs and his packages.

Buying the gifts had lifted his lagging spirits and he hoped there might be good news waiting for him at home, too. But the moment he stepped through the door he was met with the sound of coughing from upstairs, the rattling *kink-kink-kink* of the whooping cough. He was coming to hate that noise. It had been a week since he'd brought Meggie home. It should have been under control by now. Early on, there'd been some days when he'd thought he was winning the battle, but no longer. He'd not been winning for days now and Meggie had already been weak. Some would say it was a miracle she'd made it this long.

He caught sight of Peter on the steps leading upstairs. The little boy had thrived this past week thanks to Mrs Green's cooking and a warm place to sleep, but his face still wore a worried, wary look. Waiting could do that to a person. Waiting for his sister to get better, waiting for his father to come and snatch him away from the comfort he'd found here. Waiting to have happiness taken from him. Ferris could hear Anne's soothing tones with Meggie. He could spare Peter a few minutes.

'How are you, Peter?' Ferris sat down on the steps beside the boy.

'Scared, sir.' The boy turned thoughtful brown eyes his way. 'Meggie's been coughing all day, worse than yesterday. It sounds funny when she breathes.' The paroxysmal stage.

'Whooping cough can last up to ten weeks,' Ferris said. It was a long and lingering illness. It took strength to see it through.

'We have a way to go, then,' Peter offered hopefully. 'Do you remember the story you read to me last night, by that fellow, Dickens? The little boy in that story was very ill, but he got better on Christmas Day. Meggie will, too.'

'You are a good brother, Peter.' Ferris ruffled the boy's hair, hoping the world wasn't about to deal him a blow. The boy took his sister's well-being personally. 'Since you mentioned it, Christmas *is* coming, and I was thinking we might have a little Christmas early, just the four of us.'

'Miss Anne, too?' The boy's worried eyes brightened. 'I like her, sir. She is a good person. I've learned so much about herbs with her. I'll be able to help Meggie now if she ever gets sick again.'

'I like her, too.' Ferris rose. 'Come on, I've got boughs on the kitchen table. You can help me carry them upstairs and decorate.'

Meggie's room had become a sickroom. Bottles and vials littered the bedside table. Anne had the curtains drawn back, though, to let in the light, and the room smelled of lavender and fresh air. She had the window open. Good. He agreed with that particular theory. The little girl was propped up on pillows, smoking her rosemary pipe, but Ferris was dismayed to see that Anne had to hold it for her. 'Breathe it in, slowly, Meggie, and out, slowly,' Anne instructed.

'Hello, Meggie.' Ferris approached with a smile that hid his worry. 'I've had an idea. I thought we could have Christmas tonight, right here.' He felt Anne's eyes on him, divining what lay in his mind. 'Peter and I can put up some boughs, and Mrs Green has left some chicken soup and fresh rolls. We can sing some carols, perhaps Miss Anne might read the Christmas story to us and I have presents. What do you think?'

'Presents?' There was a short-lived spark in Meggie's eyes, but the word cost her a bout of coughing.

'Yes, presents.' Ferris sat down on the other side of the bed, catching Anne's eye while he spoke to the little girl. 'Shall I sit with you, while Miss Anne gets supper ready? I'll help you with your pipe. The smoke is good for you, it opens your airways. Breathe deep so you can tell Peter where to hang the boughs. Try hard for me, Meggie.' Ferris gave her a kind smile, but inside he was breaking. He could feel the fragility of his soul. It was exposed and vulnerable and it was not ready for another loss.

Not this angel, Lord. You already have Cara. You don't need this one, too. I can't lose Meggie, too.

Chapter Fifteen

He was going to lose Meggie. Ferris's gut knew instinctively what his examination confirmed. It would be tonight, perhaps in the dark hours before dawn when physicians of old believed, and not without merit, the human humours were at their most susceptible. Perhaps sooner.

Let there be time for one last Christmas. Let them have this one last thing.

His plea had been reduced to simply that: not more time, just *enough* time.

The little girl continued to fail. What was left to try? They'd used rosemary in a pipe and as an oil. They'd used lavender to help her sleep and a variety of poultices. They'd tried hyssop syrup, teas with honey. None of it had brought long-term results. Meggie's skin was pale and waxy, her eyes over-bright. The fever was back. It meant the infection was no longer in abeyance. He pressed a hand to her forehead. She was burning and could barely breathe. If she were the child of a family he attended, he would tell them to prepare, to say their goodbyes, that it could be any time. In this case, he was her family and he didn't want to accept it.

The clink of dishes on the stairs heralded supper. Anne appeared with the supper tray, looking like Christmas itself. She'd changed her work attire for a pretty, long-sleeved day dress of forest green, a white apron tied about her waist and a matching ribbon threaded through her hair. Ferris flashed her a smile of gratitude as he took the tray from her.

Anne lay out the dinner things, complete with a candle for the centre of their little table, and Ferris's gratitude swelled at her thoughtfulness for the details. 'It looks wonderful, Anne,' he complimented, drawing up two chairs, one for Peter and one for he and Anne to share while they took turns to sit with Meggie and feed her.

'It's beautiful.' Meggie stared wide-eyed at the table. 'It's like a meal from a fairy tale.'

'I hope you like the chicken broth as much as you like the table,' Anne teased, taking a bowl and sitting on the edge of the bed. 'Breathe this in. Doesn't it smell good and hot?' she encouraged, spooning some for the girl.

As they ate supper, Ferris told stories about his day and what he'd seen on his errands. Peter joined in, talking about the things he'd done with the herbs or helped Mrs Green with. The tales made for a merry meal, even Meggie managed to smile. At last, when the eating was done, Ferris went to retrieve the Bible and passed it to Anne. How many Christmases had his mother read the story to all of them as boys? 'Now, for a Christmas tale. The one in Luke, Anne, if you please.' Luke the Physician.

She took the book with a soft smile, sadness and joy in her gaze as the unspoken words passed between them.

I know what's coming. Don't worry, we will give them a Christmas before it takes her.

Ferris's heart clenched. God, how he needed her. Anne found the pages and began to read. 'It came to pass in those days that a decree went out from Caesar Augustus.'

It was full dark outside and the candles lit Anne's features in a gentle light as she read. Ferris lost himself in the familiar words, in the sound of her voice. Ghosts were hovering close tonight. When she finished, she set aside the book and took Peter's hand and then Meggie's in each of hers and began to sing in a low, pleasing alto, 'Joy to the World, the Lord is come.' Ferris rose from his chair and joined them, completing the circle and adding his own tenor. They sang another and then another. Peter's eyes glistened as the words of 'Adeste Fideles' faded away. He looked from Ferris to Anne, to Meggie and back again. Ferris knew the boy's thoughts before he spoke. Hadn't he been thinking the same?

'We're like a family,' the boy whispered. 'Meggie and I, we haven't had a family for a long time. Haven't had a Christmas either.'

Take the boy, Ferris. You can't let him go.

Anne's words came back to him, loud and insistent in his mind, just as they had been in the toy shop. His throat clogged. He wasn't sure he could speak. He cleared his throat and found his voice. 'Time for presents,' he announced only a little gruffly while Anne turned away for a moment, wiping her eyes with a corner of her apron. 'It's not Christmas without sweets. We *must* have sweets,' he teased, handing the children their treats. 'Even you, Anne.' He passed her the chocolate bar with a wink, doing his best to summon every ounce of joviality. 'Fresh in from Birmingham, I'm told.' It was hard to keep up the pretence of happiness when he knew what waited in the darkness. There were some things he could do to ease Meggie's suffering as she crossed over and he would do them after Peter was tucked in.

The children were in alt over the sweets, and Anne gave him a private smile.

You're doing wonderfully, it said. *Strength*, it said.

'There's more.' Ferris mustered a grin, giving the children the paper-wrapped packages. 'Anne, you might need to help Meggie with hers.' He should have bought the doll long before this. Why hadn't he?

Peter exclaimed over the jacks and the cup and ball, immediately attempting to put the ball in the cup. Meggie stared at the doll in awe when Anne unwrapped it and put it in her arms. 'This is mine? I've always wanted a doll.' The words came out in gasps.

Ferris smoothed her hair back from her hot face. 'Shhh, little one. Don't talk. Just hold the dolly, rock her. I can see from your face how much you like her.'

'Emmeline,' Meggie gasped out, disobeying his instructions in her excitement.

'Is that her name?' Anne said patiently. 'It's a wonderful name. You and Emmeline need to rest. I need to fix your willow-bark tea so you're not so hot.'

But Meggie disobeyed Anne, too. She insisted on talking. 'Do you think Christmas is this nice in Heaven?'

'It's better. There's nothing quite like Christmas in Heaven.' Peter stepped forward. 'And Mama's there.' Ferris felt his heart crack. So the boy knew it, too, despite his courageous words earlier.

'Don't be afraid for me, Peter. You are a good brother. I'll tell Mama.' The effort was too much for Meggie. Ferris held her while she coughed.

'Peter, get my bag.' He had poppy syrup in there. He'd been saving it, hoping he wouldn't need it, but he wouldn't let her suffer like this. Poppy syrup would help her sleep, help her relax, while he and Anne fought the cough. They would not give up.

Peter delivered the bag and said a solemn goodnight to his sister, and Anne settled him in bed with a draught of lavender tea. Ferris could hear them in the other room, Anne so calm, so loving and strong. He gave Meggie a small dose of the syrup and curled her arm about her doll, pretending to give some to Emmeline, too. 'I'll be right here, Meggie. I won't leave you.'

Ferris was on his knees when Anne returned to the room. The sight of his dark head bowed made her halt in the doorway. The image of him would be burned in her mind for ever. She would never forget him like this or how he'd been tonight. It had been a stroke of pure, loving inspiration to make tonight Christmas for the children, to give them such a memorable last evening.

She went to him and quietly placed a hand on his shoulder. He roused and for a moment she thought he would get up. 'No, don't,' Anne whispered. There were tear tracks on his face and his pain cut at her. She'd fought those same tears all evening. She knelt beside him and put an arm about him, lending him whatever strength she had left, this great, strong man. 'My father says sometimes the best place to fight is on our knees,' she whispered.

They lost her. Shortly after the witching hour, the angels came to take one of their own home. They sat at the edge of the bed in disbelief for a long while, although they'd known it was coming. It did not ease the shock when it came. One moment there'd been a raspy, struggling breath and then not another. Anne wasn't sure how long they sat there, hands locked together in a tight grip.

Ferris leaned forward, his long, elegant hand brushing against Meggie's cheek. He stood, his face drawn with fatigue, failure and grief. 'I'll call the undertaker.' Anne heard his footsteps on the stairs, then moments later there came the crash of shattering glass from the clinic office. She rose and ran downstairs. Ferris was breaking, her brave, strong man was breaking. She could not bear for him to break alone.

Sharp glass shards littered the office floor along with the contents of Ferris's usually crowded desktop. Inkstand, paperweight, files, ledgers, books—all lay amid the glass that had once decorated his elegant bookcases. Ferris stood with his back to her, shoulders heaving with the effort of his exertions, of his emotions. Did she dare touch him? Would he welcome her presence? Her witness to his weakness? She wasn't sure, but she did know that grief was better when shared. Her mother never let her father bear his disappointments alone.

Anne stepped carefully over copies of Buchan and Culpeper, trying to avoid the glass. Ferris would hate himself for the destruction later when sense returned. A moan, deep and shuddering, ripped through him, an articulation of despair. Anne put a hand on his back, letting him know she was there. 'Ferris,' she whispered his name, and said no more. What was there to say? He would not want platitudes. He would not want to hear he'd done all he could, that it was God's will or that Meggie was in a better place. He wanted Meggie here, with them, and so did she. Peter was right—for a short while they'd been a little family. Her own grief cut deep. 'Ferris,' she said again, her voice choked on the word, on grief as she gave words to the obvious pain between them. 'We've lost her.'

Ferris turned then, showing an awareness of her for the first time since she'd entered the office, blue eyes full of desolation before he shut them tight, a tear escaping beneath dark lashes. 'Anne, I couldn't save her.' He heaved with emotion.

'Neither could I,' Anne whispered. Silly man, did he really think it was his job alone to save them all?

'I should have been able to...' His voice broke, his

shoulders slumped, anger giving way to abject anguish, and then he was in her arms, or was she in his? It was impossible to know who moved first.

She knew only that they cried together, clung together, their arms tight about one another, holding to each other as they slid to the floor amid the wreckage of anger as the storm of grief washed over them, consumed them, cleansed them. His head was against her shoulder. She felt the wetness of his tears, the roll of his shoulders. She comforted him even as she sobbed her own sense of loss, stroking his back, murmuring hoarse, whispered admonitions to hush.

It broke her anew to see such palpable proof of his grief, this great, confident man who shied away from nothing: not from facing down a drunk to rescue two helpless children, not from confronting a woman who was notoriously disagreeable—that woman being herself—not from owning up to his own mistakes, not from treating London's poor when others of his station would ignore them for greener pastures, not from giving two children a Christmas to remember.

He'd faced death head-on tonight, put himself between that dark spectre and the children. He'd created joy tonight, his very last weapon with which to ease Meggie, with which to give Peter a lasting memory of his sister.

She felt his breathing steady, his shoulders still, an accepting calm settle. 'It will be all right, Ferris.' Perhaps she could speak the idea into reality. Perhaps if she said it enough, it would come true. In the moment, she felt as if nothing would be right again.

He lifted his head from her shoulder, his blue eyes burning. 'If you mean things will go on, yes, I imagine they will. But will they be right?' Resignation flickered in the depths of his gaze. 'What kind of world is this, Anne, where children die and doctors don't even countenance their illnesses with research? Buchan, Culpeper, the whole lot of them did nothing. There is no cure, not even much written about the cough and children. They relegated the care of children to old women and nursemaids.'

'Shhh, Ferris.' Anne smoothed his hair, holding his gaze, willing him to find peace, solace. 'We'll make it right again, somehow.' She drew him to her, kissing his cheek the way one might kiss and soothe a small child. But he was a man in the grips of his emotions, a man seeking a desperate affirmation of life in the midst of death and loss, and she was a woman seeking the same. It was a potent and flammable combination.

His mouth was on hers, his hands buried in the depths of her hair, his words a guttural, trembling rumbling as he devoured her mouth. 'Anne, I need you.' A madness swept them, claimed them. Her hands were at his face, framing his jaw, holding him inescapably close. She didn't want to be apart from him; she wanted her body to be his body, to have nothing keep them from one another.

His mouth was at her throat, at her breast, hungry and devouring as her own hands tore at his cravat. There were too many clothes, too many layers between them. Her legs were bent and drawn up and he was between them, a hand running up her thigh beneath her skirts.

Yes, this was so much better, his hand on her bare thigh, yet she only burned hotter, her body and mind searching for something more, something to hold the grief at bay with.

Something crunched beneath Ferris's knee and he swore, distracted. 'Damn. Glass.'

'Never mind it.' She tugged him close, her mouth fixed on his once more, her body acutely aware of his hand at the warm juncture of her thighs even as it wept for more, begged frantically for more, and his body thrummed with the desire to answer the plea—she could feel it in the tautness of his shoulders. Yes, yes, yes—she rocked against him, but it was too late. Reality had already claimed Ferris.

He drew back, sitting on his heels, his arousal thrusting evident and obvious against his trousers. He scrubbed a hand across his face. 'I will not do this, Anne. I will not take you on a glass-strewn floor and use you as a tool against my grief.' He drew a shaky breath. 'I will not do it.' There was resolution in the words as if he were trying to convince himself, compel himself into compliance.

'I would not mind,' Anne said quietly.

Ferris nodded. 'But I would, and I fear that you would, too, later, once you realised what you'd done.' He looked about him, taking in the ruin of the office, a wry look quirking in his eyes. 'It's a little like breaking bookcases—one regrets it too late.' He sighed. 'I should get a broom.'

'In the morning,' Anne said firmly. 'Come to bed. We'll sleep better if we're together.' Alone, they would lay awake and torture themselves with what-ifs and could-have-beens when it came to Meggie. There would be much to deal with in the morning, starting with Peter. They would need their wits and their patience. 'We're stronger together, Ferris.'

Chapter Sixteen

They *were* stronger together. Ferris was not sure how he would have got through the days that followed without Anne. Together, they told Peter in the morning. Anne had held the boy while he cried, rocking Peter gently as Ferris recalled how she'd rocked him amid the shattered glass of the office. They took Peter out with them in the wagon when they made their usual visits with the mobile clinic, not wanting to leave him alone and preferring to keep him busy.

Ferris made his usual rounds at the soldiers' hospital and the children's asylum, instructing the nurses about their care. These children would pull through with the right care and food. They were healthier than Meggie had been and that was an enormous factor in determining survival.

His journal was full of the names of those who'd sought the assistance of the mobile clinic since mid-November. It was time to turn it in to Sir Bentley, the head of the board of governors. He took Peter with him on his trip to the hospital in Knightsbridge, making a point of stopping at the shop windows to let the boy enjoy the sights on the way back.

It should have been a trip that brought him satisfaction. He'd achieved what he'd set out to do after the board had refused to fund his proposal. He'd demonstrated clear need. They would not deny him now, not without risking looking downright callous and uncaring with Christmas bearing down on them, just three days away. But there was no satisfaction in the knowledge.

What did it matter when he couldn't save one little girl? What did it matter when the names had come at the expense of deceiving the woman he cared about? He needed to tell Anne, but the time was never right. Now was certainly not the time, not when they were grieving the loss of Meggie. How could he add this to Anne's burden when she was already bearing so much for them, keeping their spirits up?

They stopped at a bakery window that showed off a display of carefully frosted gingerbread men with currants for eyes and trimmed with white icing. 'Shall we go in and see if there are any left for sale?' Ferris offered the boy an encouraging smile.

'Biscuits before dinner?' Peter asked hesitantly as if he couldn't believe his good luck. 'What will Mrs Green say?'

Ferris laughed. 'Who's going to tell her? Besides, Anne says ginger is good for digestion. They're practically a health food.'

The bakery was warm and fragrant, a pleasant interruption from London's wet streets. Ferris purchased two of the gingerbread men and gave one to Peter. He bit the head off his and munched, but Peter just stared at his.

'It's almost too nice to eat.' Peter bit his lip. 'I wonder when I shall eat such a lovely biscuit again. Maybe I should save it to look at.'

'Shall we take some home, then? Perhaps Anne would like one and you can have another after supper,' Ferris offered.

'But you might not always be there to buy them for me,' Peter confessed. The boy swallowed hard and looked manfully at Ferris. 'I suppose you will be wanting me to go now.' His voice trembled. 'Now that it's all over and there's no reason to stay.'

Now that Meggie was gone, he meant. The boy had not said his sister's name since she'd died. He drew up his narrow shoulders. 'You and Miss Anne have been kind letting me stay so long.'

Ferris dropped to one knee in the warm bakery, his hand on the boy's shoulder. He hoped he had the words. What did one say to a grieving, scared little boy who was trying to be older than his years? Anne would know what to say, but she wasn't here. 'Stay as long as you like, Peter.'

The boy started to shake his head. 'I couldn't.'

Pride. Ferris recognised that right away. 'You're good help. Miss Anne says you've learned herbs and plants very fast. You can work with us, run errands for us, earn your keep, if that's what you're worried about. Perhaps I could even pay you a small wage.' He mentally ran through his budget. It would be a very small wage. 'Unless you want to go home, then we won't stand in your way,' Ferris added. The boy *did* have a father.

'I'd like to stay.' Something hard flashed in Peter's eyes.

Ferris rose. 'Good. Now that's settled, let's get some more gingerbread men and go home before Miss Anne worries. We'll tell her you're going to stay.'

Peter smiled for the first time in a week at the reassurance that while some things had changed, not all things had to. He had security, stability. He took Ferris's hand. 'I'm glad I'll get to stay. You and me and Miss Anne, we'll be a family.'

Ferris returned the boy's smile, hiding his own trepidation. He'd bitten off more than he'd bargained on. A family? What if Anne left? Who would help him then? Peter would be devastated. The boy had no notion that the arrangement with Anne was temporary. Now that the ledger was turned in and the numbers accumulated, there was no need to keep Anne with him. Except that he wanted her to stay for reasons that had nothing to do with his original plans. She couldn't leave them, she couldn't leave *him*, and yet how could it be otherwise?

He was scheduled to leave for Bramble in a few days. He'd thought of staying in town in spite of his promise to Frederick. He could claim the situation at the children's asylum as an excuse. Surely the family would understand. But after Meggie's passing, town held no allure. All he wanted was to get away, and the asylum didn't truly need him. They had everything they needed to nurse the children. If something did go wrong, he was only a day away. But Bramble meant leaving Anne, and if he left Anne, she'd leave him. She'd go back to Harley Street. She wouldn't stay at the clinic with him gone. He couldn't leave her, but he couldn't stay. The idea struck like a flash of lightning in a dark sky—brilliant and sharp.

Take her with you. Take Peter and Anne and go home to your family.

What would she say to that?

She should leave. Anne looked about the room that had become her workspace, the clinic that had become her home. It was quiet, the hour of the day after Mrs Green had gone home and before Ferris was due back from errands. She hadn't been home to Harley Street in weeks. But her time was up. There was nothing keeping her here now. Meggie was gone and she'd proven herself to Ferris. Hadn't that been her goal? To show him a woman could be a healer, that she didn't need a diploma to be of worth? Ferris had said nothing about her leaving, but that was understandable. He'd been taciturn this week. They were both still trying to move past the grief of losing Meggie and their sense of failure on her behalf.

You linger for him, not for any medical reason, the truth whispered in her mind. *You stay for the man. You think he will not make you choose, that he will not make the same demands of you that Robert made, that he can give you a happy-ever-after.*

No, she answered fiercely, taking down a pestle and mortar to pound some root for distraction. She wasn't looking for long term. She was just looking for now. That was the deal she'd made herself.

If she left, there would be no resolution to those lingering kisses, to those heated minutes on the office floor when she'd been willing to give herself to him, to let him use her to assuage his grief and perhaps to use him to assuage hers, because she wanted him. Oh, she'd gone and done it now. She'd fallen for a man who was openly married to his work, thinking it would keep her heart safe. Leaving him was going to hurt. Best to do it quickly and rip the scab off the wound all at once. She would go tomorrow, before he left for Bramble. She'd leave him before he could leave her.

There was a little consolation in being the one who made the first move in that direction. She would not linger like a ghost in the clinic. It would be good for her to go. There was already one too many ghosts here. Perhaps going back to Harley Street would help her shake the gloom of losing Meggie. It would be the best of both worlds, she bargained with herself. She would still see him. They would both be out in the community continuing their work, she just wouldn't live here any longer, wouldn't take her meals here, wouldn't take her sleep here, beside him in his bed, wouldn't wake to a glimpse of naked back or torso as he shaved, wouldn't wake to the sandalwood scent of him on the bed linens. In return, she could protect what was left of her heart. He wouldn't have the chance to fail her.

They had lived practically and decadently, at least for a while. She'd discreetly moved out of Ferris's room after Meggie passed. There was no reason to share when there was a vacant room, unless they admitted to the temptation between them and indulged it. But that was hardly 'taking it slow'. She wasn't sure she wanted to take it slow any more. There was no use denying it. They weren't just professionals any longer. If she were to take a lover, she wanted it to be him. He would honour her, protect her in the ways that mattered. He wouldn't shatter her reputation, or be less than discreet, nor would he make demands after the fact.

Anne pushed back a strand of hair that had fallen loose while she pounded. She sighed. What was wrong with her? One moment she was contemplating leaving and the next taking Ferris as a lover. A most decadent thought for a woman who'd never had one—a lover, that is. She'd had *plenty* of decadent thoughts lately. Being with Ferris seemed to spawn them. Another reason to leave. It was becoming clearer by the day, by the repeated circuit of her thoughts, that to stay meant to commit to a path of no return. Sooner or later, if they continued on this trajectory, they *would* consummate their relationship. A little trill of heat and excitement shot through her. Her face flushed. It was still flushed a few minutes later when Ferris and Peter returned from their errands.

Ferris took off his coat and cocked his head. He studied her, his gaze moving between her and the copious amounts of pounded root on the table before her. 'Think you have enough angelica there? Are you well, Anne? You look a little heated.'

'I'm fine.' But come to think of it, he looked a bit flushed, too. There was a near-frantic, or was that a near-manic, look in his eyes, as if he were lit from the inside. 'What is it, Ferris?' Peter had moved into the kitchen and they were alone in her workroom.

He came around the table and gripped her by the shoulders. 'I want to ask you something, Anne.' His gaze was intent on her, melting any thoughts of leaving. How could she leave this man who burned with such intensity, such passion? 'Will you come to Bramble with me for Christmas?'

Their eyes held, a hundred messages flashing between them. To stay meant an escalation of their relationship. The earlier acknowledgement swam to the fore. This was the test. To go to Bramble meant they would explore the potential that had whispered in Lady Cowden's ballroom and had sparked to life in the physic garden and again amid the shattered glass of his office. 'Are you sure, Ferris?' She would not go to Bramble as a colleague. It would be a big deal to his family; there would be a certain nuance to navigate.

'Yes.' Ferris was all bristling, fervent urgency and it was intoxicating given that Ferris was usually a very deliberate man, so seldom spontaneous. 'I can't leave you.' No more than she could leave him. The Rubicon had come to her.

They left at dawn in the ducal Cowden coach requisitioned from the town house. It would be far more comfortable than trains crowded with people going home for Christmas. A sleepy Peter wrapped in a blanket drowsed against Anne as the horses pulled away from Number Fourteen Cheyne Walk, harnesses jangling.

Ferris leaned back against the squabs and shut his eyes. He'd barely slept last night in an effort to make all the arrangements necessitated by leaving a day earlier than planned. But it was worth it. Once the idea of escaping the city had taken root, he'd not been able to shake it. He could not stay in town any longer.

Still, this felt more like a getaway than a departure, an escape from the grief that haunted him, that kept him up at night running and rerunning scenarios. How could he have saved Meggie? What had he overlooked? He hoped leaving the city would help him leave those thoughts behind, even though it would mean facing other ghosts.

He must have dozed. When he awoke, Anne was handing out breakfast rolls from a basket beneath the seat and doing her best to answer Peter's barrage of questions. The boy asked about everything outside the window and inside the carriage. 'What's Bramble like?' Peter turned his attention across the carriage, but Ferris felt Anne's attention, too, another reminder of how brave she was with this decision to follow him home. She was walking into the unknown for him. It had been difficult for her to write a note to her sister last night, explaining the sudden change in plans. He knew she didn't take leaving Thea alone for Christmas lightly.

Ferris crossed his legs and leaned back, preparing to indulge Peter in stories of Bramble. 'My brother lives at Bramble with his family and my parents when they're all in residence. There will be boys to play with and there will be gypsies.' He winked at Anne. 'They'll love your herbs and potions.'

The mention of gypsies brought on another burst of questions from Peter and Ferris spent a pleasant morning regaling them both with stories of Bramble and his childhood, of the romps he and his brothers took across the fields, the fishing in the stream, the trees they climbed in summer and the snowballs they threw in winter when they were lucky enough to have snow. Peter yawned and snuggled against Anne, still catching up on sleep.

'I don't think he's ever left London. I hope Sussex won't disappoint him,' Ferris said as Peter drifted off.

'It won't,' Anne answered him with a smile. 'You're good with him, Ferris. He admires you.' Ferris was well aware of that admiration and the pressure that came with it. The boy had become his shadow in the days since Meggie's death. It was natural—the boy was looking for stability and constancy in a world that had taken both from him.

Ferris kept his voice low, not wanting to wake Peter. 'I wanted to talk with you about that, Anne. Yesterday, on our walk, I offered him a chance to stay with me.' He watched her face light with joy. He liked pleasing her, liked being the one to put that look on her face. 'I am hoping, though, that I might find an arrangement for him while I'm at Bramble. He'd be happier there. He'd have Helena's boys and the country air is certainly healthier.'

'I'm sure the two of you will decide on something suitable, either way.' She paused, her gaze soft. 'You've done well by him, Ferris. You're a good man, a courageous man.'

The words nearly undid him. Ferris cleared his throat and cast about for a lighter topic. He took out his pocket watch and checked it. 'Speaking of courageous, Thea will be receiving your note about now.'

Anne laughed. 'It was hardly courageous of me to wait until this morning to send the note, knowing full well by the time she got it everything would be a fait accompli. I'd be miles from town and there'd be nothing she could do about it.' He'd helped her write the note, assuring Thea that her sister would be well chaperoned by the Duchess of Cowden and his sister-in-law, Lady Brixton.

At noon, they arrived at a large village with a neat-kept High Street lined with half-timbered buildings and glass-paned shops that had Peter's nose pressed to the coach window as they rumbled past. His eyes grew bigger as they approached the village common. 'A fair! Look, it's a fair!'

Ferris leaned forward and looked out, saying with feigned surprised, 'Why, so it is.' He glanced over at Anne, who was not in the least fooled by his nonchalance. 'Why don't we stop for lunch, stretch our legs and take in the fair? There's nothing quite like a Christmas Fair, in my opinion.' Although it had been ages since he'd gone to one, ages since he'd taken a day off work, ages since he'd played, and here he was attending carolling concerts and Christmas Fairs. Two more things he owed to Anne. She brought out the best in him, something that had been long hidden.

The coach pulled into the stable yard of a clean, smart-looking inn near the commons. Ferris jumped out and swung Peter down before taking Anne's hand. Her green eyes flashed with conspiracy. 'You knew there was a fair here.'

'I *hoped* there was a fair here,' he corrected with a smile. 'I recalled that there used to be. We used to come—it's directly on the way to Bramble, we could hardly avoid it.' They were just two hours from Bramble, in fact, and if he could have avoided the fair today, he would have. But to go around would lengthen the journey considerably. He had memories here, good ones, of times that were lost to him, people that were lost to him. The last time he was here had been with Cara, the Christmas before he'd graduated from medical school, the Christmas before she'd sickened beyond cure.

He pushed the memory away. He would not think about that. Today was for new memories, a new start. He wanted to see the fair through the eyes of a boy who'd never been, he wanted to please Anne, to offer her the courtship she deserved even if just for a day. He offered Anne his arm and Peter took his hand, tugging them towards the fair booths in his excitement. Ferris felt the ghosts recede at Anne's touch and a little further at her smile.

Chapter Seventeen

He dedicated his day to making her smile, to making Peter laugh. They wandered the booths, eating meat pasties for lunch that dribbled savoury juice on their chins. They wrapped their hands around hot mugs of sweet cider to sip as they strolled among the vendors and wandering carollers. The fair booths were decked in bows and evergreen swags, adding to the festive atmosphere.

They stopped at every stall, lingering over wood-carved toys and puppets that dazzled Peter, silk ribbons and soft wool scarves from Italy that caught Anne's eye. They carefully examined the excellent craftsmanship of a jeweller, Anne's gaze surreptitiously lingering on a bracelet of deep blue, lapis lazuli from the Far East. There were milled soaps from France, and delicate perfumes that caught her nose. There were spices and herbs from the Mediterranean that captivated her. She was in raptures as she sniffed them, and Ferris laughed at the sight of her so clearly enjoying herself.

Her pleasure was his pleasure and it was intoxicating, as was this day out of time, this dangerous little fantasy he'd managed to weave for himself. It was too easy to get caught up in it, in the image of seeing himself as a family man with a son, a wife, people whom he loved, on whom he could lavish his attentions, spoil with simple pleasures, and with whom he could take joy with in the ordinary. Reality intruded. It was just one day. Not every day could be like this. He had his work. But wasn't that the point? To seize the joy, the rare day, when it presented itself? What if he could have both his work and a family? What if he didn't have to compromise? What if he opened himself fully to love again? What would he find? Perhaps more days like this.

They shopped shamelessly, purchasing little gifts for family. Anne helped him select a perfume for Helena, and he bought a bottle of Vin Santo for Frederick from the Italian wine merchant. Anne selected ribbons for her sisters, a pair of well-made leather gloves for her father and a prettily carved floral soap for her mother. 'So she can duplicate it.' Anne laughed. 'She'll have no intentions of washing with it. She'll want to make it.'

Ferris asked Peter to help him select gifts for Helena's boys from the toy merchant, and the boy's eyes lit up with being asked for advice. 'What would you like, Peter? I think you should choose something for yourself,' Ferris suggested.

'I've already had so much today, sir. What more could I want? I already have the jacks and the cup and ball.' Peter looked at him, perplexed. 'There's been pasties and fairings and cider. It's been the best day ever, sir.' It had been. The boy's spirits had lifted, and for the first time he seemed to genuinely enjoy himself without hesitation or worry that it would somehow be taken away.

'Still,' Ferris insisted, 'I want you to have a toy as well.' Ferris became serious. 'Unless you're too old? Perhaps a game instead? Look at this pegboard. The idea is to remove all the pegs, like this.' Ferris jumped a few pegs and then let Peter try. 'Yes, you're getting it, very good. It's beautifully made. The wood is polished and the pegs are finely carved. I think we should get it,' Ferris said, realising the boy wouldn't dare to ask for it. What else had he dared not ask for? 'Anne, why don't you and Peter go to the chocolatier's and purchase a few sweets for Helena's boys. I'll meet you there.' He'd seen Peter eyeing a whittling knife a couple of booths back. It would be a good hobby for him and he was old enough for such a tool. There were paper twists of herbs to get for Anne. He was already imagining how her face would light up Christmas morning when she saw them.

To reach the herb vendor, he had to pass the jeweller. The bracelet was still there in its case and his eye was drawn to it. He paused, considering it. He could not give it to her on Christmas morning amid the family gifts over breakfast. It was not that kind of gift. It was a private gift. Perhaps he should settle for something simpler, a crystal heart on a silk ribbon.

'It's a lovely piece, sir,' the jeweller offered quietly. 'As lovely as your wife.'

Ferris looked up. 'She's not my wife.'

'Ah, my mistake.' The jeweller bowed in apology. 'The two of you, the boy…well, you seemed like a family.' He stepped back to help another customer.

'I'll take it,' Ferris decided. He would find a way to give it to Anne, a way that would honour the joy of today.

He caught up to Anne and Peter, just as the first snowflakes began to fall, white against a darkening sky. Was it that late already? He checked his watch, surprised to see that the day had fled. Merchants were lighting lanterns for night shopping, transforming the little market into something magical. He made another decision. 'Why don't we stay the evening and press on to Bramble in the morning?' he announced. 'It will give us a chance to take the market in at night.' It would be a chance to follow this day out of time with a night, a chance to indulge in the fantasy a little longer.

They'd finally worn Peter out. Ferris shut the door softly behind him, leaving Peter within. *They.* That was part of the fantasy, too, the idea of belonging with someone, to someone, and the fantasy continued. Anne was waiting for him, for his report, in the quiet of the corridor between their rooms at the inn. 'Peter's asleep already.' Involuntarily, his hand reached for hers. He'd grown far too used to taking her hand, her arm.

'Happiness suits you, Ferris, and it makes you happy to make him happy.' Anne's voice was quiet, inadvertently feeding the fantasy he'd spun for himself today. They'd dined in a private parlour, watching snow fall outside the window, and taken a final walk through the fairgrounds, letting the snow fleck their hair as they snacked on warm gingerbread before Peter was too tired to do any more.

'He's not had much in his life. These are simple things, simple joys, easy to give.' Ferris dismissed the comment. 'Anyone could do it.'

'But they didn't. *You* did,' Anne insisted. 'You're a good man, Ferris Tresham. I once thought you were arrogant, but in truth, you are actually quite humble.' She smiled and he laughed.

'Arrogant, was I? I suppose that's fair. I once thought you were a charlatan.' They'd come a long way since the day in Sally Burroughs's apothecary, all the way to this dim little hallway in the middle of snowy Sussex where the past and passion simmered between them. He dropped his voice, private and low, the sound of slow fiddles drifting up from the taproom. 'I didn't think it very long though, I might add. Before I thought you a charlatan, I simply thought you were beautiful.'

He reached a hand up to push back a loose strand of her hair. 'You stole my breath that night at the charity ball and, since then, you've stolen so much more, Anne.' They were standing close now, close enough for foreheads to touch. 'That night I only knew you were beautiful on the outside, but now I know you're stunning on the inside, too.' He breathed her in, the herb and vanilla scent of her, his hand sliding to the small of her back. 'Dance with me.'

Let me touch you a while longer, dream a while longer, chase away the ghosts a while longer.

'Here?' Her eyes came up.

'Right here, Anne,' he murmured. He moved them into a slow, swaying dance that turned them in a small, close circle, bodies touching, up against one another. 'Unless you'd prefer the public room?'

Her gaze held his. 'No, right here is fine.'

When had her arms gone around his neck? When had their bodies blended together, hips to hips? When had the world narrowed to this hallway, all moments blurring into one, just this one? She wanted to stay in his arms for ever, dance here for ever. Today had been intoxicating, walking the market with him, letting the daydream run rampant as they ate and shopped and spoiled Peter, letting herself get caught up in the glances Ferris threw her way. But this was something more even than that. There was nothing to distract them now. There was just them and the truth that lay between them, unexplored and pulsing with life.

His hand was in her hair, tipping her head back to meet his gaze, meet his mouth. Oh, Lord, those kisses would be her undoing and, oh, how she wanted to be undone. She wrapped her arms tighter about his neck, holding him to her. She was starting to burn, the fire in her a simmer no more. The deliberateness of his kiss gave way to a fervent urgency. A moan escaped her as she felt the hardness of the wall come up behind her, trapping her deliciously between it and the heat of Ferris's body. His mouth devoured her—her ear, her throat, her neck—the heat of his mouth pressed over the place where her pulse beat fast and strong.

'Don't stop, Ferris. Tonight, don't stop,' she breathed,

fumbling for the handle to her door. It opened and Ferris waltzed her inside. This was better, so much better. The firelight bathed the room in soft, warm colour. She reached for his necktie, untying it with nimble fingers between kisses, his own hands at the buttons of her gown. Their hands were hungry, their desire impatient, their mouths desperate. His coat followed his necktie, and then his shirt. The hungry pace slowed.

'Don't rush this, Ferris. I want to look at you,' Anne whispered.

'You've seen me without a shirt before.' His greedy mouth was at her throat, his voice hoarse.

'But not when I could touch you, too.' She traced the contours of his torso with a deliberate fingertip: the muscled roundness of pectoral muscles, the sculpted plane of rib and abdomen. '*You* are an anatomical wonder,' she breathed. 'I do not think every man is so beautiful.'

'Nor every woman.' He kissed her hard, his arm about her waist, bringing her tight against him. His blue eyes glittered like the lapis lazuli she'd seen in the marketplace. Such blue would always remind her of him after today, after tonight. Too bad she'd not bought the bracelet. 'It's my turn now, minx. I'm going to finish what I started with this dress.'

His voice was rough with desire, with need, but not his touch—that was reverence itself. He pushed the gown from her shoulders as if he were unwrapping precious glass and looked upon her as if she were sacred and rare. He took her chemise from her and stood back, the apple of his throat working as he gazed upon her. Anne raised a hand to free her hair, pulling the last of her pins loose and letting it fall in copper skeins. A thrill of power trilled through her at the notion of rendering this man speechless. She stepped forward, hands reaching for the waistband of his trousers. He covered them with his own.

'Anne, are you sure?'

She met his gaze, letting him see the sincerity of her words. 'Surer than I've been of anything, *ever*.' It was true, she realised. She wanted him beyond reason, beyond all logic. Tonight, the impossible was possible. She could have him, this man who saw her for who she was and wanted her anyway.

His eyes glittered. 'Let me.' He undid the fall of his trousers and pushed them down over lean hips. He stepped out of them, kicking them away so that he stood before her as naked as she, as exposed as she. She'd never seen anything quite so stunning—those long legs, those thighs, that rather magnificent phallus he was sporting between them. He let her look for a moment before he swept her up in his arms and carried her to the bed with its turned-down covers waiting in invitation.

He followed her down, his arms framing her, her thighs bracketing him, their bodies fitting together in a wondrous, sensual puzzle, mouths, legs, hips moulded to one another. All the while the pleasure moved through her, a slow, steady lava in her veins. His mouth was at her breast, her body arching in his, as his phallus nudged at her entrance. Her legs came up, wrapping about his hips, urging, inviting as he pressed forward, patient even as the heat of his desire flamed in his eyes, answering the desire in hers. This was what they could be together, passion and heat and completion. She gasped as he pushed forward, her body stretching to measure him, to take him full. A noise escaped her and he stilled. 'I'm sorry,' he murmured at her neck, breathing hard from effort and restraint.

'Don't be,' Anne whispered. She pulled him to her. 'Go on. I like how you feel in me, as though I'm whole.'

Ferris groaned. 'Those are potent words, Anne.' He began to move inside her, back, forth, a slip and then a thrust, until their bodies took up the rhythm, sliding together, slipping apart and sliding together again, stronger each time, moving them towards the beacon of pleasure in passion's mist. Anne wrapped her legs about him tightly, holding him to her, claiming him as he claimed her, with mouth and body.

This was what it meant to be alive, to be with *this* man, and the thrill of it rode her hard until at last she felt a change in him, the male strength gathering and mounting even as her own body began to collect itself, a warm rolling wave moving through her as he thrust hard, deep, once, twice more, a groan wrenching from him, a sound of both extreme pain and pleasure as he pulled from her and released in the sheets with a jerking, spilling spasm of completion.

He rolled on to his back, a hand thrown carelessly over his head as he looked up to the ceiling, his chest heaving. 'Goodness, Anne, you're going to kill me.' He exhaled with a laugh. Then he pulled her to him, drawing her into the nook of his shoulder. He pressed a kiss to her hair and they said nothing more, preferring instead to bask in the drowsy quiet that followed.

This was peace. Anne sighed. To lay here, naked with him, skin to skin, the fire warming the room, their bodies warming one another, their thoughts lingering quietly on pleasure's shore, the worries and grief of London far from their minds. All that mattered was now, and there was all night for it, for them, and they made the most of it, sleeping, waking, lovemaking, exploring one another until they knew the other's body as well as their own.

Dawn intruded as Anne yawned in his arms for the last time. She would sleep once more and when she woke, the fantasy would be over. They would put on their clothes, they would leave this room and continue on to Bramble, and then what? What else would continue? Would this? What would they become in the light of day? Would there be awkwardness, would they be unsure of how to navigate this decision to consummate the passion that lay between them? Would once be enough to quench the burning or would tonight merely serve to fan the flames, create a wanting that went on and on?

She shifted in Ferris's arms, glancing at his face in repose, the dark lashes that swept his cheeks. He was asleep already. Did thoughts of tomorrow haunt his sleep? Did he feel the same as her, that one night of the fantasy would not be enough? Or would he be sated? It was a cooling thought indeed to think he might not feel the same, that it might be over for him. And yet, that was the safe choice, wasn't it? Hadn't she told him as much that day in the physic garden, that she wasn't looking for a marriage?

Better that Ferris see this as one night out of time than something that required him to make the offer honour demanded. She'd not come to bed with the expectation of such an offer, with no expectation truly except to taste the passion that had been licking at them. They were troubling thoughts to fall asleep on and not at all what she would have preferred to have ended this extraordinary night with.

Those thoughts were not gone when she awoke, although Ferris was. The pillow was cold. He'd been gone for a while. Before she had time to sort through what that meant, she heard him in the hall, laughing with Peter, and a knock on her door.

'Anne, are you awake yet?' This was followed by more laughing. 'Get up, we have things to do, the day awaits!'

'I'm coming!' she called. Anne laid back against the pillows with a smile. He wasn't gone, he was just up. There was a difference, and that difference chased away her earlier thoughts. Perhaps there was no need to complicate things with overthinking, with worrying about something that lay in the future—days from now, weeks from now. Perhaps it was simply enough to be in the moment, to get out of bed and see what happened next.

She dressed quickly, brushing down the green travel ensemble she'd worn yesterday, humming as she made short work of her morning ablutions. She twisted her hair into a simple knot at her neck. She fastened her small gold earrings and checked her appearance in the mirror above the wash basin. She wanted to look neat and respectable. She was highly cognisant of the fact that she'd be meeting Ferris's family in a few hours, that she'd be a guest in the home of people she'd met only once and only briefly.

Anne stared a moment longer at her reflection. Yes, she looked neat and respectable, certainly, but there was something more at her eyes and about her mouth: happiness. With that came the realisation that she'd not been happy for some time. Content, perhaps, at moments, with her family, with her work, with her life, but content was not the same as being *happy*. She'd nearly forgotten what happiness could feel like—a true lightness of being, the brightness it could bring an ordinary day. But today wasn't ordinary was it? It was Christmas Eve and she was spending it with an extraordinary man. Anne laughed as she gathered her things. Everything was extraordinary when one was happy—that was how happiness worked.

Anne stopped at the door, her hand on the knob. She took a moment to look back at the room. Last night she thought she'd be sad to leave the place, sad to step into the morning, because it would mean stepping away from what happened here. She wasn't worried now. She was remembering that happiness couldn't be contained. It went with you and spilled over into everything.

Ferris and Peter were waiting for her downstairs, Ferris looking clean-shaven, bright-eyed and handsome, Peter looking excited. 'We're to get new clothes for me,' Peter announced with a mixture of pride and awe.

Ferris's hand rested on Peter's shoulder as his eyes met hers, offering her a private 'good morning' as he offered her his free arm. 'Should have done it in London, clothes are long overdue.'

They spent the morning combing the shops for clothes and shoes for Peter, a most enjoyable task amid the snow-dusted rooftops of the High Street and the general festive atmosphere of last-minute shoppers who flocked to the Christmas market. Ferris's hand had spent the morning at her waist, her elbow, the small of her back as he escorted them from shop to shop. There was a sweet tenderness to those touches today, reminding her of other touches, other private intimacies they'd shared, as did the banked blue heat of his gaze when their eyes met.

Peter delighted carrying his packages, and his joy over the purchases was infectious. They made one last trip through the Christmas market for gingerbread men and then they were off on the last leg of the journey to Bramble. A few days ago, the prospect might have been a cause for worry—how would Ferris explain his unexpected guest? What would the family think of her? What would happen between her and Ferris? But today, those things didn't matter as much as the happiness filling her and taking everything one joyful moment at a time.

Chapter Eighteen

~~~~~

What a difference a day made. Ferris stretched his legs across the interior of the coach and smiled. He couldn't help it. He'd been smiling all morning. Was it only yesterday they'd pulled out of London, a demoralised three-some brought low by grief and futility? London felt like a lifetime ago. It wasn't that the loss of Meggie was diminished in the Christmas spirit, but it was balanced with hope and possibility. He'd lost Meggie, but he'd saved Peter. Anne was here with him, bravely willing to celebrate Christmas at Bramble among strangers for *him*, and he was going home for Christmas, something he'd not done for years.

Ferris caught Anne's gaze and felt her squeeze his hand where it lay on her lap. 'You're sure they won't mind you've brought a guest?' she asked.

'Well,' he teased, 'it's too late to do anything about it if they do.' He rolled his eyes and she playfully swatted at him. He dropped the teasing. 'They will love you, Anne.'

As I do.

He loved her. There was no avoiding it, no mistaking it, and he wasn't afraid of admitting it to himself on this bright, snow-frosted morning. Today was Christmas Eve, the one day of the year when love ruled, when anything was possible, even for him. For the first time since losing Cara, he believed such magic might indeed be possible if a man like him who'd sworn not to risk himself on love again was willing to try. The lapis-lazuli bracelet was a warm weight in his coat pocket. He should give it to her tonight, after everyone had retired and they were alone.

The coach turned a familiar corner and Ferris leaned forward to peer out the window, gripped with the excitement of homecoming and the anxiety of it as well. What would it feel like to see Bramble again? 'Look, you can see the house at the end of the drive. We're nearly there.' What would be waiting for him? Ghosts or greetings? What did he *want* to be waiting at the end of drive? The past or the present? Perhaps it was up to him to decide, perhaps it always had been. Perhaps it was time to let go of the fear and embrace the possibilities.

Bramble did not disappoint. The clean, stately lines of its pointed roofs decorated with snow were as he remembered it, a majestic red-bricked queen overlooking immaculate parklands. Even in winter, there was a neatness to it that appealed to him. Bramble was an orderly and decorous host and the ghosts were not out today, only the nostalgia of homecoming. Perhaps he owed that to Anne and Peter, whose excitement was a joyous thing to behold. To see Bramble through their eyes was a pleasant surprise and a warm one. It was maybe the closest thing he would get to the fantasy he'd once entertained of bringing his own family to Bramble for Christmas—a wife and a child of his own to join with his or her cousins.

His family waited for him on the top step: Helena, Frederick and the boys, and beside them, his parents. His heart was full as he handed Anne and Peter out of the coach. Everyone he loved was here. He was home, and the profound sense of fulfilment that surged through him begged the question—why hadn't he come sooner? What had he been afraid of? He glanced over at Anne, looking like Christmas in her green travelling ensemble, and his heart snagged.

Perhaps you were waiting for her...perhaps Anne gives you a reason to be brave.

Ferris made the requisite introductions, his mother and Helena exclaiming over Anne, easily recalling her from the ball. 'Of course I remember you, Miss Peverett, you were the only one my son danced with all night.' His mother laughed. Ferris could see this pleased Anne and eased her nerves. Within moments, Helena had taken Peter under her wing and looped her arm through Anne's as if they were sisters already.

A suggestion whispered through his mind: *They could be sisters in truth.*

Could he make that happen? Could he convince Anne to rethink her position on marriage? He'd have to proceed carefully, for both their sakes. They'd both been hurt. He would scare her off if he rushed her. The best way forward was to enjoy the moments he had and see where they led.

There are things you still have to tell her. Do not let her reticence become your excuse. You owe it to her to tell her about Cara and you owe it to her to come clean about the mobile clinics.

Yes, yes, he knew that. He thrust the reminder away. Not now, not yet. They'd only just arrived. They'd been through a difficult week. They both deserved a chance to reclaim the joy of the season.

Frederick shook his hand and pulled him in for a brotherly embrace. 'I'm glad you're here, that you've brought your herbalist and the boy. Having someone to fuss over will keep Mother's mind off Fortis.'

'Has there been word?' Worry instantly intruded.

'No,' Frederick assured him, clapping him on the back. 'You're just in time. Bramble festivities are about to begin and I was thinking I was going to have to lead the cutting of the Yule log all by myself. What a treat it will be for the tenants to have two Tresham boys at the saws this year.'

Frederick hadn't been joking about being 'just in time'. Ferris had no sooner changed into a work shirt than a Yule cutting party was assembled in the wide front hall of Bramble. Those who wanted to brave the cold followed Frederick and Ferris into the forest, while others stayed behind to enjoy the warm hospitality of Bramble. The public rooms were open to all in celebration of Christmas, and Bramble's cook had spared nothing in lading the long dining room table with festive delicacies: ginger cookies, miniature chocolate cakes and lemon tarts, tureens of soup and a roast from which Cook carved thin, savory slices.

It was all as Ferris remembered it: the house festooned with greenery, velvet ribbons and candles, the open house, the food, the Yule log cutting. Later, there would be games in the ballroom for children, organised by his mother and Helena, while adults ate and drank and carried on leisurely conversation. There might even be country dancing later—the very best kind, Ferris thought—before everyone paraded down to the midnight church service. But that was hours away. There was much to do before then.

It was a whirlwind of a day and Ferris was caught up in all of it. So was Anne. The tide of festivities had quite swept her away. He caught a glimpse of her as he and Frederick returned at the front of the Yule log phalanx and carried out the tradition of presenting it to their father. She was surrounded by women, her ever-present basket at her feet as she showed the women a lotion.

Helena swept by to give Frederick a quick kiss, her colour high from excitement as she turned to him to add, 'Oh, Ferris, your Anne is a wonder. Everyone adores her. She knows the most interesting things. Did you know angelica root suppresses the urge to drink?'

Ferris laughed. 'Yes, as a matter of fact, I did.' He made his way through the crowd to reach Anne—a very slow progress, everyone wanted to stop and talk and welcome him back. Even when he did reach Anne, he had to wait until the women dispersed. 'You've made more conquests, I see.' It did funny things to his heart to see her here in his home, among the Tresham people as if she'd always belonged here. Desire, intense and sure, rose sharply.

She stood and took his hand, a little smile playing at her mouth. Did she guess what was on his mind? 'Show me around? Maybe we can find a quiet place and take a breather just for a moment from all of this.'

Just for a moment? He had rather more than a moment on his mind. 'I know exactly where we can go.' And exactly what they could do.

'The stables?' Anne breathed in the warm comfort of horses and hay in winter. Their getaway from the party had been successful if rather gradual. Ferris was well liked and it had been ages since he'd been home, something she'd pieced together over the course of the afternoon. She was bursting with questions, but also with something else—she was craving him, his touch, his presence. She'd known the moment he'd entered the hall, she'd felt his return in her bones, and she'd wanted nothing more than to run to him, throw her arms about him and laugh with him, celebrate this joyous day, celebrate her happiness with him.

Ferris gave a nod, indicating a ladder. 'Up there, hayloft. Are you game?'

She managed the ladder, skirts and all. Getting down would be another story, though, but that could wait. She fell into the piles of soft hay with a sigh. 'This is glorious!' She moved her arms and legs, making a hay angel as Ferris flopped down beside her.

'*You're* glorious.' He picked a piece of hay from her hair. 'I walked into the hall and saw you sitting with the women and I just went hard, Anne, unbelievably hard. I had to have you. I've never been so jealous of so many women before. They had your attentions and I wanted them for myself.'

Anne reached a hand between them, finding his length, hard and as ready as he claimed. 'I think you speak the truth,' she said with a laugh. She lowered her voice. 'I knew the moment you came in and I wanted you, too.' She undid the fall of his trousers and slid a hand inside. 'I love the feel of you, I love knowing that I do this to you.' Last night they had been bold with their bodies; today, they were bold with their words, more sure of one another, and it added to the headiness of their happiness.

Ferris chuckled and rolled her beneath him, his gaze looking down at her, intense, burning and blue. His hand slipped beneath her skirts, pushing them back. 'I love the feel of you, too, when I'm inside you, all that wet, warm perfection surrounding me. I can't wait to feel you again.'

She reached for him, drawing him down and kissing him hard. 'Then you'd best get on with it.'

Before someone missed them at the party...before someone came looking.

The risk of discovery added an erotic urgency to the already heady exigence of their desire. They came together fast and furious, trying and failing to muffle their pleasure, passion's end taking them in an overwhelming wave of completion that left them gasping in the hay.

She snuggled close to Ferris, idly picking hay from his hair in the aftermath. 'We'll have to be careful not to give ourselves away. Haylofts can leave a lot of telltale evidence, but they're nice. What better place to be on a Christmas Eve afternoon?' Although she thought she'd like to be here any afternoon if it was with Ferris. She levered up on one arm, all the better to see his face. 'Are you happy to be home?'

'Of course, why do you ask?' His tone was casual, but she'd not missed the flicker of something else in his gaze.

'You haven't been home for Christmas in several years. Why?' she asked tentatively, feeling suddenly as if she were prying. She knew the Ferris Tresham of London, the serious, stoic physician, but today had shown her there was more to him than that and she was admittedly…curious.

'You've been listening to gossip,' Ferris replied drily but not unkindly, and she relaxed. 'I was wondering the same thing today, too. I saw my family on the steps waiting for me. I felt something of a prodigal and I wondered why I hadn't come home sooner.' His chest rose and fell beneath her ear. 'I was afraid of ghosts, I think.' He pressed a kiss to her hair. 'But I needn't have.'

Ghosts? He could *not* leave the conversation there. One did not casually drop that kind of information and then walk away from it. She was about to press him for more when Ferris put a finger to her lips with a warning hush. There was someone below them.

'Ferris, are you up there?' It was Frederick. Anne froze and flashed Ferris a wide-eyed look. Great. They'd only been here a handful of hours and were about to be caught by his brother. The family wouldn't like her so much then. Ferris shook his head, counselling silence. Frederick called out again, unconvinced by the silence. 'If you're in here, Ferris, hurry back. Mother's been asking for you. Games and dancing are underway.'

They waited a few long minutes to assure themselves Frederick had left. Ferris crawled to the edge of the loft and peered over. 'It's safe,' he affirmed, and then broke out laughing. He flopped back into the hay beside her. 'Sweet heavens, I feel like I'm thirteen and sneaking out with my father's good brandy.'

'Did you do such a thing?' Anne feigned shock as she began putting her clothes aright. 'I can't believe it.'

'Yes, all three of us, even Fortis, who was much younger. We met up here and passed it around. This has always been our favourite hideout. Probably why Frederick knew where to look for me.' Ferris tucked an arm behind his head, in no hurry despite Frederick's warning. 'We got pretty sick. Father decided that was punishment enough, and it was. We didn't drink again for a very long time. Fabulous deterrent, one I am sure Frederick will remember for his boys as they grow.' He chuckled. 'I haven't thought about it in years.'

'Tell me more, Ferris. I want to hear all about your childhood.' Anne snuggled up against him, undoing her recent attempts at restoring her clothes. 'Did you always want to be a doctor?'

'I'd always wanted to help people,' Ferris answered slowly. 'Second sons are expected to make a life away from the estate and I knew the military wasn't for me. I thought about the church, but I couldn't imagine boring people every Sunday with my prosy thoughts. I wanted to save lives, not souls. My parents were involved with hospitals, as you know, so it was a natural avenue and an idealistic one, I soon realised.'

He turned to look at her, his blue eyes thoughtful. 'I run the scenarios at night when I can't sleep. What should I have done for Meggie, how could I have saved her? Surely a doctor with a degree from Edinburgh should have been able to save one girl, but then I realised it was more than me failing, that society had failed her.'

It was the first time they'd talked of it since the night it happened, the first time he'd opened his heart about the hurt. She gave him time to find the words, to put his thoughts together. 'It's the needlessness that bothers me, Anne. A healthy child would have recovered. If she'd been fed and housed as she should have been in order to thrive, she would have made it through.'

'We're changing that, Ferris, one person at a time, with your mobile wagon,' Anne offered.

He rolled to face her, a gentle smile on his face. 'But not fast enough for my taste.'

'Give us time, Ferris,' she murmured. This must be what it felt like to be on a honeymoon, Anne thought as they held one another in the warmth of the hayloft, reluctant to return to the party, wanting only to be together, to share their bodies and their hearts. Sharing about Meggie had not diminished the happiness that had buoyed them today—if anything, it had contributed to the sense of completeness between them. Knowing and loving were two sides of the same coin. The more one loved someone, the more one knew them, and the more one knew, the more one *could* love. This, Anne thought, was what it meant to be in love, to know someone inside and out, secrets and all, souls and bodies laid bare.

Chapter Nineteen

He'd nearly laid his soul bare in the hayloft. Ferris poured himself a cup of the Christmas punch at the refreshment table, watching Anne with Helena and his mother across the room, gathering the children for the reading of the Christmas story. Anne *thought* he had, though.

He wondered which was worse, leading Anne to believe he'd shared deeply with her when he knew better, when he knew that the real secret was still locked within him, or having not told Anne. Perhaps he shouldn't have pulled back. She'd made it easy with her questions about why he hadn't come home, why he had become a doctor. He'd had two openings and he'd almost taken them. She'd not pressed him about the ghosts. Perhaps it would have gone differently if she had, if Frederick hadn't interrupted. Or not.

He did admit to some fear in naming the ghosts and bringing them to life of his own volition. He hadn't talked with Anne about Meggie in London for that very reason. He hadn't wanted to bring to life his own hurt, his own grief. And yet that decision hadn't stopped the grief, the mourning. The loss had weighed on him nonetheless. Instead, it had felt good to share his feelings over losing Meggie with her, perhaps because she'd been there, because she understood, she had her own sense of loss. Speaking of it with Anne had not summoned ghosts, but healing and inspiration in him. It reminded him why he fought, not because the fight was futile as he'd been feeling in the wake of Meggie's death, but because there was hope as long as he did fight. Most of all, he didn't fight alone. He had Anne now.

But for how long? Ferris took a swallow of punch. He'd promised himself he wouldn't think of such things, that he'd just enjoy the moments. The problem was, he wanted more moments, he wanted all the moments for always. That scared him. What if he lost Anne? There were so many ways to lose her. She'd been painfully clear on her desire not to marry and her reasons for it. Or he could lose her as he'd lost Cara—turn away for a moment and she'd be gone.

He and Cara had been just four months from their happy-ever-after that last Christmas. In the spring he would have had his diploma, been able to practise medicine. They'd celebrated their engagement here in the drawing room at Bramble, surrounded by family, friends, neighbours, amid the Christmas festivities. His gaze rested on the piece of handmade lace draped at the end of the piano. Cara's lace. She'd made it for his mother, part of the tradition at Bramble to make homemade gifts. The ghosts of Christmas Past swarmed.

He'd celebrated his victory too soon. The ghosts were still here.

Frederick was beside him, a friendly hand on his shoulder. 'A word, brother? We haven't had a moment alone since your arrival.'

They went to a small room towards the back of the house Frederick had claimed as his own office as he helped his father with the estate business. It had been redone since Ferris was last here. Now, it boasted walls panelled in smooth golden oak, neat bookcases and a desk by the window, two chairs by the fire. A wooden toy sat before the fender, proof that Helena and the baby sat here while his brother worked.

Frederick motioned to the chairs and poured them each a brandy. 'Cheers, brother.' He passed a tumbler to him. 'Love looks good on you—at least it did up until a few minutes ago. How's the hayloft? As accommodating as always?' Frederick slanted him a knowing look.

Ferris shook his head. 'I felt thirteen again, thanks to you.'

'At least it was just me.' Frederick raised a brow. 'What if it had been Father or someone else?' What had seemed harmless fun in the moment seemed dangerous in retrospect. He and Anne would have been caught in a most compromising situation. Compromising situations demanded matrimonial satisfaction. Well, that would be one way to settle the question, and not an unpalatable one. The brandy made him warm and the ghosts from the drawing room receded, pushed back by more pleasant and more recent memories.

'I am prepared to marry her, Frederick.' He spoke

the realisation out loud, spoke it into life. He was prepared to be Anne's husband, to be a father to Peter. He'd thought Frederick would greet the news with enthusiasm, but his brother said nothing. 'What? No congratulations? Isn't this what you've wanted? To see me happy, to see me married?'

'Are you truly prepared to marry her? Because I saw your face in the drawing room, the way you stared at the lace. You've not let Cara go. Does Anne know? Have you told her?' Frederick was relentless.

'It hasn't come up.' It was a poor excuse. Anne had told him about Robert, not just the facts and details about breaking it off so close to the wedding, but the betrayal she'd felt, how hurt she'd been, how the event had changed her, how it had shaped the choices she'd made going forward. He had not reciprocated in kind.

'Hasn't come up? That *should* strike you as problematic given the status of your relationship. You've taken her to bed, you're acting as if you're on a honeymoon, you say you're ready to marry her, to walk into an instant family with a woman you've only known for six weeks, yet you've not laid any groundwork for that marriage to be a success. Instead, you're keeping secrets. That should tell you something about how *ready* you are.'

Frederick leaned forward, a hand at his knee. 'Ferris, listen to me. We all loved Cara. We all wanted that dream for you. But *we've* moved on. Mother puts the lace out at Christmas to remember her fondly, not to mourn her. We see something that reminds us of her and we tell the story to each other, or to the boys. We laugh and cry with her parents when they visit. You need to do the same. Carry her with you as a memory, not as a chain that fetters you, that holds you back from happiness. Until you can do that, you will not be free, Ferris, and Anne will end up competing with the ghost of something that never came to pass. It's not fair to yourself or Anne if you idealise a ghost. The ghost will always win.'

'There are other considerations.' Ferris played with the stem of his glass. 'She's not sure she wants to marry. She has her own ghosts.' Although she'd shared them.

'Then convince her.' Frederick managed a sly smile. 'Is that why you decided to come? To let the magic of Bramble persuade her?'

'Not purposely, but… I suppose yes. I couldn't imagine spending Christmas without her when it came right down to it.'

They stared at the fire for a long moment before Frederick spoke again. 'The two of you have a lot in common, both healers, both middle children. She's a doctor's daughter. She understands your work, your life. She's grown up with it.' Frederick shifted his feet on the fireplace fender. 'How is the mobile clinic going? Did you get your numbers?'

'Yes. I turned in the ledger to the hospital before I left. There is undeniable need for services that go to the people instead of waiting for people to come to the services.' It should have felt good to talk about work, about his passion, to move the conversation away from Frederick's marital counsel, but it felt just as uncomfortable.

'What is it?' Frederick prompted, sensing his unease.

'I wouldn't have had the numbers without Anne,' Ferris admitted bluntly.

'Ah, I see. Another secret,' Frederick said shrewdly. Perhaps it didn't matter, though. He and Anne were together now in a way entirely different than any he'd imagined when he'd first offered for her to join him. Even then, he'd offered her something in exchange.

But you didn't tell her about the ledger and what you needed it for. You were not entirely forthcoming.

But the ends justified the means, Ferris argued with his conscience. Anne wanted to help people and so did he. She'd want the mobile clinic to succeed.

So why didn't you tell her? Why did you hold back? You didn't tell her when it might not have been a big deal and now you've waited too long. All she can do now is forgive you.

If she found out.

Frederick shifted in his seat. 'There is one more thing I wanted to speak with you about.' Ferris was instantly alert, laying aside his own concerns. 'Helena is expecting.'

Ferris studied his brother carefully, noting the prideful twitch of impending fatherhood at his brother's mouth. It was good news to Frederick, then. 'When?'

'We think mid to late August. Certainly, it's early yet, we could be wrong. But a man with four children knows when his wife is breeding and her courses are two weeks late. It's not like her.'

'With your permission, I'll have Anne speak with her before we leave. She'll have something to help with morning sickness, and I'll leave a diet for her to follow for nutrition, especially during the early months and in winter where fresh food is not as available.' It was his turn to give the advice. He smiled at his brother. 'Congratulations.'

They finished off their brandies and rose in unspoken accord. It was time to get back to the party. The Christmas story would be finished, young children would have been bundled off to their homes by now for sleep. Guests would be in the process of putting on coats and cloaks, well fortified with Christmas punch and warm food. Frederick put a hand to his shoulder as they stepped into the hall with a final admonition. 'Tell her, Ferris. She will understand, she will help you heal.' Perhaps his brother was right. The time had come for Christmas Present to do battle with Christmas Past for the sake of Christmas Future.

Even so, a wicked voice whispered from deep in his mind where fear lived, *telling her is no guarantee. You could give her everything and you could still lose her. Are you sure you're ready to risk such a love again, such hurt again if you fail?*

This time the answer was yes. He was ready to risk it, *more* than he was ready to risk losing for lack of trying.

In the great hall, he helped Anne with her grey cloak, pressing a surreptitious kiss to her cheek when he was sure no one was looking. She was flushed and pretty as she drew her hood up, her gaze soft on him. 'Are you all right?' she asked, taking his hand.

'I am. Frederick wanted to talk.' He was all right, he realised. His mind was settled on a direction and it was time to take the next step on that path. 'Would you come with me, Anne? There's something I need to do at the church before the service and I'd like you to be there. In fact, I *need* you to be there.'

It was time to tame a ghost in the silence of the night. Ferris held the wrought-iron gate that led to the cemetery open for Anne and followed her through. It had started to snow again, dusting the grey headstones with white icing along their edges. There were evergreen wreaths and candles shrouded in glass chimneys at some graves, their flames giving the graveyard a solemn glow appropriate for a night that celebrated holy, eternal love.

Ferris gripped Anne's hand and felt the peace of that light settle on him. He'd not expected to feel this way in this place. He'd expected to be pummelled with the past, assaulted with the pain of his loss. But it was not here. Only peace was here. He halted before Cara's stone, a beautifully carved slab of granite that read simply,

Cara Bradford
Beloved Daughter
September 7th 1822—January 20th 1842

'I was not entirely honest with you today, Anne. I need to tell you why I haven't been home for Christmas in years.' He shot her a sideways glance, watching her face as he pressed on. 'I need to tell you about the ghost of my Christmas past.'

'You can tell me anything, Ferris,' she encouraged

softly, and it was all the prompt he needed, but where to start? How to begin?

He closed his eyes and the simple words came. 'I loved her all my life. I don't remember a time when I didn't. I grew up with her.' Memories unlocked, poured out from the confines of their treasure chests, glowing all the brighter for the telling of them. How he and Cara spent a summer searching for Roman ruins, digging up his father's fallow cornfield in their conviction that a Roman legion lay beneath it. They'd found some non-descript shards, but nothing more. How they'd nursed a hawk with a broken wing back to health one winter and set it free in the forest that spring; how they spent their days riding the breadth of the land searching for people and animals to help. 'I was destined to marry her, there was no other path for me but her. We were to wed as soon as I finished medical school. We were young. I was twenty-one, she was nineteen, but we'd waited long enough.' Ferris stared at the headstone with its deep carved dates. 'She's still young, nineteen for ever.' And he was growing older, time was passing for him, and with it opportunity.

'We celebrated our engagement on Christmas Eve with the understanding we'd wed in the spring when I graduated.' It had been hard to leave her to return to Edinburgh when the term began, as if some unconscious part of him had known he would not see her again. For years he'd wished he hadn't left, that he hadn't insisted on waiting to make love to her until the wedding, on being so bloody honourable about it even though he went to bed burning every night, frustrated by kisses that could go no further because he'd decreed it.

'She died a few weeks later of a lung fever. She'd gone out to rescue a horse stuck on the ice. The ice was thin and it broke. She went in, but not before she got the horse to safety.' It was just like Cara to put the animal ahead of herself. 'She pulled herself out eventually and rode the horse to Bramble, but the weather had already done its worst.' He'd pictured her so many times in his mind, making that ride, soaking wet, freezing from ice water and January cold. His parents told him she'd arrived draped over the horse's neck and unconscious. She was too weak to move and they'd kept her at Bramble. She'd lasted only a week before she succumbed. 'She was dead before the letter even arrived that she was ill,' Ferris ended softly. 'I set out immediately from Edinburgh, but I met the other courier halfway. There was no point in coming home. I couldn't save her.'

Anne's gloved thumb drew circles over the back of his hand, soothing through the leather. 'And so you finished your studies and joined Frederick on his Grand Tour because it took you further from home and, you hoped, further from the pain. Did it help?'

Ferris faced her, looking at her fully for the first time since he'd begun to speak. He raised a hand to her face, cupping her jaw gently. 'No. I threw myself into my work when I returned, helping others as we had planned to do together. It helped a little. I was busy, distracted. There was less time to think about her.'

'Perhaps that was a mistake,' Anne said softly. 'Grief

isn't meant to be bottled, but to be shared, and you, my dear man, you've been alone for far too long.'

Ferris gave a wry smile. 'That's what Frederick said to me today.' He drew a breath for the rest of what he had to say. 'It hurt to lose her, Anne. I've never felt anything like it and it hurt for so long. Some days, I couldn't even remember what it was like not to hurt. When it began to numb, I knew I never wanted to feel that way again, to hurt like that, to feel like I was shattered into a thousand pieces that could never be whole. Then I met you and something happened. Those pieces and things inside me I thought were dead, maybe even hoped were dead, came alive again. And I've been scared, Anne, because I feel for you the way I felt for her, only perhaps more intensely, more deeply, because I know how precious and rare such a feeling is.' He raised her gloved hand to his lips and kissed it. 'But I'm more afraid of losing you than I am of loving you. So, at great risk to myself, Anne, I love you.' There, he'd done it. He'd laid his heart at her feet. Now, it was up to her what was to be done with it. In the distance, the sound of singing floated on the air as the parade of villagers and tenants made their way to church.

Anne's eyes held his, glistening with emotion. 'You, Ferris Tresham, are the bravest man I know.' She kissed him then, a warm touch against the cold night. It wasn't exactly an affirmation, but it was enough.

Chapter Twenty

Ferris Tresham loved her. He'd laid his soul open for her.

It was all Anne could think about as they took their places in the Tresham pews at the front of the candlelit church, as the vicar gave the Christmas message about the power of love. Ferris loved her and he was letting her decide what to do with that love. A man only confessed such depth of feeling when he wanted something, and she feared she knew where Ferris's declaration was leading: a proposal, marriage, a marriage to her. Or a marriage to replace the one he'd lost years ago? No, not the latter. Tonight had been an exorcism of sorts for him, a chance to purge his grief and to recalibrate the memories, a finding of perspective, perhaps, or balance as he'd done with Meggie.

But for all the balance it may have brought him, she was unsteady, reeling from the potency of his disclosure. Had she said the right words in response? Done the right thing? Had he expected her to say the words back to him? *I love you, Ferris.* She felt them; it would not have been a lie.

She did love him, but she held back because of what those powerful words might have meant to him—that perhaps she'd changed her mind about marriage, when she had not. It would give him false expectations. It was easier to let the kiss do the talking, to embrace the joy of that love and not the jeopardy. She would be happy in the moment and perhaps, if she could string enough moments together, the future would work itself out. It was, admittedly, risky thinking and hopeful wishing.

They filed outside afterwards, to the pealing of the midnight bells ringing in Christmas. Ferris's grip on her hand was tight, his face awash with rare emotion as he looked to the night sky. 'I'm free, Anne. At last, I am free.'

A star winked in the sky, cutting through the parting clouds. 'Quick, make a wish,' Anne whispered. 'A Christmas star is lucky.' They closed their eyes and wished, laughing at the childish pleasure.

'What did you wish for, Anne?' Ferris asked as they began the walk back to Bramble with the others.

'You're not supposed to tell or it won't come true,' she scolded. Her wish had been simple: if Ferris could dare to give himself over to love again, perhaps she could, too.

Christmas Day at Bramble reminded Anne fondly of Christmas mornings at Haberstock Hall. The Treshams gathered at the long table in the dining room set with the heirloom silver and the best china, the table lined with a breakfast to end all breakfasts: sausages, racks of toast, compotiers of jam, bowls of fluffy scrambled eggs and flat-bottomed dishes of shirred eggs, platters of kippers and smoked salmon, and, at the centre, a pyramid of carefully stacked oranges that had Helena's boys in awe. At each place setting, a twist of ribbon-wrapped paper awaited, holding nuts or peppermints. A family tradition, Ferris told her with a wink, holding out her chair before sitting next to her, with Peter on his other side. Across the table, Frederick was already busy peeling oranges for his two oldest boys while Helena helped the others.

Breakfast went on at length, everyone leisurely filling their plates, assisting the children and exchanging stories. Yesterday had been about celebrating with friends, but today was private, meant just for the family. They were eager to hear about her own family. The Duke and Duchess nodded solemnly as she told them about William serving as a doctor with the troops in the Crimea, his decision resonating with them in the absence of their own son.

When breakfast had been demolished, the Duchess ushered everyone into one of the private sitting rooms, where a tree had been decorated for the children. A carved Noah's ark sat beneath it, animals set two by two were interspersed with presents, some of which Anne recognised from the Christmas market. The children's eyes were wide with surprise and excitement. Peter was hesitant, not knowing what to make of such a spectacle.

'I'll go first.' Ferris strode to the tree and brought

forward his gifts, handing one to each of the children. 'They're from Anne and I.' The announcement caught her unexpectedly and she felt a strange, emotional lump form in her throat. Every Christmas could be like this, surrounded by children, by family. Hertfordshire wasn't so far from Sussex that the families couldn't join together. What a party that would be and, oh, how active her imagination was today, already leaping ahead to Christmases future. Perhaps it was what happened when a good man said he loved you and spent the night showing you the truth of that in every way before sneaking back to his own bed before dawn.

The children exclaimed over the toys from the market and Peter was in awe over the whittling knife, a perfect gift for a boy who wanted to be older than eight. Emotion threatened again. Sweet heavens, all this familial goodness was turning her into a watering pot. But it was more than that. It was the vision of what she could have if she reached out for it, things she'd once thought she'd have to give up to have the other thing she loved—her work.

Anne rose, needing to give herself something to do. 'I have gifts, too.' She reached for the basket she'd brought downstairs with her. She'd meant to give the gifts at breakfast, but was glad she'd waited. She had hand lotions for Helena and the Duchess, and a masculine-smelling salve of cinnamon and sandalwood for the men. 'Use it on your hands,' she told Frederick, who sniffed at it sceptically. 'They looked a little raw after chopping the Yule log yesterday. The lotion will soften calluses in no time.' She felt more in control talking about the remedies, and the tightness in her throat receded.

The rest of the morning and early afternoon was spent playing with the children in the 'Christmas Tree' room with their new toys. Ferris helped Peter with his new knife while Frederick taught the younger boys animal sounds with the Noah's ark. Anne drew Helena aside to offer herbs to help with impending morning sickness. She liked Lady Brixton. The woman was easy to talk with and a dedicated wife and mother.

'Tell me about you and Ferris,' Helena said as they chatted. 'I've never seen him so smitten. I confess to wanting to see my brother-in-law happy, but I'd given up on it. You saw him at the charity ball, polite and distant. I've never known him to be otherwise, but with you, he's come alive, a whole new person.' She smiled slyly. 'Should we be expecting an announcement soon? Frederick told me about the hayloft. It's comfortable, isn't it? We've used it a few times. Before and after we were married.'

Anne blushed. 'We've only known each other a short time.' It was an inadequate answer, especially given that *everyone* seemed to know what had happened in the hayloft.

'You have misgivings?' Helena picked up on her reticence. 'Well, that's to be expected. It's difficult to marry into a ducal household. I had misgivings, too, although my parents didn't. They practically threw me at Frederick. Fortunately, he caught me and we sorted it all out together.'

'It's just that I have my work and it's very important to me. It's part of how I've been raised, to devote my life to bettering my community and...' Anne trailed off, unable to find words to complete her thought.

Helena patted her hand. 'You worry that there won't be room to be a mother, a wife and to be yourself, to pursue your passions.' She nodded understandingly. 'I had dreams like that, too, dreams that I thought Frederick wouldn't understand or that our marriage wouldn't have room for.' She leaned close and whispered, 'I wanted to be a special kind of teacher and work with young children, five and under. I just love babies and watching their minds develop. I wanted to teach them to read and count and play. I'm intrigued with the idea of what a childhood is and how we can make sure every child has one. I know it's not ladylike to be interested in such things, especially not for a future duchess. Peers don't raise their own children, let alone take interest in someone else's.'

'And what happened?' Anne was intrigued.

'Frederick and I are setting up a kindergarten on the property here at Bramble for the village children. We went to Germany for our honeymoon and met with Friedrich Froebel, who had established a kindergarten a few years prior. It was wondrous, and since then we've been in contact with him—well, until he died last year—but he was quite instructive about how to make a kindergarten here. We'll open it soon.' She squeezed

Anne's hand in assurance. 'So, you see, you can have your dreams and your love for Ferris, too.'

Anne nodded, but the old worry came to her. If something sounded too good to be true, it probably was, and Robert had proved it.

There was a cry of frustration from one of the younger boys and Helena rose. 'Naptime, I think.' She took the boy from Frederick and gathered her brood. 'I'll settle them and then we can be off to the gypsies.'

Anne shot Ferris a questioning look and he came to her aid. 'Another Tresham custom to be upheld, my dear. A Christmas Day visit to celebrate with the gypsies. Best refill your basket. You'll have work aplenty.' Something warm blossomed inside her, doing battle with her worry. Ferris understood her, he knew exactly what she needed because he needed it, too, to be of use to others, to their community. She had no doubt that his black bag would accompany him as her basket would her.

This was a glimpse of Christmas Future. He and Anne among the gypsies, she with her basket, the hood of her grey cloak pushed back to reveal the copper of her hair as she worked among the women. Was it possible to love her more? His own heart swelled with pride as he watched her work. Vano, the leader for the caravan, stood with him and his father, nursing a mug of vodka mixed with Benedictine—a potent combination. One had to be careful to sip it slowly.

'We have not seen you in years, Lord Ferris,' Vano said. 'Now you are back with a boy and a beautiful woman by your side. That is good. You are too old to be alone.' He winked as Frederick strolled up to join them. 'But you will never catch your brother. Now there's a man, your brother. Four fine strong boys in eight years.' He poured a drink for Frederick.

'And another on the way—' Frederick beamed '—for you to celebrate this time next year, Vano.'

Vano raised his mug. 'We must drink to three generations of Treshams and four decades of friendship.' He clinked his mug against the Duke's. 'It has been over forty years since the first winter we came to Bramble and received your welcome.' Vano sobered. 'And there will be many more. Long after we are gone, our sons and their sons will continue the tradition. To longevity!'

To longevity. Ferris drank the toast, his eyes seeking out Anne. Did she see it, too? This glimpse into the future, this look at what they could be together? What did she think of it? Did it appeal to her? Did it frighten her? He'd given her the words last night, *I love you*. He'd not expected her to say the words in return. He'd promised her they'd take things slowly and that was part of it, giving her time to process the words. She would say them in turn when she was ready. Her response last night had touched him, given him hope. She'd understood how momentous it was for him to take that step, just as he understood how momentous the next step would be for her.

Yet he didn't want to go slow, not now that he was sure of his heart. He could think of no better way of persuading her than to show her, to put her into the midst of it all and know that there was a place for her, that he wanted her beside him, a partner in all ways. He excused himself from the group of men to join Anne and Helena with the women as a gypsy with long black curls and a bright turquoise scarf approached. Selina, the fortune teller.

'Lord Ferris, you've come home.' Selina took his hand and turned over his palm. 'You must let me read your palm.'

'You know I don't believe in that. I'm a scientist.' He laughed off the offer. He shouldn't believe it at any rate, but Selina scared him. She'd correctly predicted the gender of all four of Frederick's children. There was only a fifty-fifty chance she'd miss, but one would think at least one would have been a girl. It *did* unnerve him. He'd prefer Selina kept her opinions to herself.

'Lady Brixton isn't afraid.' Selina turned to Helena and Helena offered up her palm. 'You're expecting, again.' Selina's dark eyes danced as she studied Helena's palm. 'It will be a boy in late summer.' She flashed Ferris a confident smile. 'See how painless that was. Now for you, milady.' She reached for Anne's hand and looked around. 'Avaline didn't come? Your other brother's wife?'

'No, but you'll see her before you leave,' Ferris assured her, but Anne's hand had already claimed her attention. Anne threw him a disconcerted look. 'Perhaps she doesn't want her palm read,' Ferris tried to intervene.

Selina looked up. 'Too late, I've already done it.

You're very sweet in love, Lord Ferris, so protective. But this lady doesn't need protection.'

'I don't want to know,' Anne said, snatching back her hand. Selina split her gaze between them and sauntered away with a smug look.

Ferris led Anne to the perimeter of the camp where they might have a moment alone. 'I'm sorry I didn't stop her sooner. She can be tenacious.'

'It's not that. I just didn't want to know.' She held his gaze and he saw the desire and uncertainty in them. 'I want to find out for myself, in my own time, how this ends between us.'

'Ends? That sounds quite fatal. Does it have to end, Anne?' Ferris murmured. It was hardly the endorsement he was hoping for. He wrapped his arms about her and held her close. 'Anne, I wish you could see what I see. What a life we'd have together. Can't you see it?' He was being bold, far bolder than he'd planned to be, but the magic of today that worked on him so powerfully had worked differently on her. When he saw her with his family, with his nephews, with the gypsies, he saw the future he wanted, but she didn't.

'Don't, Ferris,' she whispered. 'I just want to enjoy now. I don't want to ruin it with thoughts of what can or cannot be.'

'Fair enough.' He smiled and reached into his pocket, thinking to move the conversation back to better ground. 'I have a present for you. I've been waiting for the right moment, but it's been hard to get you alone.' He gave her the long, slim box tied with a pale blue ribbon and watched her eyes light with pleasure as she opened the lid.

'It's the bracelet from the market. When did you do it?' she exclaimed, and the smile on her face made him want to buy her a thousand bracelets. This woman who gave so much of herself to others deserved a gift herself. Ferris could not begin to articulate how much she'd given him. 'May I put it on? Perhaps if I wore it beneath my glove.' Because they both knew the gift might draw speculation and expectation from others here.

She tugged off her glove and he took the bracelet from the box. 'Allow me.' He fastened it about her wrist, his fingers lingering on the tender underside of her skin. He wanted to say, *I love you, Anne*. But she would hear those words alongside the gift and feel pressure, not persuasion. Despite her passion and her open desire for what they had, she was as skittish as a cat around strangers. One wrong move would see her dashing for cover. He would not lose her.

She turned her wrist, admiring the bracelet. 'Thank you, Ferris, it's lovely. I've never had such a pretty piece of jewellery.' Probably not. He'd only ever seen her in practical pearls and gold earrings.

'Lapis lazuli is symbolic of wisdom, strength and courage, all the things you have, Anne. Now, you have a reminder of that every time you wear the bracelet.' And hopefully a reminder of much more—that there was a man who loved her. He kissed her then, slowly and deliberately as he liked to kiss her. 'Anne, are you in a hurry to get back to London?'

'No.' She smiled against his mouth.

'Good. I thought we might stay a while.' Long
enough to woo her, long enough to exorcise her ghosts
as she'd exorcised his, long enough to convince her
that his love was enough and that she could trust him
with hers.

Chapter Twenty-One

How long could a honeymoon last? They'd been at Bramble for thirteen days. Christmas had slid past and so had New Year's, far longer than he'd intended to stay. He'd meant to be back in London on the twenty-seventh. But Ferris hadn't the will to pull himself away and perhaps he feared breaking the spell of happiness that had woven itself around them. In the end, it was decided by a letter forwarded from Sir Bentley by Mrs Green. It lay in the salver on the console in the entry like a hot coal, daring him to touch it. He put it in his pocket and went for a walk in the gardens and tried to ignore it. But the truth was, touching it was a very short step to opening it, to reading. Ignoring didn't last long.

Ferris found a bench in the garden and sat down, bracing himself for what was within. What did he want to be in the letter? He wasn't sure. A rejection of the project meant he could stay here ad infinitum if he wished, walk away from London and establish a practice here at Bramble. But even as part of him hungered for that, part of him recognised it as a cover for failure. A rejection meant he'd need to regroup, take his father's and brother's offers of money and get back to it. If there was acceptance in this letter, then it meant returning to London immediately before Dandridge and the board could change their minds. Either way, he reasoned, things between him and Anne would have to move forward. Whatever the answer in this letter, the honeymoon was over.

He opened the letter and unfolded it. Three lines only—Sir Bentley was an efficient man.

The board requests your presence at our January meeting on the seventh at three o'clock, at which time we will discuss the merits of your proposal.

He was also a non-committal man. Did discussing merits suggest they'd approved it? Or were they still only in the considering phase? Today was the sixth. If he meant to act, he needed to act now. They'd need to leave tomorrow at dawn to make the meeting, or even leave this afternoon, which would take them halfway before dark and make the next day easy travelling. It was only ten now, they could be underway by two, but Ferris could raise little enthusiasm for leaving in a rush. There were decisions to make. He folded the letter up and went to find Anne.

She was in the nursery with Helena and the boys. The sounds of their laughter and play rang through the third-floor corridor with merriment. Ferris stood back and let it wash over him. He closed his eyes, wanting to remember the sound of it, wanting to remember the sight of Anne, carefree and happy on the braided rug in the nursery, the Noah's ark from beneath the Christmas tree spread about her, Helena's youngest on her lap gnawing a wooden giraffe. This was what he wanted. Anne, with children, *their* children, making a life with him, a family with him. He did not think he'd made any progress in that direction despite his best efforts day *and* night to convince Anne such a life was possible without compromising her dreams.

He stepped forward into the doorway and Anne looked up with a smile that halted when she saw his face. She handed off the baby and rose. 'What is it? You've had news. No one's ill, are they?'

He shook his head and took her hand, leading her out into the hallway where they could talk. 'Sir Bentley has written. The board wants to discuss the mobile clinic.'

'That's wonderful!' Anne was immediately pleased for him. 'When?'

'Tomorrow.'

'Ah, I see.' Her smile dimmed. 'We had to go back sometime, Ferris.' She drew a breath and squared her shoulders. 'I'll tell Helena. I can be packed within the hour. We can leave after luncheon and stay at an inn tonight or push on if you prefer.' Ferris's heart swelled. Was it possible to love this woman any more than he already did? Was there no end to her understanding and self-sacrifice? Here she was, ready to pick up and go with him on a moment's notice.

He grabbed her about the waist and pulled her close,

stealing a quick kiss. 'Thank you, Anne. But it's not necessary. What I prefer is to leave tomorrow morning and have one more day at Bramble with a proper goodbye.'

She gripped the lapels of his coat, demanding his attention in earnest. 'This meeting is important. This is about your dream getting the recognition it deserves. You will not risk it on rutted winter roads trying to race to London tomorrow. A broken wheel, a broken axel, a horse pulling up lame is all it would take to ruin your schedule and your opportunity.' Anne provided the voice of reason. She was right, of course. Winter roads, even dry, posed all kinds of hidden dangers. 'We can't leave it to chance.'

'Is everything all right?' Helena came out into the hall.

No time like the present to share the news. 'We have to leave this afternoon, I'm afraid,' Ferris explained, but Helena took the news in her stride.

'I'll have your mother serve luncheon early.' Helena smiled. 'But what about Peter? I was wondering if he might like to stay with the boys. I know he's older, but London in winter is dismal for a child. He could learn his letters, some reading. I could teach him,' Helena offered. 'I'm starting with our oldest.'

It was settled over a soup lunch while maids and valets hurriedly packed trunks upstairs. Ferris and Anne would return to London. Peter would stay with the family until the Duke and Duchess came up to London for the Season, although he was welcome to stay longer if he liked. Ferris suspected he might choose to stay indefinitely. Bramble had enchanted the boy. The loss of his sister had become more manageable for him here amid the boisterous household and the younger boys looking up to him. But there were still tears from him when Ferris left him with promises to write and tell him of London.

'You'll miss him,' Anne said as the coach rolled down the drive and the family waved from the top step, Frederick's hand on Peter's shoulder.

'I hope it was the right decision. He's had a lot of upheaval in a short time. Coming to the clinic, losing his sister, coming here and now staying here without us.' Ferris was second-guessing himself. Perhaps they should turn the coach around and fetch him.

'Bramble will be good for him, he will be loved there, he'll add to those who care for him. He won't forget you, Ferris.' Anne cut through to the real worry. 'You can visit any time you like. You needn't wait until spring to see him.'

Something in Anne's tone grabbed his attention. He'd been talking about *us* and *we* when it came to Peter, but today, she'd talked of the singular. *He* could come visit Peter. 'Will you come with me?' Ferris asked.

Would she? Sometimes simple questions were the hardest to answer. 'If I have time,' Anne prevaricated, taking refuge in the excuse of work. Now that they were headed back to London, there were issues that must be addressed. They were no longer wrapped up in the idyll of Bramble, weeks out of time, weeks of living a fantasy that required nothing from them but the moment. It had occurred to her that she could not keep living at the clinic, not now that she was his lover, that there was no more health crisis that demanded her constant attendance.

'I cannot risk bringing scandal to my family by living openly with you, Ferris. I need to return to Harley Street and Thea.' Perhaps some space would be good for them both. It would give them time to think about what they really wanted without being surrounded by the festive, family perfection of Bramble at Christmas and without the exigence of a medical emergency throwing them together. Those circumstances had created an intense, insular world for them that didn't necessarily represent reality.

The arguments held little sway with Ferris. 'I wouldn't ask you to live with me in that fashion.' Ferris stretched his long legs and crossed his arms, settling in to do battle. She had to go carefully here. She did not want a proposal today when emotions were running high over the hasty farewell and the impending hospital meeting. Ferris would see marriage as a quick fix—a step towards an instant, permanent family for Peter, a way to set aside her concerns about living with him so they could go on as they were. She wasn't sure that was the best course of action, one that they wouldn't regret sooner than later.

'We don't need to settle it today, Ferris. There are other things that take precedent. We have time. How do you think the children at the asylum are faring? We've

had no word, so I'm inclined to think it's going well.'
Anne changed the conversation, focusing on a positive
topic related to going back.

They spent the afternoon in pleasant speculation
about their various patients: was Mr Burroughs still
taking the angelica root? How did they think Lieutenant Stroud's lavender protocols were working? How was
Mrs Fulton getting on with her father-in-law's rheumatism? How big was little Thomas Fitzsimmons? He'd be
a little over a month old now. The talk sparked reminders of things she needed to do. Anne took out a small
notebook and made notes about the remedies she needed
to make up. She'd need to make a trip to the physic garden for some of the herbs, her own supplies running low.

A small chuffling snore caused her to look up. Ferris had fallen asleep as the conversation had dwindled
to fits and starts while she made her list. The afternoon
had been a pleasant diversion from the dangerous topic
of their future, at least where Ferris was concerned. She
had succeeded in distracting him, but not herself. This
afternoon's conversation had been a quiet trap she'd
inadvertently sprung. It had shown her what a day in
the ordinary life of *them* could be, amicably discussing
patients and cases as they drove along.

She did understand the enormity of that luxury. They
had the capacity to share in both the public and private
lives of one another. Like Frederick and Helena. Helena's story about the kindergarten resonated strongly
with her as she watched Ferris sleep. It was proof that
she could be a wife, a mother and a healer, with Ferris

at her side, that Ferris wanted those for her as much as she wanted them for herself. The dragon of hard-earned caution raised its head. What if she was wrong? She'd been wrong before. Distance was still the best counsel, distance to think through her thoughts and for him, too. She didn't want Ferris to feel obligated to propose, or to propose as a reaction to solving immediate problems. He had to ask for the right reasons and she had to accept for those reasons as well.

Ferris seemed to recognise it, too. This return to London was an ending as much as it was an opportunity to open a new beginning. That recognition was riding them hard with a sense of desperate urgency as they climbed the stairs to their room at the inn, the same inn they'd stayed at on the trip to Bramble. How much had changed since then and how much still remained unresolved.

'Shall we eat in?' Ferris asked, setting their travelling valises on the bed. His voice was a low growl that indicated his preference.

'Yes.' A tremor rippled through her. Tonight, they'd made no move to hide that they were together, from others or from themselves. Tonight they would stay in this room as man and wife. There would be no sneaking in and out of rooms, no more cold pillows. There would be, however, the bliss of waking beside each other in the morning light.

Dinner was set on a table placed before the fire, the covers removed and the door shut behind them once more. The smell of a braised venison roast, mingled with winter potatoes done with butter and rosemary and fresh-baked bread, invited them to the table. Ferris worked open the cork of the wine bottle and poured glasses for them. It was a cosy supper in an intimate setting that relaxed even as it ratcheted the anticipation of what was to come.

'What do you think they're doing at Bramble right now?' Anne sipped from her goblet.

'Helena will be herding the boys to the table for supper.' Ferris laughed, both of them remembering the chore of getting eight little hands and four faces washed for supper. 'It's worth it, though, to have them at the table when the family dines in. They'll grow up more at ease with suppers and manners. My brothers and I did.' His eyes were burning blue coals, his voice low. Her blood began to hum as he moved to her side of the little table. 'For instance, I learned to hold a chair for a lady...' he knelt before her, taking the napkin from her lap and dropping it on the floor '...and when a lady's napkin falls, I learned I should return it.'

'What else did you learn?' Anne gave him a coy smile. She rather liked the look of him at her feet, his eyes burning as he played the supplicant.

'Let me show you.' He took her foot on his lap and unlaced her shoes. His hand slid up her leg, reaching the top of her stocking. His fingers undid the garter and began to slowly roll the stocking down until first one and then the other leg was bare to him. 'Did you know there's a sensitive spot behind the knee?' he whispered, his mouth moving to demonstrate quite effectively, too. She gasped several times in proof.

His mouth began to move, trailing a line of kisses up to the warm, damp juncture of her thighs. Whatever excitement her knees had generated was quickly elevated to something more—more heated, more thrilling, and when his tongue licked across the nub hidden in her folds, Anne thought she might go wild, abandon all sense and give herself over to pleasure.

She gripped the arms of the chair and felt herself slide down in the seat, all of her wanting to be closer to the pleasure, closer to him and that wondrous mouth that was sending her into raptures. She gave up on the chair arms and anchored her hands in the depths of his hair as if her grip could keep him close, control the pleasure. Her frenzied body didn't know what it wanted—to hold off the pleasure or to let it claim her. Perhaps the choice was never hers.

His mouth took her over the edge and she gave herself up in a cry of joy, aware not only of her pleasure, but the pleasure he experienced in the giving of it. His shoulders heaved against her thighs, his breathing coming in deep gulps as his head rested at her belly, her hands still clenched in his hair.

'You've got good manners.' Anne's joke came out in a shaky gasp of humour as the pleasure began to mellow, her body warm from the fire, from him.

He looked up from her belly, a wicked, private smile on his lips just for her. 'That's just the beginning, my love. Tonight I mean to claim you, body and soul.' He drew her to her feet with a hard kiss.

'Then we are in accord, because I mean to claim you.' Anne busied her fingers with his necktie, with the buttons of his shirt. Who would have guessed such pleasure was available with all of one's clothes on? Well, stockings excluded, and she meant to give as good as she got, to be his partner in this as she was in all else.

It was a night for seduction and decadence. Ferris's demonstration of 'table manners' set the tone as they undressed one another, divesting each other of clothes with hands on fabric and mouths on bare skin as garments fell to the floor and their naked owners fell to the bed. They came together in a furious coupling, hungry and desperate to claim each other and the passion that waited for them, desperate, too, to ensure no moment of the night go wasted.

But pleasure's oblivion couldn't keep every question at bay. When might they be together again like this, uninterrupted? When would there be another night? What decisions would have to be made for another night to occur?

Anne reached for her basket as Ferris lay beside her, recovering. She rooted about, finding a small white jar of the sandalwood lotion. 'Roll over on your stomach, Ferris.' She put a dollop of lotion in the palm of her hand and blew on it, warming it before rubbing it across his broad shoulders. She worked it in with a light pressure of her fingertips.

'Lord, Anne, that feels divine,' Ferris murmured.

'Good, just relax,' she encouraged, massaging his shoulders and the expanse of his back, working ever downward towards the narrow taper of his waist and the muscled rounds of his buttocks. Her hands gloried in the feel of him, of her man, beneath her fingers.

He could be yours always, the temptation whispered, only to be pushed aside by the darkest question of all: Would there be another night? What would she be willing to risk to secure this pleasure for herself?

Anne put the last of the lotion in her palm and reached between his legs for his sac and the rising length beyond that. She cupped and stroked. 'Does that feel good?'

He groaned. 'You minx, you know it does. You're not relaxing me, you're *readying* me.' He gave a laugh, rolled over, pulled her on top of him and the pleasure started again.

Chapter Twenty-Two

They arrived in front of Fourteen Cheyne Walk at half past one, with barely enough time. Barely enough was the watchword for the next hour—barely enough time to unload, for Ferris to change, to ready himself for the meeting with Sir Bentley and the board. Anne and Mrs Green were flying upstairs with travelling trunks and back down to iron a shirt.

'Lift your chin,' Anne instructed sharply, trying to do his tie in the hallway as the minutes ticked past. 'There…' she gave the tie a final pat '…you are ready to go get your dream. You'll be fabulous today.'

Mrs Green bustled out as Ferris slipped into his greatcoat. 'Oh, good, you haven't left. I nearly forgot in all the excitement of your arrival.' She reached into her apron pocket. 'This letter arrived this morning.' She handed it to Ferris, but not before Anne caught sight of the seal. It was from the hospital. Ferris tore open the note, blue eyes quickly scanning, his mouth narrowing to a grimace as he reread it.

'Not bad news, I hope?' Anne enquired. She hoped the meeting hadn't been cancelled after the great effort it had taken to get back on time and the sacrifices that had been made along the way.

Ferris offered her a smile she didn't quite believe. 'Not bad news, not yet, just some things to set straight today.' He tossed the letter on his desk. His gaze lingered on her. 'Anne, stay for dinner? We'll need to talk when I get back. There's not time now, I've got to go.'

She watched him go, his broad shoulders getting back into the coach and a little knot of worry forming in her stomach. She wished she could read him a bit better. If he'd asked her to stay for dinner five minutes earlier, she would have thought it was to talk over the hospital meeting. But she'd seen the light go out of his eyes as he'd read the letter. Tension had replaced his excitement, his hope, for the meeting.

Back inside, Anne took a cup of tea with Mrs Green and shared Christmas at Bramble with her. She retreated to her workroom and unpacked her basket. She busied herself with doing a brief inventory of her stores and adding to her list of oils and teas that needed replenishing. The hall clock chimed half past four. It would be at least another hour or two before Ferris was back. Mrs Green came in to say she was leaving and supper was on the stove.

Shadows lengthened outside and Anne went to light the lamp Ferris left in the front window. How had she ever thought this place was not a home? She remembered thinking there was nothing of the man in this place, just work. She didn't think that now. Looking around the parlour that acted as his office, she saw him in the bookcase with its repaired panes, in the coatrack that stood by the door, his black bag at the base, waiting for the next emergency that would take him out at a moment's notice. She saw herself here, too. Her stamp was on the herbal room, her cloak hung on the coatrack. Her basket stood at the ready in the workroom. *This is us*, she thought. This is what we could be. Together. They could make a fulfilling life that blended work and family as her father and her mother had done. For the first time, she began to believe it was possible.

She passed his desk and glimpsed the letter he'd thrown there in his haste to be off. Anne reached for it and sat down in the desk chair. Sir Bentley had written, outlining what the hospital was willing to do in support of the mobile clinic. They would supply three wagons, the necessary horses and their care. They would see the wagons supplied with basic instruments and equipment. They would help find three doctors willing to take on the recommended routes.

Anne put the letter down. Why, this was wonderful news! They were giving Ferris everything he'd asked for. They were handing him his dream. Why had he looked so grim? She turned the letter over.

However, we must ask you to clarify and re-form your current relationship with one Miss Anne Peverett.

What?

> *It has come to our attention that, perhaps in order to get the number of patients up who were treated at your wagon, you took on a joint partnership with a dangerous but charismatic herbalist, Miss Peverett.*
>
> *While we applaud your ingenuity in making the case for numbers and we believe that the numbers do indeed demonstrate a need for your project, the association with Miss Peverett is of concern.*
>
> *She is not a studied professional, and certainly this is not a field for the feminine mind, demonstrated by recent news regarding the death of one Mrs Fulton of Webber Street, who expired shortly after Christmas from an excess of poisonous mushrooms despite the best efforts of one of our physicians to save her.*
>
> *We believe she was a client of Miss Peverett's.*

Mrs Fulton, dead. She'd not even prescribed mushrooms for the woman. She'd only talked to the ladies about what mushrooms could do but only if one was careful.

The hospital had labelled her as dangerous. They could ensure she didn't work again in the neighbourhoods if word got out. It might already be too late for that. Mrs Fulton's death wasn't exactly a ringing endorsement.

The hospital was forcing Ferris to choose between her and his dream. He could have it all if he gave her up. They meant as a professional associate, but they'd certainly never tolerate her as his wife. She'd be a liability to him for ever and she'd never be able to work *with* him the way she had been, the way they'd planned. That part of the dream was in tatters. How could she be Mrs Ferris Tresham, or Lady Ferris Tresham even, if she could not also be Anne Peverett, healer? How unfair that they were making Ferris choose. How could he possibly make such a choice?

Her mind slowed down and focused on the earlier section of the back page.

> *It has come to our attention that, perhaps in order to get the number of patients up who were treated at your wagon, you took on a joint partnership with a dangerous but charismatic herbalist, Miss Peverett.*
>
> *While we applaud your ingenuity in making the case for numbers...*

No. He wasn't being asked to choose. He'd already chosen.

He'd used her. He'd lied to her about why he wanted to join forces and she'd accepted his reason. She'd settled for a chance to prove herself to him and not pushed for a more complete reason. She'd been conveniently persuaded by the offer of workspace. And by the man himself. She'd *wanted* to take the offer. Although Thea had warned her, she'd stopped looking for motives and simply accepted what was in front of her at face value. And what a face it had been—handsome Ferris Tresham with his passion for healing, with a hidden temper that flared when confronted.

What else had he lied about? Did he even mean to let her practise if their relationship proceeded to the next logical step? Or was that a lie, too, something to retract when it was too late for her? That was likely the case. He'd shown himself to be capable of doing and saying whatever might be needed to get what he wanted. He'd wanted his dream and he'd wanted her. He'd got them both and she was the one who would pay the price, especially now that he couldn't keep her. Had he ever meant to keep her? He hadn't *asked* her to marry him, he'd just hinted very broadly that such a proposal might be in the offing. And she'd been so sure she knew his mind, she'd actually panicked over him making the offer.

Oh, she'd been a fool ten times over—a fool for trusting a man she'd kissed on the first acquaintance, a man who later had insulted her intelligence and ability in her craft, a fool for believing he understood her just because he said he did. Had she truly learned nothing from the disaster with Robert? Apparently not.

How could she have misread him so completely? She'd been so focused on the man who'd wept over the loss of a child he barely knew, who'd poured his heart out to her in a graveyard on Christmas Eve, a man who said he loved her. Because she was good for business. A man might do or say anything under those conditions, she'd just thought not this man. He'd been very persuasive on that account.

Misery swamped her in stunning waves. The shock of it all was so great, she couldn't even cry, couldn't even break down. She was numb with all of it and what it really meant. She could try to blame Ferris, and some of the blame did fall on him. It was never acceptable to manipulate someone's good intentions as he had. But she had also allowed herself to be manipulated. The bulk of the blame fell on her, not only for being swayed by Ferris's too-good-to-be-true offer of working together, by his blue eyes, by his sincerity, which had never been meant for her, but also for her own naivety—something she thought she was well beyond.

Ferris had tried to warn her. How many times had he argued with her about encouraging people to self-diagnose and treat? How many times had she dismissed his arguments as the arguments of the arrogant, people more worried about preserving their position in society as gatekeepers to healthcare?

She knew now what he wanted to talk about tonight. No wonder he was grim. He was going to tell her about Mrs Fulton. He was going to say he'd told her so and as a consequence they needed to separate. Gone was the hard-won happiness of a few minutes ago, thinking she could see herself as Mrs Ferris Tresham, that they could have an honest life together. Gone was the joy she'd feasted on at Bramble, the exquisite pleasure of lovemaking and lying in his arms afterwards, feeling untouchable, feeling that what she had with him was *real*.

Would his riddance of her even have been honest? Would he have told her about the hospital's ultimatum to him or would he simply have dismissed her on the grounds of Mrs Fulton alone without ever revealing the hospital's position?

Anne rose on shaky legs. She wasn't going to stay and find out. She knew how this was going to end even if she didn't know the exact method. She needed to be gone before he came back. She didn't want to hear what he had to say, didn't want to see his blue eyes dismiss her. With trembling hands, she fumbled with the clasp of her bracelet, letting it clatter on the desktop. It would only remind her of him, of those eyes that had burned her to cinders, of the moment he'd given it to her and whispered the words that could have changed the trajectory of her life. *I love you, Anne.* She'd nearly bet everything on those words.

Good thing she hadn't unpacked. Her trunk was upstairs. Good thing she'd planned on going back to Harley Street tonight anyway. All there was to pack were her herbs. She packed them in haste, not taking time to carefully wrap equipment as she had when she'd moved them here. Now that it was over, she was in a hurry to be gone. If she stalled, she might second-guess her decision, might start making arguments on his behalf. She would go to Harley Street and then back to Hertfordshire. There was nothing in London for her any more, not work or pleasure. Better to leave furious than leave sad. Anger could sustain her.

Ferris was furious. He was *always* furious when he left the board of governors' meetings. He should stop going to them. Well, maybe this time he wouldn't go back. Ferris kicked at a pebble, sending it out into the street. He'd had enough of their small minds. Now they thought to make him choose between Anne and his dream of a fleet of mobile clinics venturing into the parts of London that needed care the most. The love of his heart or the hope of his heart? He needn't choose. He could have them both. He would set aside his pride and appeal to his father for the funds. He and Anne could recruit young, energetic doctors fresh from medical school to help.

He'd been furious even before the meeting. He'd boiled when he'd read the letter from Dandridge, who hadn't even tried to disguise the threat to withhold project funding if he didn't separate from Anne. How dare the man malign her when he barely knew her, had never seen her work. Did Dandridge even think it would be a choice for him? He'd made the case for Anne without hesitation at the meeting. He'd argued that Anne offered clear instruction on how to use the herbs and plants she recommended, how he himself had warned Mrs Fulton against picking and using mushrooms on her own. If Mrs Fulton disregarded those instructions for something she'd not even been prescribed, that was hardly his fault or Anne's.

His arguments had fallen on deaf and discriminating ears. Dandridge had simply sat at the head of the table with a dark stare and said, 'She has no training, no diploma, not even a licence. She and people like her are a liability to our profession.' Then the conversation had turned to celebrating Dandridge's imminent fatherhood. His wife was expecting for the third time and was due any day. 'You'll attend her, of course, Dr Tresham, as you have at the other births,' Dandridge said, and Ferris understood the topic of the mobile clinics had been settled in their minds. He was to go home and consider his options.

* * *

His options were fully considered by the time he reached his front door. The sight of the lamp in the window softened the hard edges of his anger. Anne must have put it there. She would feel terrible about Mrs Fulton. She needed to understand it wasn't her fault. She would be livid over Dandridge's ultimatum. He would have to break the news to her gently, help her to see the opportunity today's developments created, not the obstacles. This did not change their love.

Ferris opened the front door and took off his greatcoat, calling out for Anne, 'I'm home', only to be met with no response. Perhaps she was upstairs. That brought a smile to his face. Was she in his room? Dare he hope she was unpacking, deciding that she could stay after all? If so, he'd send for a special licence tomorrow.

He passed his office, his eye catching the glint of something blue flashing on the desk. He came to a full halt. He entered the room in trepidation, his mind starting to register what his eye had already seen. The lapis-lazuli bracelet lay on the desk alongside the letter from Dandridge. Dread took up residence in his stomach. She'd read the letter. He could see its contents through her eyes: the blame, the condemnation, the betrayal, even the liability. Even if she managed to dismiss all else, she would see the ruin she posed to him. Whether she loved him or hated him after reading the letter, her response would be the same. She would leave.

Ferris sprinted from the room, taking the stairs two at a time. Her trunk was gone. He forced himself to think. Of course it was. She'd said she planned to go to

Harley Street tonight, but that was to be after dinner. No matter how he looked at it, the missing trunk was a bad sign. He ran back down the stairs. She'd never leave without her herbs. He flung open the door to her workroom and searched it with eager eyes. His gaze was met with empty shelves. Not a vial, not a linen square or sage ribbon in sight. She was gone, then. Gone and angry, a woman who believed she was betrayed twice now by men who had professed to understand and honour her. One of whom had taken her to his bed and declared undying love. The dread in his stomach moved upwards, becoming a rock of tight emotion lodged in his throat.

Ferris sagged against the door frame. He'd been back in London for five hours and his world was crumbling. His dream had become negotiable and the woman he loved had fled. He would go after her. He knew where she was, at least for now. She'd be at Harley Street with her sister. There was explaining to do, and with luck they'd put the pieces of this debacle back together.

A knock sounded loud and insistent on the front door. For a second he thought it might be Anne. But Anne would just come in. It was likely a patient, someone who'd seen the lamp. Ferris straightened. He wasn't eager to treat anyone, but medical emergencies didn't wait until one was in the mood.

He answered the door. A hulking brick-worker teetered on the front step, drunken rage in his eyes, a loaded slingshot in one hand. Peter's father. Good lord, could tonight get any worse? 'You're home at last, Doctor,' the drunken man roared, trying to push his way inside. 'Where the hell are my children?' Something sailed towards him, missing him, but shattering the newly repaired bookcase. Better the bookcases than his head. Otherwise, he'd be out cold on the floor right now, useless.

Explaining things to Anne would have to wait. He was going to have to explain himself here first. 'Let's calm down and talk this through,' Ferris said, but he was already rolling up his sleeves. Drunken men swung first and talked later. Right now that suited him just fine.

Chapter Twenty-Three

The fight didn't last long. Drunk irrationality was no match for furious anger, although it did pack a mean punch that would leave Ferris with a bruised jaw in the morning. What did take a while was the discussion that followed afterwards. There was bad news to break to this man and news Ferris hoped he would be happy to hear.

The fight had sobered the man up considerably and hot coffee did the rest as Ferris sat him down in the kitchen with a mug in his hand. Whatever this man's story was, Ferris was not without compassion. He told him gently about Meggie, about how they'd tried to save her. 'I have the address of the cemetery in Brompton, not far from here.' It was relatively new, having opened thirteen years prior as part of an attempt by Parliament to make burial more sanitary. In the spring it had a park-like feel to it with large trees and clipped lawns. Ferris liked to think of her in such a beautiful place—perhaps it would bring her father peace to think of it, too.

The big man across from him began to shake and then collapsed on the table, sobbing. Ferris let him cry. In his experience, there was a thin line between anger and sadness, merely just two different ways grief manifested itself. From what he'd gleaned from Peter's occasional remarks, the man had experienced plenty of grief in the past five years, losing his wife and now losing his daughter.

Ferris couldn't condone how the man had dealt with it, choosing alcohol and violence with the consequence of neglecting his children, but he could understand the grief. He'd lived with grief for years, choosing to combat it with hard work and sealing off his heart, a heart that was yearning to go after Anne, but he could not leave this man. Peter's future demanded it of him and so, too, did his oath.

In purity and in accordance with divine law I will carry out my life and my art...into whatever homes I go, I will enter them for the benefit of the sick...

This man needed him.

There was still Peter to advocate for. While he had taken Peter to Bramble with his best interests in mind, Ferris was aware of how that might appear to the boy's father. Never mind that he had not shown up for weeks after Ferris had claimed the children.

Ferris suppressed a nugget of resentment. This man was legally Peter's father, although he was not fit to be, not emotionally or financially, yet despite that, he could take Peter from Bramble simply by right of biology. There was resentment forming, too, for a society that didn't do near enough to protect children, nor its citizens. What more could have been done to save Peter's father years ago when there'd been a chance? What could have broken the cycle?

Ferris cleared his throat. 'Peter has a choice, sir, to rise above his circumstances.' He made his case and waited. The man was silent for a long while afterwards.

'He's happy there? He has food and clothes?' he asked at last. 'This costs me nothing?' Ferris could see the wariness behind the man's eyes.

'Nothing, sir. We are happy to have him, happy to see his bright mind educated.'

The man nodded slowly. 'Then, I guess he can stay.'

Ferris nodded gravely. 'Thank you, sir. I will tell him you said so the next time I write. He'll come up to town for a short while this spring and you can see how well he does for yourself.' There was bravery in this man yet. It was no small thing to turn over one's son to the care of others. He'd felt only a modicum of that worry when he'd left Bramble, and it had been enough to have him second-guessing the choice of leaving Peter there with his family. This man had his pride, too, and Ferris knew he'd been gingerly stepping on its edges all night. A stranger had taken over this man's children because he had failed to care for them.

No matter how delicately Ferris explained it to him, he would live with that for the rest of his life. The man would drink to that, too. That knowledge would be a primary motivator on dark nights to continue getting foxed, the only protection the man had against remembering and pain. It was hard knowledge to send him out into the night with. How did he help him change? If he gave him money, there was no guarantee he wouldn't drink it away out of habit and lack of focus, lack of a plan, and now lack of a family.

'Do you enjoy working at the brickyard? What do you do there?' Ferris asked, an idea forming.

'It's work. I drive a wagon, make deliveries sometimes, loading and unloading,' the man grunted. No doubt his head was starting to hurt if it wasn't already. Ferris could feel his jaw beginning to ache, in need of a cold compress.

'Is there something else you'd rather do?' Ferris was eager to conclude the interview, but he could not end it in good conscience without trying to do something for this man, without trying to break the cycle of destruction he was on for Peter's sake. The charity of the Christmas season was only a week behind them, and he would not so quickly let go of the redemption the season offered.

If he had the power to see this man redeemed, he would do it. Anne would want him to. What had she said about Peter, all those weeks ago? He couldn't save them all, but he could save this one boy. And he had. He would make a difference where he could. It was one more way in which Anne had changed him, shaped him, into being a man who focused on what was in front of him.

Interest flickered in the man's eyes. 'I used to like working with horses when I was a boy, but then my family came to the city looking for work. Driving a wagon is as close as I get to horses now.' It was the tone of a man whose dreams had expired a long time ago.

'What if I could get you a position working with horses? You'd have to stay sober, of course. We can do a trial here in London.' He explained about the horses that would pull the mobile clinics. They'd need care, feeding and brushing and harnessing. 'If you liked it and did well, you could move to Bramble, work in the stables there, be near Peter. But only if you're sober.' Ferris couldn't emphasise that enough. Without that, the plan fell apart. The man had to want it.

Ferris rose. 'You take some time and think about it. Let me know what you decide.' He ushered the man to the door, pausing at his black bag lying beneath the coatrack. He rummaged through it and came up with a small linen bag. The last of Anne. 'This is angelica root. Brew it, put it in a tea. It helps with not wanting to drink. Come see me in a few days.' Hopefully sober.

Ferris shut the door behind the man and leaned against it. The good deed had cost him. It was too late to go after Anne tonight. It wouldn't help his cause to roust her and her sister out of bed or call attention to them by banging on their door at this hour. Perhaps it would work out for the best to go in the morning. Anne would have time to think, time to look past her anger and her hurt. The morning would bring fresh eyes. But until then, there was still a long night to contend with, the first he'd spent without Anne beside him in a while and he hoped one of the last.

Ferris arrived on Harley Street at ten o'clock, a box of chocolates in hand to sweeten the discussion. Ten was the earliest he dared make a call, but he was not willing to wait any longer, not after tossing all night and giving up sleep altogether at five. Her sister answered the door, her face taking on an impassive expression when he extended his card.

'I know who you are, Dr Tresham.' There was no welcome in her tone. 'We met at the charity ball and Anne has talked of you quite a lot.' She wiped her hands on her apron. 'You're the arrogant man who called her a charlatan, then changed your mind about that and invited her into your practice. You used her popularity for your personal gain, then decided you loved her and then again to give her up for your projects.'

She cocked a sardonic dark brow in his direction and he braced for a barb. Thea had a sharp tongue, sharper even than her sister's. 'What have you changed your mind about this time?' She glanced at the box of chocolates in his hand. 'Have you come to beg? To explain why you betrayed her all the while you were seducing her?'

Put that way, he sounded like an absolute cad. But he wasn't here to appease Thea. The only one he had to explain himself to was Anne. 'May I see her?' he asked, trying to catch a look inside to see if Anne was lurking nearby. She'd not let her sister fight her battles for her. Anne was quite capable of standing up for herself.

Thea's grim mouth softened slightly as did her tone. 'I suppose I would let you see her if she were here. You're too late. She's gone. She left this morning to go back to Hertfordshire on the train.'

'When? When does the train leave?' Ferris's mind

began to race with questions, with actions and plans. He'd go to Hertfordshire if that was what was needed.

'At half past eleven.' Then Thea added, 'From the Bishopsgate station on Shoreditch High Street.' Had she offered the information to help or hurt? The information was valuable, but Bishopsgate was nearly across town from Harley Street. In the morning traffic of slow drays and people bustling to work, it would take a half hour or more to make the trip, and then there'd be the effort of finding her. Bishopsgate was a big, busy station.

'Thank you.' Ferris gave a curt nod and turned to go. He'd have to hurry and even then there were no guarantees, but Thea halted him with a hand at his arm.

'Be careful with her, Dr Tresham. You've broken her heart.'

Ferris heard the scold in it for him. *She was doing fine until you came along and ruined it for her.* Only he hadn't meant to ruin it. Now, he had one chance to mend it.

There were no herbs or oils for mending a broken heart. She ought to discover some since it seemed to be a recurrence with her. Twice now she'd thought to believe the impossible, thought to find love, to *have* love. Twice she'd been disappointed.

Anne bought her ticket and went inside the station, leaving her trunks with a porter. She kept her basket on her arm. She tried to cheer herself with the thought that perhaps this would be the first in a long string of train tickets she might purchase. Perhaps, after some time at home, she might travel on her own, see some of those far-off places with their exotic herbs. She'd love to see the lavender fields of Provence and smell them, too.

But even the thought of travel, which had once inspired her imagination, left her feeling glum. Thinking of Provence made her think of Greece, of Ferris and his stories of the Grand Tour. She looked at her bare wrist. It felt naked without the bracelet. Everything, it seemed, reminded her of him. She didn't want to think of him. She wanted to think of what came next; she wanted to look ahead, not back. That's how she'd got through Robert. It's how she'd get through Ferris. She'd travelled to London to forget Robert. She'd have to travel a lot further than that to forget Ferris.

Did she want to forget, though? Anne found a spot on a bench and sat down to wait. She had twenty minutes before the train left. She would have to board soon, but she wasn't in the mood to be sociable just yet. The trip to Hertfordshire wasn't terribly long, but it would require making conversation with those around her. In the close quarters of the train, it was difficult to escape talking with one's travel mates. Usually, she enjoyed the meeting of new people, but today she wanted to be alone.

Or are you waiting for him? the little voice in her head prompted. *Are you still holding out hope that he'll come after you, that there will be a magical explanation? Are you truly prepared to believe anything he says? Are you willing to be disappointed again?*

She really ought to give up the fantasy. If he was going to come, he would have come last night. There had been plenty of time. She'd told herself she was glad he hadn't come, that there was nothing to say. But it had hurt. He hadn't even tried to reason with her. She'd taken it as proof that he had indeed meant to end their relationship that night. And yet apparently, hope sprung eternal because she'd awakened this morning with hope that there might be a note, an explanation—perhaps the hospital meeting had run late.

She'd hoped, looking up and down Harley Street as she loaded her trunk in the cab. She'd hoped all the way to the station, at the ticket booth and all the way to the platform. She was hoping even now as she put off boarding, although she wasn't sure what she was hoping for. What happened if he came for her? Was it simply that she wanted to see him one last time? Did she want him to change her mind?

'Miss, we leave in fifteen minutes.' A young conductor approached her politely. 'You'll need to board soon.'

Anne nodded her thanks and picked up her basket. She could put it off no longer. She might as well get on the train and get it over with. She'd just put her foot on the last step when she heard it.

'Anne!'

She turned to look and froze. There, cutting through the crowds in his usual dark coat, the one with the faded cuffs, was Ferris. Her heart pounded. He'd come. What did she do now?

'Anne! Wait.' He reached the carriage, out of breath as if he'd run some distance. There was a dark bruise along his jaw.

'What happened to your face?' The words blurted out before she could think through them. How easy it was for her heart to worry about him, to care what happened to him even when her mind counselled that she shouldn't, that she ought to proceed with caution and protect herself.

He put a reflexive hand to his jaw. 'It's why I couldn't come last night, but it's a long story for another time.' The train gave a warning blast of its whistle. There was panic in his blue eyes, panic she'd put there. 'We need to talk, Anne. I need to explain so much, apologise for not telling you sooner. I know what you're thinking.' It was hard to hear him amid the station noise—his sentences were a jumble of pleas.

'Five minutes!' the call went down the line.

'Anne, get off the train,' Ferris begged. 'If you don't like what I have to say, then you can catch the next one.'

How could she do that? Her own thoughts were as muddled as his sentences. 'But I have a ticket, my trunks are already loaded.' It was no use. It was too late. 'You have your dream now, Ferris. You don't need me any more.'

'You are my dream, Anne.' He was talking fast now. 'I've turned down the hospital. I won't take a penny from them.'

No, she could not allow him to give that project up. That project was his soul. It was part of his way of honouring Cara, of honouring Meggie. 'I can't make you happy, Ferris, not if I'm the reason you give up your dream.' It had occurred to her in the long night that even if they resolved their differences, there was more to what kept them apart than that. When people kept those they loved from achieving their dreams, resentment grew. Her own resentment of Robert had taught her that. She knew where it led. It would be a shame to put Ferris through that pain after he'd opened his heart to her. She could not bear to watch him come to regret his decision as the years passed and she became the reason doors were closed to him. It would hurt him now, but he would thank her eventually.

'No, Anne, you don't understand. I'm *not* giving it up. You and I will do it on our own. Please.' It was the grimmest, most desperate exhalation of the word she'd ever heard and it moved her, just enough to want to hear what he had to say. The hesitation must have shown in her eyes, given her away. Ferris grabbed a porter and shoved some coins in his hand. 'Quick, sir, we must have her trunks. Two of them, labelled Peverett.' He turned towards her. 'Anne, if you bear me any love, get off the train, or I will get on it.' It might have been a single step, but to Anne it was a leap of faith and she took it.

Chapter Twenty-Four

~~~

They found a quiet tea shop near the station and it struck Anne that some of their most important negotiations had taken place over a pot of hot Assam. Their first had and perhaps their last. She was acutely aware that this conversation did indeed have the strong potential to define the future of their relationship. No, not potential, it absolutely would. Either she would be on the train to Hertfordshire or she'd be with Ferris. There was a lot riding on this pot of tea. The next train was at two.

'You didn't tell me why you really offered me space in your clinic,' Anne said. This was the most important issue. Nothing mattered as much as that. They could have all the mobile clinics they wanted, but if he lied to her and she could not trust him, there was no point in being colleagues or anything more.

Ferris held her gaze, his blue eyes steady and unblinking. 'No, I did not. It was poorly done of me. I had convinced myself that you were the enemy at the time, that I owed it to my clients to keep you under surveillance without curtailing your right to practise as you pleased. I had also thought there would be merit in the old saying, if you can't fight them, join them. Joining you seemed the path of least resistance towards my own goals.'

'And later, when I was not the enemy? You could have told me then,' Anne argued gently. He'd shared so much at Bramble: his boyhood memories, the defining power of his first love, his grief over Meggie. But he'd not shared this one deception, and its omission hurt all the more for it.

'I convinced myself it didn't matter, that the ends justified the means, and that you wouldn't have minded. You wanted the same things I did. You would have done whatever was necessary.' He paused. 'And I was afraid of losing you, that I'd waited too long to tell you.' He flashed her a wry, rueful smile. 'Seems as though I might still be right about that. I don't want to be right, Anne.'

His fingers drummed on the table, his mouth pursed as he carried out an internal debate. 'I cannot take it back, Anne. I cannot undo my poor choice. I can only apologise for it, and I can plead my case. I can weigh my other qualities against the one misstep in order to convince you to forgive me. But I have to ask—this mistake seems small compared to all else that we've shared with one another. Why does this matter so greatly to you? Why is this omission the one thing you are determined to judge me by?'

Her hand tightened around the teacup. She didn't enjoy saying hard things to people she loved, but she would not back down from the truth either, not when everything depended on it. 'It matters because it was a lie, Ferris. You misled me by obscuring a whole truth to use me to get something *you* wanted. What other omissions might you be willing to make to get what you want?'

Those potential omissions had become inconsequential when she'd thought he'd meant to separate from her and take the hospital's offer. But now they were back with increased value. If he'd thrown over the hospital's offer for her, he'd be intent on the proposal he'd hinted at so heavily at Bramble. She had to consider what else he might be willing to promise in order to secure her hand. He knew her misgivings, he knew the arguments he had to overcome. Would he say anything to do that? He wouldn't have been the first. That was why it mattered.

She thought he was Robert. *That* was why it mattered. The implication might as well have been spoken out loud. Ferris felt his heart sink. His happiness was to be at the mercy of a man he'd never met. His fists clenched on the tabletop, his disappointment growing, not just in himself, but in her as well. 'I am not Robert, and I find I am resentful of being judged as if I was.' Robert was a man who by her own admissions had not understood her, had not seen her for what she was. He'd either not understood her ambitions or had simply ran roughshod over them, thinking them unimportant and easily set aside.

'I have given you no reason to believe that I don't value you as a healer, that I don't want you beside me in this new medical venture, that I would in any way not allow you to continue your work as my wife. You know I want us to be partners in all ways.' It was not the romantic proposal he'd have preferred to make, and a train station teahouse was hardly where he'd wanted to make it, but he might not get another chance to state his intentions so bluntly. 'I am counting on you, Anne, in every way. For starters, I can't possibly undertake this new venture without you.' Or the rest of his life. He supposed he'd find a way through it, but it wouldn't be the same. If he lost her, the emptiness would remain.

She was silent a long while. He hoped she was recalling all the ways in which he'd embraced her expertise, from Mrs Fitzsimmons's difficult delivery to serving beside him at the mobile wagon, and at the gypsy camp. He couldn't help himself. He had to speak again, had to find a way to change her mind. He reached for her hand, desperate to touch her, and a public display of affection be damned. 'As someone who held on to the past for far too long and who was held back by it, I would counsel you to do the same. Let Robert go.'

Anne bowed her head. 'Even if I did, it's too late for us, Ferris. Even if I forgive the lie, understand the lie, and you give up the hospital funding—'

Ferris interrupted. '*Gave* up the funding. Past tense, Anne. There's no going back.' His letter to Sir Bentley this morning had minced no words about the feelings he harboured over the situation the hospital had put him in. He'd even signed it Dr Lord Ferris Tresham, a form of address he never used for himself. He'd used it today, wanting to remind the man who he was dealing with.

She lifted her face and he could see tears on her cheeks. 'Then you'll have to go on alone. You seem to have forgotten that I'm a liability to you. The board of governors will not tolerate any association with me. I have no more choices, Ferris, except to go home and then perhaps go abroad until the hospital decides I'm not worth worrying over, and until they decide, they aren't going to punish my father or you for this.'

'Anne, they can't—' Ferris said, but this time she was the one who interrupted.

'Not officially they can't, but they can make things difficult unofficially. They can use their influence with the Royal College to not publish my father's papers or to quietly tar his reputation. They might limit opportunities for William when he returns.' Anne wiped at her tears. 'Why are you smiling? It's not funny, it's serious. They could do those things if I don't go quietly.'

'You, go quietly?' Ferris crossed his arms over his chest. 'I've never known you to retreat the field, Anne.'

'My family could suffer. I should have listened to you about encouraging people to take their care into their own hands.'

'Well, listen to me now. I should think Sir Bentley and his cronies would think more than twice about taking on Lady Ferris Tresham and the Cowden dukedom. They might be able to pressure Miss Anne Peverett, but they cannot even begin to pressure Cowden if that's what it comes to.' He made a dusting motion with his hands. 'Now that's settled, Anne, it's truly up to you. I love you. I want to spend my life with you. Do you want the same?' Pregnant silence ensued, full of meaning and expectation—his life, *their lives,* hung in the balance of her decision. For a man who liked being in control, he'd never felt so out of that control. Would she understand he was putting his trust in her to make the right decision for them and how much that meant?

'Dr Tresham! Dr Tresham!' A boy dressed in Dandridge house livery burst into the tea shop. 'I've found you at last. Sir Bentley says you're to come at once. It's Lady Dandridge's time and she's doing poorly, sir.'

The Dandridge household was a flurry of panic and a flutter of activity when they arrived. Maids ran up and down stairs with hot water and linen. Dandridge strode forward, florid with a temper borne of worry. 'Where have you been, Tresham? My boys have been all over town looking for you.'

'I'm here now, sir. Tell me what's happened.' Ferris gripped the man by the arm to calm him.

'She's been in labour since midnight, but didn't tell anyone out of concern for everyone's good night's sleep.' Dandridge scoffed at the notion. Nothing was more important to him than his dear wife's health. The world could go without sleep for all he cared. 'She wouldn't let me call for you because she didn't want to keep you here all day with nothing to do.' Dandridge snorted again at the notion that delivering another Dandridge heir would ever be considered 'nothing'. 'But now the contractions are coming quickly.' There was a sharp moan from behind the bedroom door to punctuate the truth of it.

'We'll take a look and see what's to be done,' Ferris assured him, but Dandridge blocked the way. He pointed an accusing finger at Anne.

'She's not going anywhere near my wife.'

Ferris met Dandridge's gaze. 'I want her with me. She is skilled in assisting a birth,' Ferris growled. 'If she goes, I go. You can call another physician to attend your wife.' He hoped it wouldn't come to that.

'Like the deal with the hospital? You're willing to risk everything for her?' Dandridge turned icy, his temper finding a convenient new target.

'Yes, like the deal with the hospital.' Ferris stood firm. Dandridge was angry and not thinking straight, now was not the time for further discussion. He grabbed Anne's wrist and pulled her with him as he went around Dandridge. He shut the bedroom door firmly behind them. 'No one else is to come in except by my instruction,' he ordered the maid as he rolled up his sleeves and washed his hands with the fresh ewer of hot water. He wished he had his chlorine lime soap. He wished he had a lot of things. He felt naked without his bag. Anne was beside him.

'I have some of your soap.' She handed it to him with a quiet smile. Just as he'd had some of her angelica root in his bag last night. They'd rubbed off on each other well. Did she see it, too? He forced his mind off the question left unanswered in the tea shop. He had a patient to focus on now. A woman in pain needed his absolute attention.

He turned to Lady Dandridge labouring on the bed, her face soaked in sweat, his tone calm. 'We'll have a new baby shortly, don't worry about a thing.' To the maid he said, 'Send a boy to Number Fourteen Cheyne Walk, I'll need my bag.' It would take an hour for the bag to make it back, though. Until then, there was only what Anne had in her basket.

He did a quick examination. Nearly fourteen hours of labour had left Lady Dandridge exhausted. She was in her late thirties, certainly an older woman for birthing, and this one was taking its toll and its time. It occurred to him she'd not had a contraction since he'd entered the room. Ferris took his watch out, timing the space between contractions. Over two minutes. Far longer than he'd liked to have seen for an 'imminent' birth.

'Labour seems to have stalled,' he said in low tones to Anne as she dried her hands.

'I think it's too late for black cohosh and ginger to be effective.' Anne sorted through her basket, packed full and tight for the train trip. 'We'll try ginger and ginseng…it's known for stamina and energy.'

The tea seemed to help. Contractions came closer together and Lady Dandridge appeared to be revived. But it was telling that his bag arrived before the baby made an appearance. An hour ago, he'd not thought it likely. Despite the ginseng and ginger, labour was not progressing logically. He checked again to see that the baby was turned. Perhaps he'd misread the baby's position? But, no, that wasn't the case. 'Some babies just take time, Lady Dandridge,' Ferris assured her, but he was worried. He wasn't sure Lady Dandridge had the energy to give more time. For a third child, this baby was taking longer than usual to make an appearance.

* * *

By four o'clock, he was certain of it and he was becoming concerned about the child as well. Was it breathing? Had the cord become twisted? Lady Dandridge was no longer in control of the labour, unable to push cohesively, and her emotional leash was slipping. He had to act now, only there was nothing in his bag that could help.

'We can try life root, false valerian,' Anne offered. 'Just a small amount.'

'I don't know it.' Ferris racked his brain, but couldn't recall a passing familiarity with it.

'It speeds up labour.' Anne hesitated. 'It regulates the uterus.' In other words it was also an abortifacient in other circumstances. 'Small doses should be fine for our purpose.'

Lady Dandridge moaned from the bed.

'And if small doses aren't fine?' Ferris asked.

'What choice do you have? This baby isn't going to deliver itself, as this afternoon has demonstrated,' Anne said sharply.

What if they were wrong? He didn't speak the thought out loud. Anne was never wrong. Mrs Fulton had been the author of her own demise, a demise she'd been warned about. 'Fix it,' he instructed, but not before Sir Bentley burst into the room, having finally got past the servants.

'What are you giving her? Why isn't the baby here?' He started towards Anne and the mixture. 'You're not to give my wife anything, you poisoner!'

Ferris stepped in between Dandridge and Anne. 'Labour has stalled, the child and your wife are now at risk. We must act now so that we don't lose them both.' He ushered the man quite forcefully back towards the door.

'If you're wrong, if I lose either of them, I will have your credentials, Tresham. You will not practise medicine anywhere ever again.'

'That will not be necessary, sir. All will be well.' Lord, he hoped so. He might still lose them, life root or not.

It took another hour, but shortly before six, the latest Dandridge slipped into the world, helped along by life root and a timely application of comfrey oil. Ferris presented the child, a girl, to Sir Bentley with immense relief. The babe was healthy and whole, as was the mother. Dandridge invited him for a drink after the babe and mother were settled comfortably.

'You did well, Tresham. My wife swears by you and apparently for good reason. You came through in a crisis today.' He raised his glass to Ferris, but Ferris shook his head.

'I cannot take all the credit. Much of the credit, as your wife will tell you, goes to Miss Peverett. It was she who suggested the ginseng and ginger to restart the labour and it was she who suggested the use of life root when it seemed all was lost. She saved them both, Sir Bentley. After her actions today, I would say there can be no doubt that the tragic death of Mrs Fulton cannot be laid at her doorstep. Mrs Fulton made an unfortunate choice, through no fault of Anne's.'

Sir Bentley cleared his throat. 'Well, perhaps you're

right and I am in a forgiving mood. The hospital will re-entertain the mobile clinics and, of course, you needn't separate yourself from Miss Peverett.'

Ferris shook his head. 'All I want is the hospital's good opinion of Miss Peverett. She is to be my wife.' At least he hoped so. Perhaps this last development would remove her remaining concerns over that. 'As for the clinics, I will establish them on my own.' If the appeal to the hospital had taught him anything, it was that there would always be a battle, a political agenda to contend with, in regard to funding. He didn't care for those hidden motives and agendas, he just wanted to heal people. He should have broken with them a long time ago.

'Then you shall have it, Tresham.' Dandridge offered his hand. 'And if you decide to reconsider the mobile clinic funding, let me know.'

Ferris left soon after that, eager to be away with Anne, eager to share that she needn't worry about persecution, implicit or otherwise. 'You can truly decide now, Anne,' he told her as they strolled through the gaslit physic garden.

She turned to face him, love shining in her eyes. Her hand cupped his sore jaw. 'I had already decided, before we were interrupted at tea. This afternoon proved I decided correctly. What you did for me today, how you stood up for me against Dandridge…' She was fumbling for words, her face flushed, and Ferris's heart began to pound. 'I was wrong to doubt your love, your commitment to me. You were willing to risk it all for my validation, not just because you love me, but because you *believe* in me. I am moved beyond words, Ferris.'

Ferris took her in his arms. 'Perhaps you might be moved to just one word?' He needed to hear her say it. 'Marry me, Anne.'

She laughed up at him, her arms about his neck. 'I'll give you four words. *Yes*, and *I love you*. Goodness knows you've waited long enough to hear them.'

Epilogue

Anne waited outside the church doors of St George's, in the spring sunshine of a May morning, her sisters fussing with her wedding finery: Thomasia with her veil, Rebecca with her bouquet and Thea standing by giving instructions. It was good to be surrounded by their chatter. It eased her own nervous excitement. Soon, she'd walk down the aisle to a future she'd once thought impossible, with a man she loved, who treated her as a partner in all ways.

She'd waited four months to marry Ferris, although time had flown. There'd been a trip to Bramble in February to celebrate with both of their families and to set the initial wedding plans for a date in early May at the top of the Season. It had been a joyous week filled with rounds of dinners and parties celebrating their engagement and watching both families come together. There'd been conversations with her father and with Ferris's about the mobile clinics, which had then led to months of work and purchasing in London. As a result, three additional clinic wagons had rolled out last week, each one manned by young physicians with a heart for service newly graduated from reputable schools and sent out to the neediest neighbourhoods.

It had been a giant undertaking along with keeping up their own visits in the original wagon. But she and Ferris had done it, side by side, except when she'd been getting fittings for her wedding gown and setting up their home. They'd decided to purchase Number Thirteen Cheyne Walk, next door to the practice, when the lease had come up.

She was adamant that they were to have a real home, a place to retreat when the day was done, although the lamp in the window would always shine, a reminder that help was never far away. There'd been a honeymoon to plan, too. That had been Ferris's job and he'd kept it a secret until last night. He'd outdone himself and she could hardly wait. After the extensive wedding festivities that befitted the marriage of a duke's son were over, she and Ferris would set sail on a private yacht for the Greek Isles and the south of France for a few months where she could collect lavender and hike about looking for herbs to her heart's content.

A carriage, driven by none other than Peter's father, with Peter riding postilion, pulled up to the kerb, and Anne's father hopped down. She waved to Peter. That was another miracle Ferris had effected in the New Year: seeing Peter and his father reunited and safely established in a cottage at Bramble.

'You look beautiful. Are you ready, my dear?' Her

father kissed her cheek, earning a scold from Thomasia, who'd just got her veil settled. She nodded. She was more than ready. Today, all the waiting and the planning came to an end and the life she and Ferris would make together would begin. She slipped her arm through her father's as her sisters made their way inside to sit beside their mother.

At the back of the church, Anne paused, letting her eyes and her nerves adjust as she took in the scene before her; the white ribbon garlands with their bright yellow daffodil bouquets swagged the aisle and the pews were full of people she didn't know. Society had come out for this first important wedding of the Season. In the front sat Ferris's family sans Fortis and across the aisle, her family, sans William. Both families were missing loved ones. In the Treshams' pew, Helena's hand rested on her belly. Her sister-in-law was just starting to show. Anne smiled at the thought. She'd be a new aunt by August. Ferris had promised Frederick they'd be back from Greece in time for the birth. The Peveretts had plans to remain in town, Thomasia and Rebecca both being of an age to enjoy a Season under the guidance of Ferris's mother.

'He's a good man, Anne. I couldn't have asked for more in a husband for my daughter.' Her father patted her arm.

'Yes, he is. The best.' Anne's gaze landed last and lingered longest on what mattered to her most as she and her father made their way down the aisle: Ferris, waiting for her at the end.

* * *

She was here at last. The waiting was over. Ferris felt his heart swell as Anne came forward on her father's arm. He wanted to remember this moment for ever, in all its glorious detail: his bride, his beautiful Anne, radiant in white, in a gown that spoke of simplicity and easy elegance, a look that suited both the occasion and her. Spring wildflowers were embroidered at the hem in blues and yellows, and she wore the lapis-lazuli bracelet about her wrist. Her hair hung long and loose beneath her veil. The sunlight streaming through the windows caught the copper skeins and turned them to burnished fire.

Some might think Anne looked innocent as she made her way down the aisle. But he knew better. She looked *happy* and that was far better than innocent. Happiness had to be fought for, claimed even against the sadness of the world.

She reached him and he took her hand, leaning close to whisper at her ear, 'I love you.' They were going to change the world and they were going to change each other, both for the better. The past was finished and gone. The future began now.

* * * * *